Praise for *Final Moment*

"A truly gripping and profound spiritual journey. Sue Montgomery takes readers to the very edge of life, where all the noise fades and *Final Moment* asks the only questions that matter. Her concept is genius, delivering a dramatic tale of regret and redemption through the eyes of a troubled teen. This book doesn't just tell a story; it challenges you to examine your own life and the choices that define it."

~Katie Vorreiter
author of *No Turning Back*, and *Fifty Days*

"Sue Montgomery delivers a profoundly moving and emotionally resonant story about how our choices shape us, how our most fragile moments can transform us, and how God's mercy finds us in the most unexpected places. *Final Moment* is a story that will linger long after the last page."

~Ashley Schwartz, Literary Editor

"Montgomery's heartfelt stories and vivid writing reflect the author's deep nursing experience and unique compassion gleaned from her many up-close end-of-life experiences in the critical care and hospice settings."

~Jennifer Odom
Co-Founder, Ocala Chapter of Word Weavers International

"*Final Moment* is riveting. In it, Sue Montgomery demonstrates her gift to quickly transport readers into her characters' circumstances as they make marginal life choices. Though the circumstances may differ, the reader often deeply relates."

~Michael Anderson
Co-Founder, Christian Authors Guild in Atlanta

FINAL MOMENT

It is appointed unto man once to die...

Hebrews 9:27

Final Moment

a novel

Sue Montgomery

WordCrafts Press

Scripture quotations taken from The Holy Bible, King James Version, public domain.

Final Moment

Hardback ISBN: 978-1-967649-26-6
Paperback ISBN: 978-1-967649-27-3

Cover concept and design by Mike Parker.
Hourglass image by BCFC licensed through Adobe Stock Images.

Published by WordCrafts Press
Cody, Wyoming 82414
www.wordcrafts.net

To my beautiful parents,
who each taught me how to live a life most prepared
for my final moment.

James R. Scott
1928–2000

Betty J. Scott
1930–2015

To my wonderful husband, Dave,
who always supports the dreams God plants within me.

And to Blue, our precious rescue, who fills our days with joy.

Chapter 1

100 Maple Valley Road
Ripple Creek, Vermont
Friday morning

*I*f Charlie had been mature enough to understand that big decisions are just the sum of all the little decisions that precede them, she may not have died that day. She took a long drag on a joint, held the sweet cloud in her lungs, and then let it drift into the naked branches of a mulberry tree. She rolled her nose ring between her left thumb and forefinger as she eyed the abortion clinic across the street.

The gravel parking lot was dotted with cars and surrounded by a chain-link fence that was meant to stand at six feet all around, but sagged in places as if unable to do so much longer. A security guard stood beside a *Coming Soon* sign announcing the construction of a new facility in spring. Outside the lopsided gate, a quiet gathering of people seemed to be praying.

Charlie propped the joint between her lips and tugged the report from her back pocket. Her hands trembled as she unfolded it and stared at the results, wishing for the millionth time there had been some mistake other than the one she'd apparently already made. It wasn't that she had any big plans of her own this would ruin—though she wished that also wasn't true. She dreamed of escaping Ripple Creek someday and didn't see how she'd ever manage that with a baby in tow. Even more, the buttoned-up expectations of her church-lady mother meant this was something she could never find out.

Charlie refolded her bad news, jammed it back into her jeans, pinched her lips together, and inhaled long and hard. Then she snuffed out the roach and tucked it into her pack of smokes, which she shoved into the hollow of her waist. She pushed her sunglasses onto her nose, pulled the hood of her jacket down onto her face, and crossed the road, keeping her eyes on the dirty concrete beneath her tennis shoes. When she got to the gate, the security guard held it open. "No phones or purses," he said.

Charlie nodded and held out her empty hands. As she passed through the gate, she glanced at the evidence of the recent merger with a network of women's clinics. On the new sign, the pink letters read "Ripple Creek Women's Center. Where women come first." Below it, the previous **CASH ONLY** sign included an additional sticker of credit card payment options.

Charlie hurried across the lot and up three wooden steps that dipped a little in the middle and were splintered with wear. When she opened the door, she was met with the antiseptic, coppery smell of the nurse's office at school. Overhead lights emitted a low hum, providing all the warmth of a warehouse. In the waiting room, the blue fabric chairs were occupied by women of various ages who gazed at her with empty stares.

Charlie poked out her chin and stood a little straighter, then sank into the seat closest to the door and reminded herself to breathe. If she had any certainty about who the father was, she would've made him come with her.

"You have to check in." A young woman two chairs over pointed to a frosted sliding window at the front of the room.

"Think I don't know that?"

The woman shrugged. "Just trying to help."

"Whatever."

"First time, huh?"

Charlie glared at her without speaking.

The woman returned to her magazine. "I mean, most girls who come in here with that big ole chip on their shoulder…" Then she looked at Charlie again. "All full of tough, but really just full of scared."

Charlie stood, and her chair scraped against the speckled tile. In the corner, someone on the television won a jackpot, and the audience cheered. She headed for the window, not looking back.

A clipboard on the counter held a sign-in sheet filled with the loopy signatures of the young. There were three columns of visit options from which to select: Routine Visit, Birth Control, Abortion. Charlie swallowed hard as she placed a checkmark below the others in the abortion column and scribbled her name.

The sliding window rumbled open, and a woman with light green eyes looked over her glasses. Three long strands of black hair sprouted from beneath her generous chin. She reached for the clipboard. "Do you have an appointment?" Speaking made the hairs come to life, and they danced like a bobbin with a fish on the line.

Charlie nodded. "At nine."

The woman examined the clipboard, then looked up, her tone softening. "Not that it matters, but can I ask how old you are?"

"Sixteen." Charlie tensed beneath her gaze, assuming judgment for her purple hair and nose ring.

"Would you like to talk to a counselor?"

Charlie looked away. "No."

The woman attached a packet of papers to another clipboard and handed them through the window. "You'll need to fill these out. We're out of pills, so the procedure's your only choice."

Charlie's heart sank. She'd read that the pills were quick and easy, so she'd been hoping for that option. But taking them also meant she'd be having her abortion at home. Maybe this was best.

"Is anyone with you?"

Charlie shook her head, wishing it wasn't true.

The woman gave her a compassionate look. "You drive? 'Cause you can't drive yourself home."

"Walked."

"You won't be able to do that either. We'll call you a cab when you're done." She nodded at the stack of papers. "Now go find out what you're about to do. If you decide you still want to go through with it, then sign and bring them back."

Charlie's stomach rolled. She put a hand to her mouth and gagged.

The woman gave a sad smile, handed her a plastic basin, and closed the window.

Charlie grasped the container and headed for a chair in the corner, where she settled in with the tome of papers she'd been given. She scanned the questions and filled in what she could, her gaze hovering over the last: *Method of Payment?* She fingered the cash in her pocket she'd pilfered from her mother's stash. She hoped there'd be enough left over for the cab.

The last page in the packet was titled *Consent to Treat/Release of Liability.* The sentences were so tightly packed it looked like a square blob of ink.

She hated to read anyway.

Putting her pen to the last line, Charlie signed in a neat cursive that would've made her mother proud.

~

If there was anything good about the morning, it had to be the drugs.

The thought kept rolling around in Charlie's mind as she savored the sedative that had been injected into her IV.

"Here we go, honey. One in here…" She felt the nurse picking up her feet. "And one in here."

The metal stirrups were cold against her heels, and she figured her toes were blue by now.

"Perfect."

Charlie gazed at the poster of the waterfall on the ceiling. She drifted in and out, trying to keep her knees from wobbling back and forth and her feet in the stirrups. She heard the clatter of a cart being rolled next to the table and looked over. It held a computer monitor and a device that resembled the head of a snake that was attached to a cord and hung from the side of the cart.

"Is that for an ultrasound?"

The woman nodded as she occupied herself with turning things on.

Charlie's pulse picked up. She didn't want to know anything she didn't already know about this pregnancy she'd been promised would soon come to an end. "I thought I didn't have to have one."

The nurse gave her an impatient look. "Technically, no. But we need to see how far you're along. For…" The woman's voice wandered toward the screen.

"For?"

"Your procedure. And billing. We need to know what to charge." The woman grabbed the bottle of lubricant from the cart, squirted an ice-blue mound onto the head of the snake, and lifted Charlie's gown. "This will be cold."

Charlie nearly shot off the table.

"Hold still."

"I'm trying, but—"

"Breathe in and hold it."

Charlie took a deep breath and listened to her pulse throb in her ears and her justifications roll through her mind.

It's just a piece of tissue, like the website said.

My body and my right to do what I want with it.

A medical procedure that girls do all the time.

My mother would want me to do this, even if she doesn't know it.

The monitor let out a faint swishing sound.

"Okay, breathe."

Charlie exhaled and lifted her head from the table. "What's that noise?"

"It's nothing." The nurse adjusted something on the monitor's computer and the noise disappeared.

"But it sounded like—"

"Artifact. It's normal." She held the device in place with one hand and used the other to work with the computer keyboard on the cart.

"Okay, all done." The nurse wiped the lubricant off Charlie's belly and pulled down her gown. "The doctor will be in shortly to do the procedure."

As if on cue, Charlie heard a male voice in the hall outside her door. The latch clicked, and the tiny room was overcome with the weight of cheap cologne. The doctor already had his mask on, and she could see mostly blue. A blue cap on his head, a blue mask on his face, and tiny blue eyes peering from within all that paper fabric. A few strands of wild gray hair were trying to escape the cap, winding their way around his ears, which were also full of the same.

He glanced at Charlie as he flipped through her paperwork. Then he moved to the cart and clicked through a few screens on the monitor. "Charlene Welks, is it?"

"Yes." Her mouth was so dry she could barely utter that single word.

He turned the monitor off and moved to her feet.

Charlie swallowed hard, hoping not to puke. For the briefest of seconds, she thought about sitting up and clamping her legs together.

Instead, she squeezed her eyes shut.

"Here's more medicine in your IV, Charlene," the nurse said.

A paper drape swooshed across her body.

Instruments clanked on the table at her feet.

Someone laughed in the hall.

As Charlie drifted off, she heard the snap of a switch.

And then the suction machine gurgled to life.

~

"Stop. Drop me off here."

The cab driver eyed her in the rearview mirror. "This ain't the address you gave me."

Charlie gazed out the window, too tired to argue. "I know. But it's far enough."

The man shrugged. "Whatever. That'll be twenty even."

She eyed the tattered bills in her hands. A ten. A five. Two ones. "I don't have enough," she mumbled.

He turned and looked at her. The bill of a beat-up Brooklyn Dodgers cap perched at an angle over eyebrows that had never met a tweezer. His voice softened. "You know, I get calls to that place all the time. Girls just like you. Young. Alone. Pale. Girls who should be in school."

Charlie didn't respond.

The man sighed. "Let's just make it ten, kid."

She folded all four bills together and handed them to the man.

"Look at me." His tone was gentle, and Charlie met the gaze of his deep brown eyes.

"What's your name?"

"Charlie."

He nodded. "Well, Charlie…me and my wife? We're gonna be praying for you."

"Whatever." Charlie pulled on the door handle and climbed out of the car.

Chapter 2

252 Spruce Street

The latch turned beneath her key, and she eased the door open. Charlie didn't expect anyone to be home but tiptoed into the hallway, just in case. The grandfather clock in the corner ticked each second of silence that blanketed the house. She closed the door behind her and slumped onto the white linen bench next to the umbrella stand.

On the opposite wall, a portrait of the three of them hung between two glass sconces with ornate fixtures and fake candles that flickered on after dark. In the picture, her mother gave a perfect lipstick smile with every hair tucked neatly into place around her beautiful, thin face. Beth's eyes were blue, not the deep brown Charlie had inherited from her father, and she hated it when Charlie referred to her by her first name—which is exactly why Charlie often did so.

The most recent husband stood beside her, a goofy grin displaying a hollow space behind his left upper canine. Dan's freakishly huge frame wasn't accustomed to the confines of a suit, so the material bulged in unusual places, like it was trying to escape the agony of being worn. He wasn't fat, but his whole body seemed to have too much of itself, like it had been built on the wrong chassis.

She gazed at her image in front of the pair. Her mouth formed a tight line beneath a nose that looked like it belonged on an elf. Her eyes held so much disdain that the photographer probably thought it was something he'd done. Well, there *was* the fact that he'd wanted her mother and Dan to each put a hand on her shoulders. Since she wasn't having any of that, the three of them stood there straight as nails with their hands at their sides. Two smiling strangers and the kid who didn't belong. And after this morning, that was especially true.

Charlie shook her head and sighed. Then she leaned toward the floor, put her tongue between her lips, and gave a dry spit. She did it every time she walked by the picture. *Every* time.

She stood from the bench, kicked off her shoes, and placed them in the rack by the door. Then she padded through the house toward the back porch. The white carpet was soft and thick beneath her feet, and the muted aroma of of her mother's favorite perfume clung to the air. She told her mother she wore too much and pretended to be disgusted by it. In truth, Charlie loved the smell, simply because it was one of the few constants in her life. And it gave her hope that the mom she once knew would one day return.

But she doubted it'd be today.

She pulled the pack of cigarettes out of her waistband and eased herself into a lounge chair by the pool. The cushions were stored for the winter, and the surface was cold beneath her scrawny butt. She didn't care. She only had a few hours before her mother made her grand appearance, and she needed a smoke and maybe a nip from Dan's stash before heading to her room for a nap.

She tugged the joint from between the tightly packed cigarettes, lit it, and pulled long and hard before blowing a thick cloud toward the dingy blue pool cover. A cramp rolled through her lower abdomen, and Charlie pulled her knees to her chest. Ibuprofen. She needed that too.

After the pain passed, Charlie stretched her legs onto the chaise and pulled her shirt up to expose her belly to the frigid air. She gazed at it as she ran a slow hand over its flat terrain, letting herself wonder what he would've looked like. If Charlie knew who the father was, it'd be easier to predict.

Or she. A little girl would've been cool. A little girl named…

Charlie yanked down her top and swung her feet to the pavement. *Nope.* In her universe, there was no possible scenario in which the baby of a sixteen-year-old unmarried daughter would be able to play on her grandmother's perfect white carpet.

She stared into the bright blue eyes of the stone Virgin Mary that stood in the center of the meticulous silk landscaping behind the diving board. She held the woman's gaze as she took another drag on her joint, blew out a cloud of grey smoke, then leaned over and gave a dry spit.

~

The house began to rattle when the opener kicked on for the garage door. The noise startled Charlie awake. Her room was dark, except for the soft blue glow of the alarm clock. Six-thirty. Since the legal office her mom worked for closed at five, she must have stopped at the store.

The floor beneath her filled with the car's vibration as her mom pulled into the garage. Then the house rattled once again as the door slowly descended. A final thump confirmed its closure and the end to Charlie's pleasure of being left alone.

She heard the car door slam and the rustling of plastic bags. The seal on the house was so tight that Charlie felt a movement of air when her mother opened the door between the garage and the house. She heard the thud of groceries hitting the counter and waited.

"Charlie?"

Charlie rolled onto her side and stared at the wall. She pulled the covers higher in hopes the woman would think she was asleep.

The thick flooring always muffled her approach, but Charlie was certain the sole of her foot had already graced the bottom step of the stairs.

She heard the turn of the knob, and light from the hallway seeped into her room.

"Charlie?" She felt her mother's gaze on her back. "I know you're awake."

Charlie didn't have to look to know she had her hands on her hips. Then she heard the click of the switch, and the room exploded with light.

"Mom! I'm trying to sleep."

"Why are you sleeping?" Her mother moved to the bed and placed a palm on Charlie's forehead. "Are you sick?"

Charlie continued to stare at the wall. The cool skin of her mom's hand felt better than she wanted to admit, and the aroma of her perfume lingered on her wrist from the morning's application. She gave Charlie's shoulder a gentle tug. "Charlie, look at me."

Charlie sighed and rolled onto her back. She looked up in resignation.

"Have you been crying?"

"No. I just woke up."

"How long have you been sleeping?"

"I don't know. I was tired. I just wanted to sleep."

Her mother eyed her, unconvinced. "How was school today?"

Charlie rolled back toward the wall. "Fine."

This time, the tug on her shoulder wasn't quite as gentle. "Did you even go to school?"

Charlie pushed the hand away and suddenly sat up. "Yes. Leave me alone."

She threw back the covers and jumped out of bed. That's when she heard her mother gasp. Charlie took one look at the circle of bright blood on the bottom sheet and headed for the bathroom.

~

Charlie reached for the knob and made the hot water hotter. She tilted her head back and let it pummel her skin and dilute her tears. Her shoulders heaved as the rising steam hushed her sobs and carried them away.

There was a tap on the door and then her mother's muffled voice. "Charlie?"

She didn't bother to answer, since waiting for permission wasn't something her mother ever did. Charlie felt a cool rush of air push its way over the shower door and into the stall. She reached for the knob and turned it toward red. Her skin turned as pink as bubble gum and then began to sting.

"Charlie?" Just like that, the shower door was open, and her mom was standing there.

Charlie's hands flew to her chest. "Seriously?" She grabbed the handle and slammed the door so hard the glass shuddered.

Her mother's voice faltered. "It's just…"

She heard the tap of the toilet lid being shut. Through the haze, Charlie could see her sitting on the commode, elbows on her knees. It was an unusual posture for her proper mother.

"Honey, I just…I've never seen you do that. Is your flow getting harder? Oh, I bet you're out of tampons." Her mother stood as she spoke, apparently embracing this reasonable explanation for so much blood. Charlie watched her shadow as it bent down and rummaged through the cabinet beneath the sink.

She turned back to the water and this time let it beat against her face, ignoring the pain and the other person in the bathroom. She didn't know how long she'd been standing like that when a rush of cool air signaled her mother's departure. Charlie slid the door back an inch and confirmed her suspicions. Then she turned off the water and stepped out of the shower onto the thick blue shower mat on the floor. A fresh towel of the same color was lying in a perfectly folded square on the lid of the toilet seat. Charlie reached for it and then realized that something was very wrong.

In her rush to the shower, she'd left her blood-stained jeans in a pile on the floor—with the contents of her day in the pockets. She snatched open the lid of the hamper. All her dirty clothes were gone. Charlie wrapped the towel around her and descended the stairs as if her soles were on wheels.

The laundry room was adjacent to the garage, on the other side of the guest bath in the hall. She heard the rush of water as the washer filled. Charlie slowed as she approached the door from the side, hoping against all odds that her meticulous mother hadn't checked every pocket before throwing in her clothes.

When Charlie turned the corner, she froze.

Her mom was slumped on the floor, leaning against the washer with her eyes closed, her head moving back and forth in a slow moan of movement as two trickles of mascara crept down her cheeks. The papers were scattered on the floor beside her, damage already done. The expletive Charlie mouthed echoed into the bottomless pit of her stomach as her world dropped from beneath her. She took three silent steps backward and slipped up the stairs.

Once she got to her room, she closed the door, turned the lock, and dropped the damp towel. She grabbed whatever clothing was within reach and tugged it on, her fingers trembling over every button and snap. She grabbed her phone, her smokes, and a bottle of whiskey she'd stolen from her stepfather's stash. She put her ear to the door. If her mother was standing outside, she wasn't breathing. Charlie quietly turned the little knob of the lock, eased open the door, and padded down the stairs.

The bottom of the staircase emptied into the entryway hall. It was the halfway point between the reality of the laundry room and the escape of the front door. Charlie leaned toward the sound of the chugging washer and looked for any sign of her mother. When it seemed the coast was clear, she eased around the banister and toward the front door.

But there she was. Sitting on the linen bench, staring at the family portrait. A thin line of muscle formed a ridge along her jaw.

Charlie stopped mid-step, uncertain of what to do. She held her breath and tried to blend into the wall.

"I know you're there," her mother said. She continued to stare at the picture in front of her. The rumpled woman in the laundry room had been replaced with this one, who sat with posture perfect enough to balance an egg on her head. Her legs were crossed lady-style, and her always-manicured fingers were folded into her pompous professional lap. The evidence of the day sat in a neat two-paper stack on the bench beside her, a weapon at the ready if needed.

Charlie slumped onto the bottom step. She stared at the floor and rolled her nose ring between her fingers.

The silence between them was as thick as a snowdrift.

Finally, her mother spoke. "You could have come to me."

Charlie shook her head, wondering how two people could occupy the same living space every day and experience it so differently.

"If you say so," she said to the floor.

Suddenly, her mother was before her, hands on her hips, her face twisted in an emotion Charlie didn't recognize. "What's that supposed to mean?"

Charlie looked back down as she suppressed the urge to dart around the woman like a field mouse. "Nothing."

"Look at me." There was no tenderness in the voice.

She hesitated and then looked up. Her mother squinted as if protecting her eyes from the sun. "Who's the father? Oh, no, let me correct that. Who *was* the father?"

Charlie shrugged.

Her mom grabbed the banister to steady herself. She lowered herself onto the step and put her head between her knees.

Charlie didn't move. Instead, she tried to tell herself that doing something bad enough to make your mother almost pass out was normal.

Eventually, the woman beside her sat up, but only enough to

put her elbows on her knees and her face in her hands. "How can you *not* know who the father is?" she said into her palms.

Charlie didn't respond.

Her mother turned to her. "How long have you been sexually active?"

"Apparently longer than you knew."

"Don't you dare get smart with me." She stood from the step and looked down at her daughter. "I've tried to teach you to—"

Charlie's heart pounded as she stood to meet her mother's glare. "Oh yes. Let's talk about what you've tried to teach me, Beth."

"Don't—"

"About how many men you can parade in and out of our lives? How many husbands you expect me to call *Dad*? How many times you've given me up for someone else?" Charlie savored the pain that rippled across her mother's face, the circles growing wider with every word.

"We all make mistakes, Charlie."

If it had sounded like an apology instead of an excuse, Charlie might have let up. "Oh, I see. So now I'm supposed to cut you some slack while you stand there and judge me?"

"I've turned my life around. I have a good job. I married a good man. We have a nice home. We go to church. We are respected in this community."

Charlie laced her words with as much bitterness as she could muster. "Ah yes. You and your most recent husband are pillars of the church. Pillars of the community. And you're afraid your disgrace of a daughter is going to ruin everything."

Her mom shook her head like she was trying to stop a departing train. "No. That's not true."

But it was no use. Charlie's words held a full head of steam. "And what exactly would you have done if I *had* come to you, Mom? Throw me a baby shower? Invite all your church friends? Put balloons in the yard to welcome us home from the hospital?"

Her mother reached for her arm. "Charlie, I—"

Charlie yanked it away and headed up the stairs, her voice rising with each step. "No. You don't get to do this. You don't get to pretend you're someone you're not." When she got to the top, she swung around and jabbed her index finger into the air, hurling each word on its tip. "And you definitely don't get to pretend you care about me."

Then she dropped her arm to her side and gazed at her mother, a wistful gesture of final attack. "I wish you had died instead of Daddy."

~

Charlie glared at the back of the locked door of her bedroom, inhaled long and hard on the joint, then held her breath while the buzz trickled into her system. Instead of taking all her usual precautions to hide the smell from her mother, she blew a thick cloud of smoke into the drapery she hated and took another swig of whiskey. Then she glanced at the clock.

Dan would be home soon, and she'd lose her chance. Since he belonged to a carpool to get to his sales job in Montpelier, there were days when his car remained on the right side of the driveway.

Charlie was in luck, since today was one of those days.

She put everything she needed into her backpack, put on her coat, then unlocked the door and eased it open.

The house was still.

She took a deep breath, tiptoed down the stairs, slipped the keys from the hook, and headed out the front door.

Chapter 3

The second curve on Yellow Birch Lane had a reputation for tragedy. By the time Charlie saw the flash of her headlights on the bark of the tree, it was too late. She yanked hard left on the wheel and held her breath. There was a thud of impact, a grating of metal, and the weightless moment of a rollercoaster peaking and dropping into nothing. The rooftop landing was that of a plane with no wheels, a grinding display of fireworks shooting in all directions.

When the car finally slid to a stop, she was hanging upside down. Debris pattered around her like rain on a pond, and the musky aroma of fresh dirt engulfed her as if it were being shoveled from above. She tasted blood. And smelled smoke. Her eyes wouldn't open, and her arms and legs wouldn't move. Something warm and wet trickled across her forehead. Needles of pain shot through her chest with every attempt to breathe.

Then, quiet settled in like an unwelcome guest. Charlie could hear the ticking of the hot engine. The creaking of branches in the wind. The throbbing of her heart within her ears. The shifting fabric of her coat against the shoulder strap as the limp weight of her body tested its strength. The distant wail of a siren.

The sound grew toward her in slow crescendo until it reached a deafening climax and then cut off into silence. She heard doors slamming. Movement on the pavement outside Dan's car. The click of the door latch.

"It's jammed!"

Charlie heard a grunt, the scrape of fabric, and the crunch of glass. "Miss?"

A blast of icy air pelted her cheeks with grit. The voice moved closer, and Charlie smelled garlic.

"Miss, can you hear me?" She felt a rough hand on her shoulder, shaking her. "I can't get her to respond."

"Is she dead?"

"I think she's breathing. But I can't get to her, and this thing's gonna blow any minute. Where's the fire department?"

"Listen. I hear them."

The wail of additional sirens grew louder and then stopped. Gravel crackled beneath tires on the pavement. Air brakes gave a *whine* and *whoosh*. More doors slammed.

"What happened?" A different male voice.

"Hit the tree and flipped. She must've been flying."

"Miss?" The new voice came closer. His cologne was a welcome change from dirt and garlic. Charlie felt the touch of his hand on her cheek. She tried to lean into it. To let them know she could hear them.

Then he was gone.

"She's bad, guys. Get the hydraulic—and somebody deal with that smoke."

Charlie longed to move. To twitch. Anything. She let out a scream that started in her toes and blew through her scalp. But silence filled the air around her.

Hello, Charlene.

Charlie's breath caught. She must've banged her head pretty hard.

Yes, you have a head injury, among many others.

She tried to open her eyes. *Wait—what?* The voice was too

close to be one of the medics. Somewhere in the front seat. But that couldn't be. Maybe it was all the pot.

It is your spirit that hears me.

The taste on Charlie's tongue reminded her of the penny her daddy fished out of her mouth when she was little. *But I—*

My name is Final Moment. I represent the last sixty seconds of your life on earth.

But that would mean—

Yes. You are dying.

It had to be a hallucination. That was it. From hitting her head. A trickling sound drifted from the rear of the car, reminding her of the ice maker in the fridge. Charlie had a sudden longing for home.

I know you are confused, Charlene. This is true regarding many issues in your life.

Charlie responded as if she were able to talk out loud. *I don't know who you are or what's happening to me...*

My role is to administer the Regrets Evaluation and Pliability Assessment. Do you have regrets, Charlene?

Everything was happening too fast. And too slow. The trickling sound carried with it the distinct smell of gas. *I don't know what's going on, but we're wasting time. If you're real, just help me.*

I am trying to help you, Charlene. Today alone, you have had an abortion, informed your mother you wished she were dead, and drove your stepfather's car while impaired by drugs and alcohol, resulting in this fatal accident. I will ask again, do you have regrets, Charlene?

Even as the list played out like a fast-forward film while she was hanging upside down, unable to move, and apparently near death, Charlie wanted to roll her eyes. Slam a door. Scream out loud. Stomp away. Give a dry spit at this, this, this—*thing*. Instead, she was limited to a single thought. *None of that was my fault.*

I see. That was a child in your womb, Charlene.

The words were like a bandage being ripped from her skin, abruptly exposing the raw wound of denial Charlie had been trying to ignore since she'd crawled off the table in the clinic that morning. Suppressed sensations flooded her, sweeping her back to the room. The antiseptic smell. The cold metal stirrups. The clanking of instruments. The suction machine gurgling, hesitating, then forging on once the obstruction had cleared. The certainty of knowing it was too late to change her mind.

No! A piece of tissue, that's all. The website said so. Everyone says so.

A beautiful little girl who is with the Father now. He named her Rose.

Charlie began to cry.

But I—

Your mother loves you very much.

The aroma of her mother's perfume flooded her senses, engulfing her with confusion and longing. The last time she felt loved by her mom was at the bus stop on the first day of first grade, a year after her daddy's accident. Her mom was crying as Charlie waved from the window, dressed in her little brown skirt with a matching silk ribbon tied around her collar. After that, the parade of men began, and she'd felt like an orphan ever since.

But she—

Made mistakes. A human condition. This dynamic does not diminish a mother's love. I know you have been hurt. And you miss your father.

In the torrent of sensations pummeling Charlie from within appeared a single, glistening branch of hope. Charlie grabbed it and hung on.

Wait. My father? Have you seen him?

Of course. There are many of me in the same form, continually visiting those about to leave this world.

The throbbing in Charlie's head became unbearable as tears surged and spilled into uncertain paths around her eyes and onto her forehead, tiny rivers flowing north.

I want my mom. If she had been able to speak, her words would've been a sob.

I am afraid that will not be possible, Charlene. Tell me about your relationship with God.

It was as if the emotions of the preceding seconds had never occurred. The mention of God dried Charlie's eyes and turned her heart as cold as the whip of frigid wind that surged through unseen openings and pelted her body with tiny bits of debris.

Forget it.

Little time remains. This is the most critical aspect of your review.

The smell of musty hymnals couldn't have been stronger if there'd been a stack on the car ceiling beneath Charlie's dangling head. Melancholy echoes of empty Sunday School classrooms to which her mom had not returned strengthened her resolve. *God doesn't get me. The feeling's mutual.*

He loves you very much. He knew you before you were in your mother's womb. Just like Rose.

Charlie felt a surge of panic, afraid the suction-machine noise would come back. She started to cry again.

Quit saying that.

He sent the Son to save you.

The longer she dangled in midair, the more she felt like a magician's assistant, pinned in a box about to be cut into two by the seatbelt that strained against her weight. Charlie heard the crackle of metal like a tin can in a fist, and the car shifted, releasing the latch on the door of the center console. Dan's phone charger thumped onto the ceiling beneath her.

Save me? He could start by getting me out of here.

Only a few seconds remain, Charlene. Will you accept your last chance for a relationship with the Son? He stands now, arms open, waiting to embrace you.

Charlie heard voices. Real voices of real people who would get her out. *Just leave me alone. I'm not going to die.*

As you wish, Charlene. I am truly sorry you were not ready. That your heart was not pliable enough for a final chance.

Then there were hands on her, tugging like a dog with a toy. When she popped free, cold air washed over her. She felt her body being lowered and then the hard pavement beneath her. Someone started to count, and her chest exploded with pain. Charlie tried to lift her arms to fight, but they remained limp at her sides.

Final, wait! Help me!

At that moment, she could see everything.

Uniformed bodies leaning over her.

Pulsating red lights.

The pile of metal that used to be a car.

Wha…?

You have died, Charlene.

Died? But what about my mom? How can I say I'm sorry now?

You cannot.

Charlie wiped at tears that were no longer there—which is when she realized she could move her arms. She stared at her hand, moving it back and forth, opening and closing it into a fist, like a stranger meeting a new friend. She looked below. The paramedics were loading the stretcher into the back of the ambulance, still pumping on her chest. She could see them right through the roof.

Her mother's car skidded to a stop at the edge of the scene. She made it to the back of the ambulance two steps before Dan. After one look inside, she collapsed onto the pavement.

Mom! I'm here! Final, do something!

There was only silence in response. As Charlie watched Dan kneel and pull her mom into his arms, her mind surged with a wave of regret that carried with it everything she'd ever done wrong and could no longer fix.

~

Charlie had never experienced such quiet. Or such emptiness. There was no bright light. No wash of peace. Just a cloak of nothingness draped over her senses. Dread was the only thing she felt.

Final? Are you still there?

Yes, Charlene, I am here.

Charlie didn't know if this was a good or bad sign. But she was grateful not to be alone.

I'm scared. Where am I?

We are about to visit Ian.

Another person. Maybe a real person. Charlie felt a surge of hope. Until she remembered what a visit from Final meant.

I don't understand.

I have been directed to allow you to accompany me during my visitations in Ripple Creek this night. It is an unusually busy schedule for such a small town.

But I don't want to do this. I want my mom.

Charlie knew there would be no tears to match the despair she felt.

I want to go home.

We must hurry, Charlene. Ian is nearly ready.

~

Ripple Creek Community Hospital
Room 207

The change was so immediate, Charlie felt like she'd been shoved through a door. She looked at the young man in the hospital bed and the others in the room.

Sorry, I—

They cannot see you, Charlene.

Oh. Charlie eyed the patient. *What's wrong with him?*

Ian has cancer.

Charlie had always thought of cancer as an old-people disease.

But he looks younger than me.

Yes, he is fourteen.

And he's dying? Charlie had so many questions.

Yes.

She watched Ian, lying perfectly still in the bed. A nurse walked into the room. *Can he hear us?*

Not yet. But soon.

Can I talk to him?

No. But you will be aware of everything.

"I'm giving you something for pain, Ian."

Charlie heard the words, clear as a bell. She felt the nurse at his side, touching his arm. She even smelled rubbing alcohol when the white square packet was ripped open. After the nurse injected the medication into his I.V. line, it only took a few seconds before she felt it drifting into his system.

Final, what's happening?

You are experiencing Ian's perspective as well as your own, Charlene. Just pay attention.

The thin woman sitting by the bed had deep circles under her eyes. When she leaned in, Charlie heard a single word running through Ian's mind: *Mom.*

Charlie felt his mother's lips brush across Ian's forehead like the wisp of a feather. "I'm right here, honey. I know you can hear me." The softness of her palm slid over Ian's hand. It made Charlie long for own mom. The one she'd screamed at and would never get to see again.

"Your friends are here too." The woman's voice broke. It was a few minutes before she spoke again. When she did, her words were tender, close to his ear. Her breath was warm against Ian's skin. "You're not alone. Don't be afraid."

When he inhaled a little, Charlie savored the scent of strawberry shampoo. His thoughts were her thoughts, and she knew it reminded him of cookies. The homemade oatmeal cookies his mother bribed him and the guys with to get them to do their homework around the kitchen table every night. He was thinking that without that kind of support and being dragged to church, he wasn't sure what would've happened to him. To all of them. Charlie knew Ian was longing to wrap his arms around his mom one more time. To have just a few more minutes with the one person who'd been his constant. Who loved him unconditionally despite everything he'd put her through. Who wore out the knees of her jeans, pleading for her only son. Who believed in him when nobody else would. Who never gave up on him, even when he gave up on himself.

Charlie wondered how different her life would've been if she'd had a mom like this. A mom she could love the way Ian loved his.

It's okay, Mom. I'm not afraid.

The woman suddenly sat up, as if she'd heard him. A tear fell from her cheek, and Charlie felt it land on Ian's arm. She heard his mom sniffle and then the scraping of the chair as she stood. His mother's lips brushed his forehead again, pausing in the center, trembling as she murmured against his skin, "I love you so much." A loose strand of her hair fell onto Ian's cheek, dancing along his skin in rhythm to her movements. Charlie knew he longed to reach up and touch it, and so did she. His mother's tears trickled onto Ian's face, a baptism of goodbye.

I love you so much, Mom, Charlie heard his spirit say. Then she watched one of Ian's friends move to his side.

"Hey, bro." Calluses scraped across Ian's skin, and he barely managed to grasp one of the thick fingers. "Hey, you hear me. It's Jig. We're all here, man. Finn and Zip and Skeeter—" When Jig spoke again, his words were a ragged whisper. "I love you, man." Charlie was as surprised as Ian by the peck on his cheek as his friend squeezed his hand one last time.

She listened to the low rhythm of classic rock that drifted from the corner. A chair scraping the floor. Voices murmuring. Lights humming. A patient's call bell pinging in the hall. Someone blowing their nose. She knew Ian sensed every breath might be his last.

Hello, Ian.

Charlie recognized the surge of confusion. She wanted to shake Ian. Tell him to wake up and run.

Who—

My name is Final Moment…

⌣

952 Cedar Street

The sudden transition from the warmth of Ian's hospital room to the frigid back alley was like throwing open a window in the dead of winter. Charlie heard the man hit the pavement with a thud.

Final? She stared at the unmoving form that seemed to blend into the scatter of street debris around it.

His name is Shane.

Charlie took in the dismal scene.

Wait. Don't do what you did with Ian. I don't want to feel stuff and I don't want to hear stuff. Especially all that back and forth between the two of you.

It is how you will learn, Charlene. We will not be long.

Then Charlie felt the pain of the gash that had opened along Shane's right eye and began to trickle blood. He remained motionless, each quick breath stirring the street dirt under his cheek into little clouds of dust. She saw the frozen stream of mucus that clung to his beard and felt the hairs within his nostrils that were stuck together in a clump.

She watched Shane make a feeble attempt to wrap the camouflage jacket around himself and knew what he was thinking. That it used to hang on him like a tent, but lately it wouldn't close around his belly. That the melon of his gut underneath was swollen and tight, giving his frame the appearance of fruit on a withering vine. And that tonight, it hurt more than usual, transforming throughout the day into a cauldron that now curled him like a fetus.

He made a halfhearted attempt to kick away broken glass as he inched toward a dumpster and tucked himself against the cold green metal. Then nausea rolled through him, and he heaved, spraying deep-green vomit onto the pavement. The acrid taste of bile filled Charlie's mouth, reminding her of how much she hated to throw up. Shane moaned as he settled his right cheek back onto the grit on the pavement.

It may have been the overwhelming weakness, the puking, or

the deep yellow of his skin. Whether it was one thing or everything, it occurred to Shane that he should probably go to the hospital. But he quickly discarded the idea, aware of the treatment he'd get. The long looks of judgment. The slow shake of the head. The clucking of the tongue. The nurses who argued about who would be assigned to his care.

As if anyone knew what it was like to be him. The occasional rat and the low hum of a streetlight provided all the company he needed. Other people had never done him any good anyway. When Charlie heard that clear as a bell, she realized her first impression had been wrong. Shane was a kindred spirit after all.

Hello, Shane.

The man's eyes fluttered open. Charlie recognized the thoughts racing through his head. That maybe he was finally losing it. Or that maybe this was what it was like to die.

My name is Final Moment…

320 Aspen Street

When Charlie felt the blast of hot air, she knew she was no longer with Shane. She watched the long thin fingers drumming the steering wheel in front of her with the rhythm of a pianist. They weren't the hands of her mother, whose nails were always polished and perfectly shaped to show off the diamonds of her wedding set. Instead, the simplicity of short, plain nails and a thin gold band made these hands as inviting as a familiar pair of slippers.

Final?

You are with Ruby, Charlene.

But I don't like being inside these people.

My time with you is brief. This is the most efficient means of instruction.

But I—

She was late. Again. The thought in Charlie's mind was as

clear as if Ruby had spoken it out loud. The garbage truck in front of the car chugged ahead, then stopped. Charlie watched the mechanical arm swing an oversized trash can into the air, flip it over, and make a deposit into the truck's bed.

Friday night garbage pickups. Only in Ripple Creek. Charlie felt the surge of Ruby's frustration and knew she was thinking that she'd promised her girls she'd be home to tuck them in. But at this rate, she'd never make it. She reached for her phone and punched the speed dial for home.

A man's voice came through the line. "Everything okay?"

"Got held up after the study. Are the girls still up?"

"Of course. They're waiting for you."

"Will you put them on? Traffic's at a crawl behind this garbage truck."

Charlie listened with awe, wondering what it would've been like to have a mom who worried about telling her goodnight.

"Where are you?"

"Aspen and…" Ruby leaned forward and squinted at the street sign. "Cedar."

The line went silent. Charlie was familiar with the area and wanted to hit the gas.

"I asked you to stay away from there." The pitch of her husband's voice rose a notch, but Charlie sensed Ruby wasn't the least bit scared.

"My usual route was closed for construction."

"Are your doors—"

"Locked? Yes."

"Where's your pepper—"

"Spray? In my purse."

"Your purse? A lot of good it'll do you—"

"Honey. I'm fine. Put the girls on."

His sigh was so loud Ruby lifted the phone from her ear. "Okay, just be careful."

"I will."

"And don't buy any drugs while you're there."

That took Charlie by surprise. Drugs? She sensed the smirk on Ruby's lips.

"That'd go over big."

"And don't get out of the car to pray with anyone, either."

Charlie had known plenty of people associated with drugs. And enough people who talked about prayer. But never anyone who knew about both.

"Now, that, I might not be able to resist," Ruby said into the phone.

"Ruby…"

"Just let me talk to the girls."

"Okay, here's double-trouble." There was a rustling noise on the other end of the phone. Charlie had the sudden image of two blonde-headed girls who looked like twins and whose chatter filled the line.

Ruby smiled. "I know, girls, I'll be home soon. Just remember I love you both with everything I've got."

Emotions surged through Charlie. Envy that the little girls got to have such a mom. Longing for a family brimming with such love. Regret that she'd never get to tuck her Rose in. Panic when she realized that Ruby would never make it home. She wanted to scream for her to get out of there. Instead, she heard Ruby say, "Okay, put Daddy back on. I'll see you in a little bit."

Ruby's husband came back on the line.

"I told them I'd be home soon. And Honey?" Charlie saw the image in Ruby's mind of her husband's beautiful brown eyes.

"Yeah?"

"I love you."

"I love you too. Be careful."

"I will. I'll see you in a few minutes."

No-no-no, Charlie thought. As she watched Ruby's long thin index finger tap the screen to end the call, she heard a popping sound fill the air.

Ruby glanced over her right shoulder, and Charlie saw the car that was barreling up the sidewalk, pelting the house on the corner with gunfire. A shot from within lit up the front room.

Ruby's car exploded with glass as the bullet ripped through the side window and lodged in her right temple. Neither Charlie nor Ruby felt a thing as blood gushed from the torn artery and into Ruby's brain. When she slumped forward, the car's horn began to blare.

Hello, Ruby. My name is Final Moment…

405 Pine Street

As abruptly as switching television channels, Charlie heard the clatter of an empty pill bottle, which she watched roll across a tile floor. The noise stopped when it hit a pile of dirty laundry. She eyed a well-nourished roach as it scampered under a sock, its brown antennae twitching with apparent curiosity. Through the slow rotation of dust-encrusted fan blades, she saw the woman lying on the bed beneath them.

Her name is Esta.

Did she just do what I think she just did?

Yes, Charlene, Esta has just ingested an overdose of medication.

Just as Charlie was about to ask another question, her perspective shifted, and she could hear the woman's dwindling thoughts as the medicine seeped into her system.

Fifty years old.

Fifty stinking years old.

And nothing to show for it.

All she had was a stack of bills she couldn't pay, a crappy job she couldn't stand, and a crappy condo she hadn't cleaned in a year. Charlie sensed that Esta was relieved to feel the heaviness creeping through her body. And then recognized a familiar feeling: hopelessness.

Esta was thinking about how everything had been good once. The future had been so bright. But that she'd gradually lost her way and everything had changed over time.

Charlie thought it was the perfect snapshot of her own life since her daddy's death. Since that last hopeful day at the bus stop with her mommy—the woman she'd thought she could count on forever to be there for her. Since Charlie had painfully and repeatedly discovered that not to be the case in the years since, she had contemplated doing exactly what Esta was doing more than once. She felt like cheering her on. But somehow, it didn't seem right to do that. In fact, for the first time ever, she thought about what God might think. And that maybe he didn't want people to decide on their own when it was time to die.

Once that thought occurred to her, she longed for a bucket of cold water to dump over the unmoving Esta. To startle her out of the progressive heaviness Charlie felt overtaking her body. The slowing of her heart rate. The pauses that grew longer between each breath.

Charlie knew Final was about to step in and screamed with the same silent helplessness she had from within the wreckage of Dan's car: *Lady, wake up!*

But as she watched Esta's chest fail to rise again and sensed her relief that she'd finally gotten it right, Charlie knew it was too late.

Hello, Esta. My name is Final Moment…

~

N1947B

When the flicker of Esta's ceiling fan was replaced by the flicker of a propeller against the waning horizon, Charlie realized she was in the cockpit of an airplane. Except for the glow of the instrument panel, inky blackness surrounded her, and call numbers crackled through the headset she felt over the pilot's ears.

Oh c'mon, Final. I hope this isn't what I think it is.
His name is Galen. He is a businessman.
But are we—

Charlie knew it was no use. Instead, she watched Galen's coat-clad arm reach in front of her to adjust a knob. Then his hand returned to lightly grip the cold, angular surface of the yoke in front of him that controlled the plane. His eyes shifted from the instrument panel to a cluster of twinkling lights directly ahead, and somehow Charlie knew it was Ripple Creek. It was a clear night, and the horizon was dotted with pockets of light from distant cities that glowed like birthday candles in the dark. The hum of the engine murmured beyond the headset, its vibration palpable through the leather seat beneath him. Charlie felt the chill on the tip of Galen's nose and wondered why he didn't turn up the heat.

Then she felt something else: pride. It surged through Galen like the rush of a river. She knew he was thinking his business trip had been a huge success that was going to do a lot of good for the homeless shelters in the Montpelier region. That his new plane had been worth the money and a valuable addition to his portfolio. That all of his hard work and determination over the years had paid off and his profile in the community would continue to grow. That with all of his wealth and growing influence, he'd be able to single-handedly change the world. He glanced at his gold watch to see if he had time to take his business partners out to celebrate.

With her dual perspective, Charlie saw the lights of the other plane long before Galen did. She wanted to grab his chin and turn his head to the side. She didn't understand how the plane couldn't see them or why Galen was still admiring his watch. He lifted his left hand from the yoke and pushed in one of the buttons on the side of its face, which lit up with a bright blue hue to reveal a series of numbers. When he reached for the computer tablet at his side, she wanted to scream for him to look up.

By the time he spotted the red portside light of the plane emerging from his blind spot, it was too late. Its nose ripped through the cabin, which exploded into flames. Galen's charred body shot upward into the air, a ragdoll climbing through space.

Hello, Galen. My name is Final Moment...

~

Ripple Creek Care Facility
300 Cherry Street

Charlie smelled urine. She gazed at the old man slouched in his wheelchair, staring into a plate of food that hadn't been touched.

Final. No. I definitely don't want to be in that guy's head.

Do not worry, Charlene. Your visit to Duff will be an exception. Although you will be able to hear our conversation, you will not experience his perspective.

Charlie eyed the saliva that trailed down the right side of the man's stubbled chin and the soiled bib that hung haphazardly over his concave chest.

What's wrong with him?

Duff had a stroke many years ago and is unable to care for himself.

She listened as a game show blared from the activity room. An attendant had his feet up on a table and was sipping coffee and reading the newspaper. Duff eyed him without moving his hanging head, peering over the tops of his filthy spectacles. His lips spread into a thin, drooping line.

Is he smiling?

Yes, Charlene. Duff has many dark thoughts. Currently they are about his attendant.

How long before he dies? He gives me the creeps.

It will not be long. A small piece of debris has just dislodged from a bed of plaque in his left carotid artery and is about to block the flow of blood to his brainstem.

As if on cue, Duff slumped forward, burying his beak of a nose in the pile of mashed potatoes. As gravy oozed into his nostrils, his eyes flickered shut.

Hello, Duff. My name is Final Moment…

1350 Cherry Street

The sudden transition from the cold darkness of being with Duff to the warmth and light of the home was like walking into a bakery on a sunny morning.

In the bed below, Charlie watched the woman's bony chest seesaw under her satin gown as she struggled to breathe.

Final, wait. I need a break.

I know Duff's visit was difficult, Charlene. But Anna is quite prepared for my arrival. Unlike the others, you will be able to interact with her directly.

"What is it, Mom?"

Charlie's perspective shifted to the woman's in the bed, which is how she knew the voice was that of her daughter, Patch.

It's no good anymore. Although Anna was too weak to utter the words, Charlie heard them loud and clear.

"It's okay," Patch whispered. "I'm right here."

Tender lips brushed Anna's forehead. Charlie knew she was trying to open her eyes and recognized the profound weakness that prevented her from doing so. However, she managed to turn one corner of her mouth up ever so slightly.

"You hear me." Patch opened Anna's palm and inhaled in a way that was part sob and part goodbye. Moisture trickled onto Anna's thumb. "I love you, Mom."

I love you too, Patch. More than you'll ever know.

Charlie felt a surge of warmth rush through Anna more powerful than anything she'd ever experienced.

As Anna completed the thought, a flapping sensation filled her chest and then she couldn't breathe. And neither could Charlie.

Final!

"It's okay, Anna. I'm right here. I have your medicine."

Charlie watched a woman with a stethoscope around her neck lean toward the bed. There was a gentle touch on Anna's lips, parting them slightly and then Charlie tasted something strong.

"Let's put your head up a little more, and get some air on your face." The motor of the electric bed started to hum, and a breeze began to blow as the woman held a small fan in front of Anna's cheeks. It was like opening a window to a suffocating room. Charlie felt the balm of the medication as it began to seep into Anna's body.

Hello, Anna.

Anna tried to open her eyes. *Who said that?*

My name is Final Moment.

Really? You mean THE final moment?

Yes. The mitral valve in your heart just failed. Your lungs are filling with fluid.

I'm dying right now?

Yes. I visit everyone who leaves earth during their last sixty seconds.

Mercy sakes. Sixty seconds. Out of a lifetime.

Charlie decided to try her voice.

Hi, Anna.

Why, that sounds like a child.

Anna, this is Charlene. She is sixteen.

It's very nice to meet you, Charlene.

Thanks. You can call me Charlie.

Are you—

Charlene is accompanying me this evening, Anna.

I see.

She has had much to learn.

I understand completely.

I am here to conduct the Regrets Evaluation and Pliability Assessment, though the latter will not be necessary in your case. Do you have regrets, Anna?

There was a pause, and Charlie wondered what Anna was thinking. For some reason, she had no idea.

I honestly don't think I do. Except I wish I could've helped more people know the Lord.

You have been a faithful servant, Anna, living your life with integrity.

But Charlie, I'm concerned for you, child. Why you're here. I bet you're like my Patch used to be.

Charlie was startled and touched by the fact that Anna was worried about her when she was in the midst of her own death.

I appreciate that, Anna. But there's really not much time.

If the Father has placed you here with me, there's a reason for it.

Okay, why do you think I'm like Patch?

Let's just say that Patch has always been very strong-willed. Are you familiar with the story of the prodigal son in the Bible, Charlie?

Yeah.

Well, that's me and my Patch.

What do you mean?

Opinions and circumstances couldn't separate us. Our love runs much too deep.

But the prodigal son really messed up.

That was us. When it was time to heal, we forgave each other and moved forward.

I wish I had that kind of thing with my mom.

You'd be surprised at the depth of a mother's love, Charlie. Perhaps there are things you don't yet understand.

What do you mean?

Charlie, everyone goes through difficult seasons at one time or another. I've had my own journey, too.

You mean you weren't always such a church lady?

Me? A church lady? Now that's hilarious.

But you seem so—

Loving God doesn't have anything to do with appearances, Charlie.

My mother seems to think so.

If you're a teenager, your mother is young. Perhaps she's still finding her way. The fact that you're impacted by that process doesn't diminish her love for you.

Charlie longed to curl up next to this loving woman and settle in for a long talk. Instead, she heard Final begin to wrap things up.

Anna, our time is nearly complete. Is there anything else?

Will my family be okay?

They will miss you. But they appear to be ready.

My Patch?

The Father will help her.

My sweet husband?

He is waiting eagerly for you.

What about Charlie?

What is the context of your inquiry?

What will happen to her?

If it was possible to hold her breath, Charlie did so as she listened for Final's response.

I am not privileged to that information, Anna.

Well, then I do have one more thing.

Yes, Anna?

My final prayer.

He is always listening.

Father, help Charlie. Please give her another chance.

Chapter 4

*H*ello, *Charlie.*

The voice was soothing and gentle. Nothing like the no-nonsense tone Charlie had become accustomed to with Final. *Who are you?*

My name is Grace.

Where's Final?

Final's mission with you is complete. I'm with you now.

Are you an angel?

I'm here to help you through the next leg of your journey.

Am I going to heaven now?

No, Charlie, you are not going to heaven now.

Oh.

You sound disappointed.

Well, yeah. I visited all those people with Final, and I thought maybe God might change his mind about me.

Why would he do that?

I thought maybe he'd give me another chance.

Do you think you deserve another chance, Charlie?

I don't know. I'm really confused about everything.

Are you sorry for all you did?

Absolutely.

And the Son?

Yeah, I want that. Him. However I say that. I learned a whole bunch of stuff with Final.

Yes, Final helps many people.

You know him?

We occasionally cross paths.

So if I'm not going to heaven…

What is it, Charlie?

Grace, am I going to hell now?

No, child, you are not going to hell.

Well, if I'm not going to heaven and I'm not going to hell—

God still has plans for you, Charlie. You're going back.

"Clear!" The current of electricity surged through Charlie and she bolted upright, swinging.

"Whoa! Welcome back!"

It was more like a wrestling nightmare than a homecoming. Her arms and legs were pinned to the cart and pain shot through her body. Her attempts to scream were useless and searing light blinded her.

Grace lied. I must be in hell.

"Charlie. Settle down. It's okay. You're going to be okay." The voice belonged to a man. It wasn't Final and it wasn't Grace. Someone else. Someone real. She opened her eyes in a frantic search. Two men in blue stared down at her, smiling.

"We're here. It's okay." His tone was a ragged whisper as he touched her cheek. "We thought we'd lost you."

"Charlie!"

Mom?

"Ma'am, hang on. You can see her in a minute."

"But my baby. I want my baby!"

"Honey, wait. Just let them work on her." Charlie recognized Dan's voice.

I want my mom! Charlie tried to say it but felt the tube in her throat. She ripped her hand free and yanked it out in one swift motion, creating a path of fire in her airway.

"Mom!" She felt like she screamed it, but the word came out in a croak.

Before she could try again, her mom was at her side, kissing her face, tears spilling onto Charlie's skin. "I'm here, honey, I'm here."

Charlie tried to speak, but the words were little more than fragments of sound. "I'm sorry, and I love you and—"

Her mom placed a finger over Charlie's parched lips. "Shh… it's okay. It's okay."

"But I—"

"You just rest. We're right here."

"Hey, Charlie. There's my girl."

"Dan?"

She felt the weight of his hand on her lower leg. "I'd come in there, but I don't think I'll fit."

She looked up at her mom. "Tell him I'm sorry I wrecked his car, and I've been so mean, and—"

Dan's voice at her feet was gentle. "I can hear you, and there's no need for all that. We're just grateful to have you back."

Charlie tried to move her head but couldn't. All she could see was that she was in a tiny space with medical equipment tucked into every available crevice.

The paramedic placed a gentle hand on her forehead. "It's a neck brace, Charlie. We have to leave it on until they clear your spine."

"Where am I?"

"You're still in the ambulance," he said.

"But I died in the ambulance. I saw it. I saw all of you."

"You're right kid, you did."

"What?"

Charlie heard the shock in her mother's voice.

"Yes, ma'am. Her heart was stopped for a good while."

"But how—"

"Beats me. Honestly, we'd given up. I was about to put the paddles away. But out of the blue I had the sense I should shock her one more time."

"What about her—"

"Brain? Looks like it works just fine to me."

The paramedic buckled a strap across her chest. "We've gotta get you to the hospital, Charlie."

Charlie gripped her mother's arm. "Don't leave me."

Her mom looked up at the paramedic.

"It's okay, ma'am. You stay right where you are."

Charlie savored the sweet lull of sedation. The pain that had raged through her body was a distant memory. She smelled rubbing alcohol and disinfectants. Vomit and blood. Her mother's perfume. The *ping* of monitors circled her. Distant voices floated toward her. A shiver that wouldn't stop wracked her body. Previous experience told her she must be in the emergency room.

"Mom?" Her eyelids were too heavy to open. Plus she knew there was a glaring overhead light just waiting to blind her.

She heard movement beside her and felt her mother's lips on her forehead. "I'm here, honey."

Charlie opened her eyes and looked at her beautiful mother, who was hovering over her, a frown lining her brow. Charlie felt a single tear trickle down her right cheek. "I'm so sorry, Mom."

Her mother shook her head. "Charlie, you don't—"

"For everything. For giving you such a hard time for so long."

"You haven't—"

"For being such a brat and mouthing off and hating your husbands."

"I heard that."

"Dan?"

"Right here, Charlie." He moved to her other side. He was more handsome than she remembered, and his eyes were kinder.

"I'm sorry I wrecked your car."

He nodded. "I'm just grateful you're okay."

"Why?"

"Why what?"

"Why are you grateful I'm okay?" Charlie began to weep. "I've been so mean to you." She looked at her mother. "To both of you."

Her mom took her face in her hands. "Honey, I love you no matter what."

For the first time in years, Charlie didn't feel like an orphan. "I guess Final was right."

"Final?"

She smiled. "Just some weird guy I met."

"He couldn't have been too weird if he told you how much I love you."

"Yeah, he didn't end up being so weird after all."

~

Charlie held her breath as the cart rattled beneath her. Each bump shot pain through her body, convincing her the orderly was aiming for every imperfection he could find between the emergency room and X-ray. A wave of nausea washed through her.

"Hey, can you slow down a little? I'm gonna barf."

"Oh, sorry." The cart slowed, and she opened her eyes to stare at the checkerboard of lights passing over her. She was glad to be done with the smell of smoke and gas at the wreck but now wondered if she'd ever get the stench of antiseptic out of her nostrils. Nervous laughter drifted from the other end of the hall. It reminded her of school, and she wondered why they were letting loud kids roam around in a place where you're supposed to have peace and quiet.

"Boys, shh."

"Sorry. We just—"

"You're just in a lot of pain." The woman's voice broke. It was familiar, and Charlie tried to place it. "You boys are going to be okay, Jig. God will help us."

Jig.

She knew it. They must be leaving after Ian's death. Her heart pounded so hard she was sure the orderly could hear it. As the voices grew closer, she wrapped her fingers around the frigid side rail. She tried to sit up, but the pain in her chest pinned her back onto the cart.

"Whoa. What are you doing?" The orderly put a hand on her shoulder.

"I need to talk to them."

"To who?"

"Those people. I—" She stuck a hand through the rail. Jig was closest, and she grabbed a fistful of dirty t-shirt. Charlie's cart stopped with a jerk.

"Hey! What the—"

"I saw you."

"Saw me? What are you talking about?"

"With Ian. I saw you."

The color drained from Jig's face as Ian's mother gently unraveled Charlie's fingers from the fabric. "Honey, here. Let go."

She locked onto the women's red-rimmed eyes. "And you, too. You're a great mom."

The woman's chin began to quiver. "Who are you?" she whispered.

The orderly's voice was apologetic. "She was in an accident. I thought she didn't have a head injury, but—"

"I don't have a head injury. I saw all of you with Ian. The rest of you are Finn and Skeeter and Zip, right? But Ian—"

"Died." Finn stepped toward her. "And I don't know what kind of freakin' game you're playing."

"Finn, I'm not playing a game. I...I died too."

"You..." His mom pulled away.

The orderly looked at Charlie and nodded. "She's right, lady."

"And you—"

"Yes. Ian was the first one I met. Well, after Final, that is."

"Final?"

"Final Moment. He's this guy…well, more like a spirit…that visits in the last sixty seconds before we die."

Ian's mother shook her head. Her face looked like it'd gone numb. "I don't understand."

Charlie nodded. "I don't blame you. I'm still trying to figure it out."

"I still don't get how you saw all of us," Zip said.

"It was when I was dead."

"When you were dead?" Skeeter's voice was barely audible at the foot of her cart. Charlie managed to prop herself up on one elbow to look at him.

"I know it sounds weird."

Jig glared at her. "You're weird, that's what's weird."

Zip moved in beside him. "Yeah, and if you think your accident was bad—"

"Boys." Ian's mother regained her voice and took a protective stance between Charlie and her ragged pack. She touched Charlie's cheek. "I'm sorry this all happened to you, honey. But I think maybe the trauma—"

Charlie sat up, lifted the hand from her cheek, and cupped it between her own as she gazed at the woman. "He said you were his constant."

When Ian's mother closed her eyes, little pebbles of tears tumbled down her cheeks.

"He said you wore out the knees of your jeans praying for him."

The woman's chin began to quiver.

"You made homemade oatmeal cookies to get them all to do their homework every night. And go to church. He said he made a lot of mistakes but turned his life around. And found God. And apologized to you."

Her knees buckled, and Zip grabbed her. All four boys wrapped their arms around Ian's mother. Then they began to weep.

"I think that's enough, kid," the orderly whispered in her ear.

Charlie's cheeks were wet when she fell back onto the cart, stared at the ceiling light, and listened to their pain.

Gradually, sniffles replaced sobs as she heard them move apart. His mother reached over the rail and placed her hand over Charlie's. Her eyes were puffy, but her expression was peaceful. Her voice was barely a whisper.

"Tell me. What else did my boy say?"

Charlie was too exhausted to keep her eyes open and too exhausted to sleep. She looked at her mother's long, thin fingers laced within her own, evidence of her determination never to let Charlie leave her again. Her mom's head dipped toward her chest as she nodded off, her slender frame perched on the folding metal chair beside Charlie's cart.

She wished they'd assign her to a room already. Since the nurse wouldn't let them shut the door, the only thing separating her from the noise in the hallway was a curtain she could practically see through. She longed for a real bed and some privacy so she and her mom could get some sleep. After that, maybe she'd tell her about seeing Ian's mom.

"Why'd you bring him here?" The female voice in the hall sounded irritated. A shadow of chaos passed by her curtain as radios crackled.

"This is the only hospital in Ripple Creek." The man sounded young. And confused.

"Of course it's the only hospital in Ripple Creek. Which is why people who have obviously been deceased for this long should not be brought into the emergency room."

"Oh. Sorry. We're—"

The woman's sigh was loud enough for Charlie to hear. "New. Obviously. Never mind. Just…bring him in here."

Her mom stared at the curtain as she absently patted Charlie's hand. She knew they were both thinking the same thing: it could've been her. Which gave Charlie a new appreciation for Final and Grace.

A muted conversation drifted from the room. "Do we have any idea about next of kin?" Charlie decided the irritated woman must be the nurse in charge.

"Yeah. There was an emergency notification card in his pocket. Same last name. Says it's his wife."

"Where was he found?"

"Behind the tavern. Next to a dumpster."

Charlie sat up.

"Honey, what is it?"

"Did he just say they found that guy by a dumpster?" she whispered.

"I think so."

"Can you find out what his name is?"

"Honey, I don't think I should—"

Charlie tugged her hand like a toddler. "Mom, please. It's important."

Her mother looked at her like she also suspected a head injury. "I'll try, but they probably won't tell me."

"Thanks. Just do it." Charlie propped herself up and watched her mom approach the curtain as if it might attack. She poked her head into the hallway without committing her feet.

"Excuse me."

No response from the hallway. She looked back at Charlie and shook her head. "They—"

"You didn't even try."

Her mom gave her a look that crossed practiced exasperation with the gratitude of having one's daughter back from the dead. She took a deep breath, pushed aside the curtain, and this time committed her whole body to her mission. "Excuse me, sir?"

Charlie saw a tall paramedic writing on a clipboard. When his radio crackled on his belt, he rolled a knob between his thumb and index finger to turn it down. "Can I help you?"

Her mother's body slumped with apology. "I hate to bother you, but that patient you just brought in?"

"Yes."

She hesitated and looked back at Charlie, who was vigorously nodding her head. "I know you probably can't do this, but my daughter wants me to find out what his name is."

The paramedic shook his head. "You're right, ma'am. Patient privacy. I can't give you his name."

"But I think I know him." Charlie blurted it out, mowing over any effort to be polite.

Her mother dropped her head and shook it in slow resignation. The paramedic looked over her shoulder. He eyed Charlie as he stepped into her room. "Aren't you the kid who was in the accident?"

She nodded.

"Heard you died and came back."

Her mother recovered and assumed her post next to Charlie's side. "Don't even say that. She didn't die."

Charlie looked at her, realizing it might not be possible to explain everything after all. "You know it's true, Mom."

"You were just unconscious for several minutes."

"I was dead for several minutes."

"So I heard."

Her mother glared at the man. "How do you—"

Charlie pointed at his waist. "Radios, Mom."

"Yeah, we hear everything around town all shift. It's been a busy night."

Charlie sighed. "Tell me about it."

"So what's the deal with the guy next door? You think you know him, huh?"

"Yeah, I think I do."

"I doubt it. Looked like a loner." He patted her foot and turned to leave. "Sorry, kid. No can do."

"Was it Shane?"

He hesitated but didn't turn around. Then he stepped into

the hall and gave her a final glance. "You didn't hear it from me."

As soon as the words left his lips, the hallway erupted with activity once again. Another blast of cold air and the smell of exhaust signaled the latest arrival. Her mother pulled the curtain closed.

"Over here. In six." The voice was male. Rushed. The energy of resuscitation swooshed by her curtain with intense silence, broken only by the pinging of the monitor and the crackle of radios. Someone calmly provided the details, of which she could hear every word.

"Single GSW to the head. Bullet entered her right temple with no exit wound. She was in full arrest when we arrived and resuscitation protocol initiated."

Charlie sat up, holding her breath.

"Any signs of response?"

"None. No pulse, no respirations when CPR stopped."

"Then why are we still trying to resuscitate her?"

"License says she's an organ donor."

"Oh, that's a different story. We'll need to establish brain death and talk to the family. The donation company will want the details of resuscitation efforts."

"Everything's here."

"You got a name?"

"Let's see…here it is. Her first name is Ruby."

Sleep was an impossibility. Charlie stared at the ceiling above her cart as her mind raced. She knew there must be something she was supposed to do about the fact that Shane was lying across the hall, officially dead, and Ruby was lying in the room next door, almost-officially dead.

She looked at the empty chair her mother had vacated in search of coffee. Dan had gone home, and Charlie felt very alone. She had the absurd thought that it'd be nice to talk to Final, then remembered that talking with him meant you were almost dead, so she decided Grace would be a better option.

God would be a better option, Charlie.

Grace? Is that you?

Yes, it's me.

Oh, it's so good to hear your voice.

It's good to hear you seeking guidance, Charlie.

Do you see what's happening down here? I ran into Ian's mom and friends, and then Shane ends up across the hall, and Ruby's in the room next door!

Do you think that's a coincidence, Charlie?

No, but I don't know what to do about it.

Charlie, let me introduce you to Someone else who will help you from now on.

Wait—you're leaving?

No, I will always be here when you need me. And there will be many times in your future when that will be the case.

But why can't you just stay and tell me what I should do?

That's not my role, Charlie.

But I like you.

And I you. You're easy to get attached to.

But, Grace, then—

Charlie, I have Someone very important for you to meet.

Oh, no. Not again.

Believe me, you'll be quite pleased, and I am more than honored.

Now who?

Charlie, it is my privilege to introduce you to Spirit.

Hello, Charlie.

Hey.

I understand you are seeking guidance, Charlie.

That's the understatement of the year.

Then we will be fast friends.

So you're a spiritual being like Final and Grace?

He is much more than Final and me, Charlie.

How's that?

Spirit is God.

Whoa! What?

God is Three in One, Charlie. The Father, the Son, and the Spirit.

Like a package deal?

Yes, something like that.

It's true, Charlie. Now that you have accepted the Son, I am the manifestation of God who is always with you, to guide and comfort you.

Wow. You mean we can hang out, and you'll tell me what to do?

We'll work together on that. You must also seek my guidance and listen for my voice.

I'm game if you are.

Chapter 5

An hour earlier, Charlie would've given anything to get out of the ER. Now she was afraid they'd make her leave and she'd never figure out what it was she was supposed to do. She thought about her new relationship with Spirit and wondered how all this guidance and comfort was going to work.

"Let's check some vitals, Charlie." Her nurse whipped back the curtain and held a temperature probe in front of her forehead in one swift motion. She punched a button on the blood pressure machine, and the cuff inflated to the pressure of a hungry python. Charlie glared at her and hoped Spirit didn't know what she was thinking.

"Everything looks good. You need anything?"

Charlie didn't respond. She was absorbed in watching the young woman who was standing outside of Shane's room, holding a little boy's hand. The curtain had been drawn and the door closed. She looked uncertain about going in.

"Charlie?" Her nurse looked at her and then followed her gaze. She took a few steps out of the cubicle. "Miss? Can I help you?"

The woman was thin, with short, thick brown hair, and a peaceful presence that reminded Charlie of Ruby. The boy slid behind her leg and peered up at the nurse. Then his eyes locked on Charlie, who was watching him intently.

"I got a phone call about my husband."

The nurse glanced at Shane's curtained door, then back at the woman. Her gaze drifted down to the boy. "Your husband?"

"Yes. They said you'd keep him here until we got here." She lifted a timid finger and pointed. "The lady at the desk said he's in there."

The nurse touched her elbow as her voice took on a gentle tone. "What's your husband's name?"

The woman let out a sigh that spelled a lifetime of sorrow. "Shane." She reached around and absently stroked her son's curly red hair. "His name was Shane McDonough."

The hallway outside her cubicle was oddly quiet, and Charlie knew she wouldn't have much time before her mother returned and Shane's wife decided to leave. She lowered her bare feet onto the cold tile, tied the gown around her waist, and turned off the heart monitor. Every inch of her body reminded her she was dead not long ago, but she pushed the pain aside and unplugged her IV pump. Gripping the pole for a crutch, she rolled it beside her like a scarecrow on wheels and inched her way toward the hall.

"Ruby's over here, sir. In bay five."

Charlie froze.

"Did she…"

She heard the pain in his voice. Charlie parted the curtain across her doorway and peeked through the crack. Ruby's husband was probably handsome when his eyes weren't so red and puffy.

"It was very quick, sir. I'm sure she didn't suffer."

"Can I…see her?"

"Certainly, please follow me. We'll talk more when you're ready."

Charlie took a step back and slumped into her mom's chair. She thought she might throw up.

Spirit? Are you there?

After all that'd been happening in her head in her alive, then dead, then alive recent past, the last thing she expected was silence.

Spirit?

Her room was too quiet with her heart monitor unplugged.

I could use your help. I'm a little freaked out right now.

A cart clattered past her room, and another radio crackled. She knew her mom was going to be back any minute, and Shane's wife was going to decide it was too much for the kid.

Charlie sighed. She was just starting to get excited about the idea of hanging out with God.

I'm right here, child.

Spirit? Oh, thank God. I mean—

What would you like to do, Charlie?

I don't know, but I think I'm supposed to talk to them.

Which?

Both. They're both here. That must mean I'm supposed to do something.

Do you know why you want to talk to them, Charlie?

Because I want to help them.

And how will you do that?

I know stuff they need to know.

Like?

Shane's wife needs to know that Final told him about how she'd changed and about his son.

Good. What else?

I got the feeling he was sorry for what he did to them. Oh, and that he accepted Jesus like she did. And that he got to go to Heaven.

And you want to tell her that?

Yeah, I think it'll help them.

How do you think it will help them?

Maybe she'll know he wasn't so bad after all, and the boy will grow up knowing that, too.

Good, Charlie. That's very good.

~

Since she had to duck back behind her curtain several times before the coast was clear, and a steady arctic wind was blowing from somewhere down the hall, Charlie felt like she was walking on ice cubes by the time she got to Shane's door. She lifted a trembling hand and placed her palm on the cool metal handle.

The woman and child both looked up when they heard the click of the latch and saw Charlie maneuvering her IV pole through the parted curtain. Then she stopped, her heart in her throat, her back against the door, as she stared at Shane's motionless body on the cart. Someone had cleaned him up and combed his hair and beard. A white sheet was folded neatly across his chest so that only his peaceful, ashen face was visible. When the floor tiles began to spin, Charlie decided this might not be such a good idea after all.

"Are you okay?" She felt the woman's hands on her shoulders as they rescued her from toppling over. "Son, bring Mama that chair."

Since Charlie's world had turned almost black, she was only able to imagine the tug-of-war the little guy was having with the chair that was being scraped toward her. Finally, she felt cool metal behind her knees and gentle pressure on her shoulders, sitting her down. She put her head between her knees and the merry-go-round began to slow.

"Can't you find your room, honey?" The voice was as thick and sweet as the word itself.

Charlie eased to a sitting position as the boy stared at her. She looked at Shane's wife and shook her head. "No. I'm not lost."

"But this—"

"You're Shane's wife, right?"

The woman studied her without speaking. Finally, she nodded. "Yes, that's right."

"And this is his boy."

His mother pulled him close. "Look, I don't mean to be rude. I can see you've been hurt—"

"I know this is weird, but I've got something to tell you and if I don't do it pretty soon, I'll either lose the guts to do it or pass out right on this floor."

The woman knelt in front of her. The boy peered over her shoulder from behind. Charlie took a big breath. "This will probably sound crazy…"

The woman put a hand on Charlie's knee. "Honey, I'm fairly familiar with crazy."

Charlie nodded and plunged into her news. "My name's Charlie. I died, and I was with Shane when he died." She slumped back in the chair and breathed.

The woman slowly removed her hand and leaned back on her heels. The boy watched his mother and then looked at Charlie.

"What'd you just say?"

Charlie shrugged a little. "I warned you."

"You died?"

"Yes."

The woman absorbed her words. "Apparently that wasn't the end of it."

"Apparently."

"Why were you with Shane when he died? Were you a friend of his?"

"No, I wasn't physically with him. I was with him in…spirit?"

"In spirit."

"Really, ma'am. There's nothing wrong with my head, I promise."

The woman took a deep breath and then exhaled as if propping up her resolve to listen to such a story. "Go on."

Charlie licked her lips, which cracked with the effort. "When I died, I was visited by a spiritual being named Final Moment."

"Final Moment."

Charlie was afraid the woman would bolt with the kid and call security. Her words tumbled out. "Yeah. He's this guy who visits everybody during the last sixty seconds before they die. He was with me and then we were with Shane."

The woman watched Charlie without speaking. The boy tugged at her shoulder and began to whimper.

Charlie sighed. "I know it sounds crazy."

"Honey, this is a very confusing day for me, so I really don't think I can manage much more."

"Okay, okay. I'll make it quick. Just hear me out."

She pulled the boy into her arms. "Quickly, then."

"When I died, Final went over my life with me and things didn't look so good. I don't think I was supposed to get another chance, but at the last minute, something happened, and he took me with him."

"Took you with him?"

"Yes, to see everybody else. You know, before they died."

"And he—"

"Right. He took me with him when he visited Shane."

"Honey, I don't—"

"He said Shane left you when he found out you were pregnant." She held her breath and watched as the color drained from the woman's face. The woman ran her fingers through her son's thick curly hair, her hands deftly covering his ears.

"He said Shane had a bad problem with drugs and booze and that was why he was so messed up."

A single tear trickled down the woman's right cheek. She gazed into the red mop of hair under her hand and murmured as if talking to herself. "I don't know how this is possible."

Charlie felt awful, which wasn't how she'd thought she'd feel. "I'm sorry. I don't mean to make things worse."

The woman smiled at her sadly. "Believe me, honey. You couldn't possibly make things worse."

"I think he was sorry." She blurted out the words.

"Mama…" The boy tugged at his mother's fingers as he tried to pull her toward the door. Caught on Charlie's last words, she didn't seem to notice.

"He was?"

Charlie nodded. "He didn't know a bunch of stuff about you and how you'd changed and found God and his son has a chin just like his and you were waiting for him to come home."

The woman took a quick breath and put her hand to her mouth. Two puddles of tears threatened to spill onto her cheeks. "How—"

"Final knew all that stuff. And he told Shane. That's when he started saying he wanted another chance with you guys."

"He did?"

"Yeah, but being it was last minute and all…"

"But he knew I loved him before he died?"

Charlie nodded. "Final told him."

"And he knew about our son?"

"Yeah. At first he said he was mad about you being pregnant and not going through with…" Charlie glanced at the boy. "You know. But then he was really happy when he heard about his chin and how much he looked like him."

Relief crossed the woman's face like a swell on the sea. Charlie started to feel a little better.

"What about his…soul?"

"Oh, I almost forgot. Final said that was the best part."

"What was the best part?"

"He did it."

"Did what?"

"God. Jesus. He said he was sorry and accepted him."

When the woman's hands shot into the air, the little boy took a step back and stared. "Oh, praise the Lord! I can't believe it!"

"I know. It was at the very last second, but Final said it still counted."

His wife stood from where she'd been kneeling and grabbed a tissue from the box on the bottom of Shane's cart. She patted the tears from her eyes and blew her nose. "I just can't believe this. Talk about a miracle." Then she looked back at Charlie. "Is there anything else I should know?"

"I don't think so. There was stuff about his dad, but nothing else for you."

"About his father?"

"Final knew his dad was a drinker, too. I don't know what happened, but it seemed bad. But he said he quit drinking and tried to find Shane to apologize to him."

"He told Shane that?"

"He did. Shane seemed surprised. But relieved, too. He said he knew his dad was a good man once. That he would've given him another chance if he'd really changed."

"He did change for a while. But then…"

"I know. Final said he started drinking again."

"He did. I've tried to stay in contact, but he doesn't seem interested. I still have hope he'll get to meet his grandson someday."

Charlie looped her fingers around her IV pole and gingerly stood. "My mom's going to be looking for me. I hope it's okay I told you all that."

Shane's wife leaned in and gave Charlie a hug. "You've helped us more than you'll ever know, Charlie. Thank you."

Chapter 6

Charlie knew it wasn't a good sign that she could hear her mother's voice before she even opened Shane's door to leave.

"What do you mean, you don't know where she went?"

She cracked open the door and peeked into the hall where two red-faced nurses were trying to calm her mother down.

"Ma'am, if you'll just wait in—"

"I'm not waiting anywhere! My daughter almost died, and now you people can't even keep track of her!"

"Mom." Charlie's voice was quiet. She stepped into the hall with her IV pole in tow and tried not to let her teeth chatter. She realized it wasn't the cold this time but that she was afraid she'd disappointed her mom.

"Charlie." Her mother was on her in three steps and hugged her hard enough it hurt.

"I'm sorry you couldn't find me." She mumbled it into her mom's shoulder as she tried to breathe through the pain of the frantic embrace.

Then her mother held her at arm's length and examined her. "Why weren't you in your room?" She looked over Charlie's shoulder at the door behind her. "Or maybe I should ask why you were in that room." Her voice held an edge of disappointment.

Charlie shook her head. "I wasn't doing anything wrong, Mom. I swear."

Her mother took a deep breath as if committing to a new resolution to believe her daughter. "I didn't think you were. I was just worried about you."

Both nurses glared at Charlie with none of her mother's compassion. One pointed toward her room. "Let's go. I've got to hook you back up."

Charlie guided her IV pole into her room and crawled onto the cart like an obedient child. Her mom was right on her heels. "Now, I'm not accusing you of anything, but I would like to know why you were in that room."

"As would I." The nurse continued to work as she said it.

Charlie looked back and forth between them. "Ma'am, I'm sorry I went in there. But would it be okay if I talk to my mom alone about it?"

The nurse punched the heart rate monitor back on. "Whatever." Then she tapped something into the computer and left the room.

Her mother crossed her arms, waiting.

"I'm afraid you're going to think I'm crazy."

"Honey, I'm so glad to have you back I wouldn't care if you had three heads."

"But, Mom, I'm not crazy. What I'm going to say is true."

Her mother paused, then nodded. "Okay, then I promise to believe whatever you tell me is true."

Charlie's eyes widened. She'd never thought she'd hear those words come out of her mother's mouth. "Really?"

"Really." Her mom smiled, then patted Charlie's knee. "As long as you promise what you tell me is true."

"Absolutely."

"Okay, then. Shoot."

For starters, Charlie thought maybe she should stick to her own visit with Final. She took a deep breath and plunged in. By the time she finished, her mother was giving her a wide-eyed stare.

"Is that true?"

"Mom…"

"I mean, I know it's true. But really, there's someone who meets us like that just before we die?"

Charlie exhaled with relief. "Yeah, and he makes you tell him stuff about your life, like what good stuff you did and what bad stuff, and he knows everything."

"Everything?"

Charlie nodded.

"I bet that was uncomfortable."

"You have no idea. Especially…" Charlie reached for her nose ring, which was the first time she realized it wasn't there. She ran her finger along the space between her nose and her upper lip as she thought about Rose and ached for the cool round comfort she was accustomed to finding there.

Her mom reached for the sheet at the bottom of the cart and tugged it up to Charlie's neck, then folded the top back onto itself and adjusted it into a neat line of material across her daughter's chest. "We don't need to talk about that now. And you can tell me more about this Final Moment when you're ready. You need to rest, and we've got all the time in the world."

Charlie looked up. "Actually, we don't."

"What do you mean?"

"That's why I was in that room."

"Why?"

"Because the dead guy in there was someone I met."

Her mother's mouth went slack. "Someone you—"

"I don't think I was supposed to come back. When Final did my review, things didn't look so good."

Charlie couldn't remember a time when her mother's face looked so pale.

"But at the last minute, something changed, and he got to take me with him."

"With him?"

"On his other visits for the night."

"You mean to—"

"Other people in Ripple Creek who were dying while I was dead."

Her mother sank onto the metal chair. The only sound in the room was the steady blip of Charlie's heart rate monitor as her mom stared into the hall. Then she looked back at her daughter. "So why did you go in that man's room if he's already gone?"

"His wife and son are in there, and I had to tell them some stuff I knew about Shane that would help them."

The look her mother gave her was of someone trying to place a familiar face. "And you did?"

Charlie nodded. "I was scared to death. About passed out right on the floor."

The sculpted lines of her mom's eyebrows folded into a frown. "Oh, honey. You should have waited for me. What'd they say?"

"I think she thought I was crazy at first. But after I told her everything, she knew I couldn't be lying."

"Did it help her?"

"I think so."

The pat her mother gave her was both proper and dismissive. "That's good, honey. It's good to help people."

Charlie looked down at the perfectly manicured nails resting over her hand. Then she looked up. "About that, Mom. Someone else I met is next door."

Her mother's eyes widened. "Another dead man?"

Charlie shook her head. "A dead woman. And I need your help."

~

Charlie was relieved to have her mom taking the lead on this one, though she obviously didn't know how to slide around the rules like Charlie did. She listened from her cart as her mother talked to the nurse outside the curtain.

"She saw him come in and knows his wife."

"I don't think he'd want to talk to anyone right now."

"I'm pretty sure he'd want to talk to her."

"Ma'am, I'm not going to bother him with—"

"Would you please just ask him if he'd be willing to see her?"

"Okay, okay. I'll ask him. And how does Charlie know his wife?"

She heard the hesitation in her mother's voice. "Uh, mutual friends."

The nurse said nothing, but Charlie could hear her sneakers squeaking on the tile as she walked away. Her mother pushed back the curtain and reappeared.

"Well, we'll see."

"I told you we should've just snuck in there."

"Yeah, and if Attila there caught you out of bed again, you'd never have a chance."

Charlie sighed. "I guess you're right."

Her mother smiled. "There are ways to accomplish things within the rules, my sweet rebel."

Out of habit, Charlie glared at her, and then realized she wasn't mad. A slow smile spread across her lips. "I guess I'll have to get used to that concept."

"A second miracle today."

She heard a man clear his throat outside her curtain and then thick fingers appeared at the edge, pulling it wide enough for him to step in. Ruby's husband looked like he'd been dragged behind a car for a mile or two.

"Excuse me, but the nurse—"

Her mom was out of her chair and extending her hand before he could finish, as if greeting him at the front door. "Thank you so much for coming."

He grasped the outstretched hand and looked over at Charlie, who was holding her breath. "You know my wife?"

She nodded. "I met her. This evening."

"This evening?"

"Uh-huh."

"You were at her Bible study?"

"Uh…no."

"Were you in one of her classes?"

"Classes? No."

He stepped closer and eyed her. "Are you sure you have the right person?"

Charlie nodded. "Her name is Ruby, right?"

"Yes, it is."

"And she's a preacher, and you guys have two little girls, right?"

"Yes, but many people—"

"And she was a recovering alcoholic, and you told her she shouldn't have been in that section of town at that time of night and she should get out her pepper spray and not buy drugs." Charlie took a breath and held it, watching him.

He leaned against her cart as if in sudden need of something to prop himself up. "Who are you?" he whispered.

She exhaled and looked at her mother, whose mouth was hanging slightly ajar. She was standing so still she would've blended into the curtain behind her if it hadn't been for the wash of color draining from her face. Charlie felt bad, but knew she had to finish. She turned back to Ruby's husband. "I'm Charlie. I died last night."

"You died?"

"I did. But then I got to go with Final."

"Final?"

Charlie wondered if there was a better way to say all this that didn't make her sound so crazy. "Final Moment. He's a spiritual being who visits people in the last sixty seconds before they die."

"What do you mean you visited my wife?"

"He visited her, and I was with him."

"Why were you with him?"

"I think I was his project."

"What makes you say that?"

"I think I got a bad report card on the first round and seems like God gave me another chance."

Ruby's husband looked at Charlie's mom, who was now staring at the floor, slowly shaking her head. He eyed her with uncertainty, then gestured toward the metal chair. "Do you mind?"

She startled, and then nodded. "Of course."

The rubber tips on the ends of the chair legs thumped against the tile floor when he tugged it toward the cart and positioned it in front of Charlie. The metal creaked beneath him when he sat on the edge of the seat and leaned in. "So these visits were a lesson for you?"

"Well, sort of. I mean, mostly they were for the person we were visiting."

"How many did you make?"

"Seven."

"Seven? Wow. What happened during the visits?"

"Final makes people look at their lives and finds out if they have a relationship with God. He gives them the Regrets Evaluation and Pliability Assessment."

"How interesting. To determine preparedness for death."

Charlie nodded. "I think so."

"Willingness to accept the Son."

"That seemed to be—"

"A final chance for salvation."

Charlie gave an impatient sigh. "Mister, don't you want to know what your wife said?"

Ruby's husband leaned back in the chair and smiled so peacefully Charlie thought maybe he was in shock. When he spoke again, his tone was as gentle as balm on a wound. "I already know what she said."

Charlie didn't know how she could be so irritated with a man who had just lost his wife. "How could you know what she said?"

"Because she'd said it many times."

"What, that she loves you?"

He nodded. "And she didn't want to leave us." His eyes shimmered. He blinked hard and looked away. Then he cleared his throat and looked back at Charlie. "I bet she had some advice for you."

Charlie hesitated. "I wasn't allowed to talk to her."

"Well, if she could've, she would've offered some. That's why I loved her so much." His gaze drifted toward the floor. "She was always trying to help someone else."

"She did seem like a nice lady."

"Did visiting her help you?"

The question took Charlie back to the front seat of Ruby's car. To the cracked sidewalk in front of the abortion clinic that Ruby envisioned during her review. To Charlie's Rose. And Ruby's Andrew. She wondered what it was like when Ruby met her boy for the first time. And if their children played together. And if there was any possibility Ruby could take care of Rose until Charlie got there.

"Charlie?"

She looked down at her arm, where Ruby's husband had gently placed his hand. Then she lifted her eyes and held his gaze. "We both did the same bad thing." Somehow she knew Andrew wasn't his child. That Ruby's abortion happened in her former life.

The way he nodded and gently squeezed her arm confirmed that she was right.

When she looked over at her mother, there were tears trailing down her cheeks in two crooked, glistening paths that she made no effort to wipe away. Then she looked back at the man. "But Final said God forgave Ruby the very first time she asked him to, even if she couldn't forgive herself. But I think she finally did. Maybe someday I can, too."

Chapter 7

Saturday

"You're sure she's ready to go home?"

Charlie's mother looked at the nurse doubtfully. The woman was young and had already admitted she'd only recently received her license. She wore a pen behind her ear and a stethoscope around her neck as if they provided proof she knew what she was doing.

Charlie swung her feet to the floor. "Mom—"

"You almost died." Her mother lifted her ankles back onto the mattress and tugged the sheet up to Charlie's neck, folding the fabric just so before stepping back.

Charlie looked at the nurse and rolled her eyes. The girl's smile was all the permission she needed to fling the perfection of her mother's linen arrangement onto the floor and stand up. Her mom gathered the pile of sheets with both hands and glared. "What are you doing?"

"I *did* die, Mom. And now I want to go home."

"Your injuries need time to heal."

The nurse tapped her stack of discharge papers together and shrugged. "That has everyone shaking their heads. If there's nothing to treat…there's nothing to treat." She patted Charlie's shoulder. "She'll be better off at home."

"I knew I liked you. Now, where are my clothes?"

Her mom shook her head. "Your clothes are history. They had to cut everything off."

Charlie swung in a circle, searching the room. "My new jeans?"

"Oh, settle down. We'll get you another pair."

"But—"

"Charlie, do I need to remind you that we're looking at things from a new perspective these days?"

She sank back onto the bed. "No."

Her mom handed her a bag. "Good. Then put these on."

Recognizing the logo of the department store, Charlie handled the bag as if it were a snake. "Put what on?"

Her mother began to pack the contents of her bedside table. "Don't start."

"You bought me clothes from—"

"Your discharge was a bit of a surprise. I didn't have time to run home. Or to the mall. It was the closest store that was open."

"But what if someone sees me?"

Her mom sighed and turned around. "I'd hope they'd be happy to see you alive."

Charlie stared out the window and tried to remind herself she was supposed to be grateful not to be dead, but putting on those clothes would test all of the new good stuff she'd been trying to think. And having to wear them in public would most likely push her over the edge.

"You haven't even looked at them."

"Mom, I know—"

"Good afternoon, ladies." A physician breezed in and rescued them both. "And how are we doing today?"

Charlie frowned. "Don't ask."

He looked back and forth between Charlie and her mom. "Well, regardless, I'm happy to say you're ready to go home. Just be sure to follow-up with your doctor in a week, and call sooner if you start to feel poorly."

Charlie flopped against her pillow. "I feel poorly alright."

"Really?" The man glanced at her paperwork. "I thought—"

"She's fine, doctor. Thank you. We're grateful she's coming home."

"If I didn't wish I was dead."

Her mom raised an eyebrow and looked at her. "Charlie."

She raised her hands in surrender. "Just kidding."

The vibration of his phone distracted the doctor. He glanced at the screen. "Excuse me, I have to take this. Enjoy your day."

Charlie watched him walk from the room. "Unlikely."

"Young lady—"

She held up her hand. "Listen."

Outside her door, Charlie heard a familiar name as the man answered his call. "Esta's sister? Tell her I'll be right down."

She looked at her mom.

"What's wrong?"

"Grab him."

"What?"

"Just do it."

Her mother gave her an exasperated look and poked her head into the hall. "Excuse me, doctor?"

"Yes?"

"My daughter wants to speak with you a moment."

He was tucking the phone back into the holster on his waist when he stepped into the room. "Yes?"

Charlie pointed to his waist. "That call?"

He followed her finger and then looked back up. "What about it?"

"Did I hear you say, *Esta's sister is downstairs?*"

"Why?"

"Well, I ah…I knew Esta." She glanced at her mother, whose eyes were saucers.

The doctor crossed his arms. "You knew Esta."

"Sort of. And I'd like to talk to her sister, if I could."

He shook his head. "I don't—"

"Did they just find her?"

"Who?"

Charlie swung her feet to the floor and stood up, hoping it would make her seem more credible. The sudden breeze on her butt reminded her it might not be possible. She yanked the edge of her gown for cover and looked up at the man. "Look, doc. I know about privacy and all that stuff, but I know some things, so I'll just say them, and then I'll get my answer, okay?"

"Honey—"

Charlie frowned her mother away.

The doctor checked his phone again as if he'd heard enough. "I have rounds—"

"She killed herself last night, right?"

He looked at her and didn't say anything.

"Okay, that's a yes. Did they just find her today?"

The doctor stood still as a stone.

"Another yes. So…is her sister here to identify her body?"

The doctor gave a sigh of resignation.

"Got it. Thanks, doc."

The man rolled his eyes and walked out of the room.

Her mother waved her right index finger like a flag in battle, slowly shaking her head. "No, you're not."

"But, Mom, I have to."

"Charlie, I think you've talked to enough families. You've got to think about yourself."

Charlie started to giggle. Her mom watched her and then began to giggle too, until they were both laughing so hard her mother let out a snort. Charlie fell back onto the bed. "Did you… just…*snort?*"

Her mothered covered her mouth and nodded, still laughing.

Finally, they were both quiet. Her mother took a cleansing breath and looked at Charlie. "I don't even know what we're laughing about."

Charlie smiled. "What you said."

Her mom shook her head, trying to remember. "What'd I say?"

"That I need to think about myself."

"Well, you do. What's so funny about that?"

"I can't believe you don't know."

"Know what?"

"Mom, until I died, the only person I ever thought about was myself."

~

If Final would've told her getting dead and then undead would've meant she could convince her mother to sneak toward some creepy morgue in the hospital's basement with her, she would've signed up long ago.

It was at that moment, with her mom tiptoeing behind her down a dim, cold hall that she realized she needed to start a journal.

She felt her mother's hand on her shoulder.

"Honey," she whispered.

Charlie stopped, scanning the hall ahead as if it were a battle zone without turning around. "What?" she whispered back.

"Why are we whispering?"

Charlie turned around. "I don't know, you started it."

Her mom stood straighter, as if suddenly coming to her senses. "Well, I—"

"You're as freaked out as I am."

Her mother smiled. "It is a little…awkward." Her expression changed as she gazed over Charlie's shoulder.

Charlie turned to look. Her doctor was talking to a woman who looked to be in her mid-fifties. She lifted a tissue and dabbed at one eye, then extended a hand. He shook it and nodded. When he started to go, he saw them and stopped. He paused a moment, as if making a decision. Then he turned back to the woman and said something. She looked in their direction. Then his heels clicked on the tile as he walked toward the elevator.

Neither of them budged as the woman approached. She walked with her head down, as if lining up questions on the squares of the flooring beneath her feet. Charlie pried her mother's vise grip from her shoulder.

"The doctor said you knew my sister." The woman said it when she was several feet away, as if she was afraid they might dart.

Charlie nodded. "I met her."

Her mother patted her shoulder. "Maybe we could find somewhere more private than the hall."

The woman pointed behind her. "There's a family room down there."

They were silent as they walked, as if waiting until just the right moment to open an envelope.

The area supposedly meant for families was nothing but metal chairs and battered side tables. A bare bulb barely lit the room, and the smell of stale coffee filled the air. Charlie's mother sat in the closest thing that would hold her. Charlie sat next, and Esta's sister slowly eased into a chair across from them, eyeing them like a couple of hostages.

"Where did you meet my sister?"

Charlie cleared her throat, and her mother looked away. "It's a little complicated."

"Well, that would certainly explain anything related to Esta."

"I know, she was kind of—"

"A mess."

Charlie looked at her hands. "I didn't want to say that."

Her sister sighed. "It's okay. It's the truth. I guess you know she…died."

Charlie nodded. "Yeah. Killed herself." Her mother jabbed her side and she jumped. "What? The lady knows she killed herself."

"Yes. Unfortunately, it's not the first time she tried to commit suicide."

"I know."

The woman looked at her as if she'd suddenly returned to

earth. "Wait. Who are you? Esta didn't have any friends who were kids. She barely had any friends at all."

"Except the one who tried to get her to go to church with her."

"How do—"

"And I know you called her on the phone while she was dying."

"How could—"

"And that your mother was depressed too, but she got better and tried to help her, and Esta told her she hated her before she died, and that made her depression worse."

Charlie could see the fillings in the woman's molars.

"Uh, lady, maybe you should take a breath."

Esta's sister inhaled and exhaled as if it were a new experience. Swallowing, she shook her head. "How could you possibly know all of that?"

"Because I died too, and my spirit was there with Esta when she died." She watched and waited.

The woman blinked hard, absorbing her words. "You died?"

Charlie nodded.

"And you—"

"Came back to life? I guess. Final—well, I guess it was God who made the decision—gave me a second chance, and I keep running into the families of the dead people I met, so I think I'm supposed to tell you some stuff."

"You've met other families?"

"You're the fourth."

The woman's molars reappeared. "How many people did you meet?"

"Seven."

Esta's sister propped her elbows on her knees and her head in her hands. "I can't believe this." Her voice wandered toward the dirty tile.

Charlie felt the sudden need to touch her, which was a surprise because she usually hated that kind of stuff. She moved to the chair beside the woman. It was cold as a Popsicle against her bony butt, and she was certain the crappy discount jeans were at fault. She hesitated, then rested her hand on the woman's back as if it might bite. "She wanted to tell you she was sorry."

The woman sniffled but didn't look up.

"And that she was too ashamed to let you help her."

Charlie felt the woman's shoulders begin to bob.

"And that she wanted to tell you all that she loves you and should've left a note."

The woman straightened and looked at her. "She did?"

Charlie nodded and then felt bad. "Well, the note part I added because I thought it was a lousy thing for her to do, not leaving you one."

The woman's smile was sad. "You're a nice young lady."

"If I am, that's something new."

Her mother finally chimed in. "Honey, that's not—"

"True? You know it is, Mom." She turned back to Esta's sister. "I've done a lot of stupid stuff so far in my life."

The woman nodded. "Most of us did when we were your age."

"Well, my poor mother didn't deserve it, and you didn't deserve the way Esta treated you."

Her sister's words were a sigh. "I just wanted to help her. We all did."

Charlie took her hand and held it tight. "She knew that, and she was grateful."

"She was?"

Charlie nodded. "She wanted you to know that. Final said maybe God would send somebody to tell you. Guess that somebody was me."

The woman squeezed Charlie's hand and smiled. "I'm glad it was you. Thank you." Then she slipped the loop of her purse over her shoulder and stood. "I guess I should go."

"There's something else."

Esta's sister eased back down into the chair. "There is?"

Charlie glanced at her mom, who appeared to be holding

her breath. She looked back at the woman beside her. "Esta went to Heaven."

The relief that washed over her sister's face had the effect of a wiper clearing a windshield of rain. "I thought she didn't want anything to do with God."

"That's what she said too, at first. But when Final told her it wasn't too late, she changed her mind. It was kinda last second, but when she said she wanted Jesus, Final said Heaven started cheering."

Esta's sister put both hands over her mouth and closed her eyes. Charlie watched a single tear slip from beneath her right eyelid and trickle down her cheek. She hesitated, but then plunged ahead. "And Final said somebody special was waiting for her."

The woman opened her eyes, dropped her hands into her lap, and gazed at Charlie. "Who?"

"Your mom. He said your mom was waiting to welcome her home."

Chapter 8

Sunday

Charlie tapped her mom's phone to end the call and stared out the window at the snow. It had been falling like the aftermath of a pillow fight since early morning. She smelled her mother's approach as she sauntered into the living room with a cup of steaming coffee.

Charlie raised an eyebrow as she watched her curl into the corner chair as if learning a new skill. "Beverages in the living room?"

Her mom shrugged. "Seems we're making some changes." Taking a sip, she eyed Charlie over the cup's rim. "How'd it go?"

"I don't think she believed me."

"That you were sorry? Which, by-the-way, you still haven't explained."

Charlie waved her hand in dismissal. "You don't want to know."

Her mother nodded. "I'm sure you're right." Then she took another sip, adjusted the wooden coaster on the antique table beside her, and placed her cup on it with the care of handling an egg. She looked back at Charlie and smiled. "Maybe your friend just needs time to get used to the new you."

Charlie sighed. "I have a feeling she might not like the new me. Which might be true of all my friends."

"Sometimes it takes a while for people to come around."

"But you guys forgave me right away."

"We're your family. Usually that means the process is easier."

"Yeah. I guess." She stared out the window and tried to remember enjoying the snow as much as the two little boys who were screaming and throwing snowballs across the street.

"Charlie, look at me."

She looked across the room at her mother, wondering if this happiness with each other would last, or if it was just a post-dead thing. And what would happen if her abortion ever got talked about.

"The important thing is you said you're sorry and meant it. You can't control how people respond."

"So I've heard. Dad said it's like sweeping your own side of the street."

Her mother had picked her cup back up and now choked mid-sip. "What'd you say?"

"Well, if you keep your side—"

"Dad?"

Charlie shrugged. "I thought I'd try it for a change. *Dan* is so formal. I'll also have less explaining to do when I introduce him to people." She smiled at her mother, who was moving toward her like a torpedo, arms open wide. She wrapped them around Charlie and squeezed her as hard as she did in the ambulance.

"I'm so proud of you," she whispered.

Charlie blinked back tears and cleared her throat. Finally, she hugged her mother back and hung on.

"What's going on in here?" Dan's booming voice filled the room.

Charlie pulled away, embarrassed.

"Oh, you know, just giving my sweet daughter some love. What're you up to?"

Charlie watched her stepfather look back and forth between them. It was then, when she saw the lack of anything to dislike and remembered her visit with Esta, that she realized he'd been an innocent bystander all along.

"Just watching the news."

Her mother got up and headed back to her chair. "Anything earth-shattering?"

"Well, those poor people."

She sat down and picked up a magazine. "What people?"

"That plane crash."

Charlie looked at her mother, who was absently flipping through the pages. "What plane crash?"

"Honey, I know you've had a lot going on, but two planes collided the other day over that little airport on the edge of town. Both pilots were killed. Makes me a little nervous about catching my flight today. I told my boss I didn't want to go out of town again just yet, but he says this client meeting can't wait."

Charlie's mom floated back to earth as she looked at her daughter. "When was that?"

"What, the plane crash? Friday evening. The first funeral is tomorrow."

As her mother began the familiar wave of her finger, Charlie crossed her arms and nodded.

~

Monday

It was a perfect day for a funeral. Charlie blew into her hands as she stood outside the car, listening to the patter of sleet on fallen leaves and waiting. When her mother rolled down her window, Charlie resisted the urge to sink her face into the cloud of warm air that seeped into the cold.

"Honey, I told you we should've gone to the funeral home. Please get in the car. They could be hours."

Charlie stared at the green canopy that whipped in the wind, waiting for the casket due to occupy the empty steel rectangle in the ground beneath it. "And I told you, there will be too many people at the funeral home."

"You don't think there will be here?"

She looked at her mother and rolled her eyes. "Not unless they're all as stupid as I am and want to freeze their as—"

"Charlie—"

"Assets off."

Her mom gestured toward the seat beside her. "At least get in the car. You just got out of the hospital."

Charlie sighed, creating a frigid cloud that hung in front of her face. She walked to the passenger side and grabbed the metal latch, which stuck to the moisture on her fingers left from blowing into her hands. She opened the door and was about to climb in when she saw a black hearse, a black limousine, and a short line of cars with little blue flags announcing Galen's arrival.

She leaned into the car and savored the warm air that poured from the vents along the dash. "They're here."

Her mother patted the seat. "You can still wait inside."

Charlie sighed and slipped in. She closed the door and watched the cars ease into a respectful line. When they stopped, an array of mourners emerged and hurried toward the canvas to huddle against the wind. From among them, six men gathered at the back of the hearse.

Charlie tilted her head as if doing so would help interpret the scene.

"What are they doing?"

"Those are the pallbearers. They'll carry the casket to the grave."

"Oh. I didn't even think about how he'd get over there. Which one do you think is his daughter?"

"The limo is for the family, so she's probably in there."

As if her words were a signal, the doors of the limousine swung open. A young couple emerged, along with several others. The driver provided the protection of an umbrella and the support of his arm as he helped an older woman through the weather. "That must be his wife."

The hearse driver opened the wide back door of Galen's ride.

The six men moved into position, eased his casket from within, carried it to the canopy, and placed it on top of the steel frame.

"Why don't they put him in the ground?" Charlie asked.

"Sometimes they do it that way. Just for the ceremony. They'll put him in the plot after."

A man stood at the front of the shivering crowd and spoke for a few minutes. When he was done, Galen's wife stepped forward and placed something on the casket.

"What's she doing?"

"It's probably a rose. I got to do that for your father."

Charlie turned to her mom. She hadn't even thought about her father and the fact that her mother may not want to be watching a funeral with her. "I remember that."

"You do?"

"Uh-huh."

For a few minutes, they both looked out the window without speaking.

Finally, Charlie turned back. "Do you miss him?"

Her mom didn't respond right away. "Sometimes."

Charlie hesitated, then figured she might as well. "Can I ask you something?"

"Of course."

"Did he have a closed casket because you had to get a coffin on sale that had a pink liner in it?"

Her mother's jaw went slack. "What in the world makes you think that?"

"You said so."

Her mom frowned. "No, I didn't."

Charlie nodded. "You said a sale's a sale and he'll never know the difference. And then you buried him in pink satin with a red flower and my baby shoes on his chest."

Her mother ran a finger around the steering wheel, remembering.

"What're you thinking?"

"I'm thinking I don't remember what I might have said. I was in so much pain, and I was mad."

Charlie turned sideways in her seat. "Mad?"

"Very mad."

"At him?"

"Yes."

"Why?"

Her mother sighed. "Because he'd been drinking when he had his car accident."

"Like—"

"Just like you. And he hit a tree, too."

"He did?" Charlie watched the pain in her mother's eyes as she relived the memory and wondered how it was she'd never known this.

"Yes. And all the sudden I'm left with a little baby and no income, and I thought he was so selfish to have done that to me."

Charlie let these new revelations sink in for a minute, then turned back to her mother. "So, it's okay to be mad at people if they're dead?"

Her mom shrugged. "I don't know if it's okay, but that's how I felt. I don't think God expects us to be robots."

"So you think you might have really said that?"

"Probably. I think it was on sale. Lord knows I didn't have any money. What we had was scraped together from our families."

"But did you have to bury him in pink?"

Her mom laughed. "Now, that, I don't think I did. It was probably the lighting at the funeral home."

Charlie nodded and sighed, relieved to have been both right and wrong. "And the closed casket?"

"It was best."

Charlie decided she didn't want to hear the details about why that was so. "Do you think he knows stuff about us now?"

"I don't know. But there is one thing I do know."

Charlie turned, eager for something else to add to her new portfolio of tidbits. "What?"

"He doesn't have your shoes."

"He doesn't?"

"Of course not. I'd never part with those."

Charlie nodded and looked out the window. "You know what, Mom?"

"What, honey?"

"I think I've been mad at him, too."

~

Tuesday morning

The newspaper crackled as Charlie spread it out on the kitchen table. She was glad her mom had agreed with her plan not to return to school just yet, because she had things to do. She ran her fingers over the two obituaries as if reading Braille. She felt her mother's approach from behind but didn't turn, knowing what was coming next when she smelled her mother's perfume at her shoulder.

"Wasn't yesterday enough?"

Charlie sighed and closed the paper. "I thought she'd want to know."

"Honey, it's probably understandable she didn't want to hear from a girl who says she came back from the dead when her father didn't. Especially when you added the fact that the conversation took place in mid-air."

"But it was the truth."

Her mom squeezed her shoulder. "I know this is important to you."

"Not just to me." She put her elbows on the table and her chin in her hands in a full-out pout. "I wanted to help them."

Her mother sat down across from her. "Galen's family might want to talk to you when they're not so raw."

Charlie looked at her doubtfully. "You think so?"

"Maybe."

It wasn't a convincing response, but Charlie knew it was the best she was going to get at this point. "Can I ask you a question?"

Her mom got up and headed for the cupboard. "Of course."

Behind her, Charlie heard the clink of a mug, the clunk of the coffee pot being pulled from its station, and the churning of liquid. The aroma that drifted from the granite countertop made her glance at her emptied cup. "Do you know Spirit, too?"

Her mother returned with a steaming mug and sat back down. "Somewhat."

Charlie propped her elbows on the cool surface of the cherry table and rested her chin in her hands. "Do you know how he works?"

Her mom took a sip of her coffee and then set it back down. "What do you mean?"

"When I first met him, we had a regular conversation. I just figured it'd always be that way, but that hasn't happened since the hospital, and I'm wondering if I screwed something up and God's mad again."

Her mother smiled. "I don't think God operates that way."

"You don't?"

"No, I don't."

Charlie opened the paper again and gazed at the obituaries, side by side, as if they had been waiting for her. "Then I have no choice."

Chapter 9

952 Cherry Street
Tuesday afternoon

The house was white with light blue shutters and two white wicker rocking chairs on the front porch. From the sidewalk, three cement steps led up to the brown grass of the yard, and then three more ended a short path that led to the door. Charlie sat in the car with her mother, listening to the purr of the engine, enjoying the blast of heat from the vent, and watching a cloud of exhaust creep around the fenders. She peered at the porch as if from a foxhole. "He molested her."

"What?" Her mom turned completely sideways in her seat.

Charlie nodded. "Sick, huh?"

Her mother studied the structure as if this new information had changed its appearance. "Honey, maybe this isn't even the right house."

"It's the right house." Charlie had been trying to will away the pit in her stomach, but nothing she told herself had any effect. If she didn't have such a strong sense that Spirit was behind this trip, she'd rather have been anywhere else, even in school.

Apparently, her mother felt the same way. She looked at

Charlie and back at the house as if there had to be some mistake. As if such a thing happening in Ripple Creek to someone who lived in a house so simple, neat, and normal just couldn't be. "But why are you so sure?"

"Mom, it's a small town. There isn't more than one person with that last name who also happened to be listed as Duff's stepdaughter in his obituary."

Her mother was still eyeing the house. "Maybe she moved."

"Would you stop? You agreed I have to listen to Spirit. I am, and this is what I think I'm supposed to do."

"But, honey—"

"Mom. Your whine is worse than mine. What? You want me to disobey God after the Grace thing and all?" Charlie cocked her head as she gazed at her mother, savoring the unusual sensation of pinning her into a self-righteous corner.

"Oh, right. Lay that one on me."

Charlie pushed against her door and slid a long thin leg out into the cold. A chime began to ding when her mother opened the driver's side with the keys still in the ignition. "I'm coming with you."

"No, you're not." Charlie said it over her shoulder, unwilling to allow her mother to change her mind or slow her down. She swung her feet to the ground.

"But what if—"

"What if you could help me more by staying put?" Charlie stepped out of the car and shut the door behind her. The engine idled against her rear as she leaned back and took a deep breath. She felt her mother's door slam shut and smirked as she imagined the pout on her face.

"Okay, Spirit, here we go…" Crunching through pellets of salt, she whispered what she thought might be prayers. When she got to the front door, it opened before she had the chance to knock.

A woman in her late forties stood in the doorway, eyeing her from within the house. Thin brown hair stopped at her shoulders, framing a plump face with no makeup. Charlie did a quick sweep of her outfit and decided her mother may recognize her from the discount store. She cleared her throat and cursed the birds flapping in her chest.

"Hi. I, ah…" Charlie wondered how a person started a conversation about meeting someone she preferred never to have met who happened to be the child-molesting stepfather of the person standing in front of her. "Are you Jacquelyn, Duff's stepdaughter?"

The woman looked startled. "Yes."

Charlie was both relieved and disappointed that her mother had been wrong. "I need to talk to you, if that's okay."

"Who—"

"I met him. Before he died. Well, actually when he was dying."

The woman put a hand on the doorframe. "You what?" She squinted at Charlie as if nearsighted and then peered over her shoulder at the car behind her.

"That's my mom."

"Oh."

"Can I—"

"Huh? Oh. Okay. Yeah. Come in." She stepped back and Charlie wiped her feet on the mat. "Don't bother. I have two dogs. It's hopeless."

As if on cue, Charlie heard barking from the back of the house. From the deep pitch, she figured they must be big and hoped they wouldn't be emerging to greet her.

"Something to drink? Coffee or…" She eyed Charlie. "Hot cocoa, maybe?"

"Coffee would be great."

"Let me quiet those two. Go on into the kitchen."

Charlie watched her go, listening to the banter she carried on with her dogs. The scent of fresh bread and spices took her by the nostrils and led her into the kitchen. She stood at the doorway and rolled the cool metal of her nose ring between her left thumb and forefinger as she surveyed the room. The sink was empty and gleaming, baskets cuddled up to each other on every spare inch of wall, and steam was escaping from a pot on the stove. She decided the dinette was as good a place as any and tugged out a wooden chair, which was no small task with the thick carpet underneath. Once seated, she rested her folded hands on the plastic tablecloth of flowers and reminded herself to breathe.

Before long, the woman returned. "Oh, good, you've made yourself at home." She moved to the cupboard and pulled out two cups. Tugging the coffee pot from the machine, she paused and looked at Charlie before pouring. "You're sure it's coffee, you want? You don't look—"

"Yes, ma'am." Charlie nodded, thinking she hadn't sounded so polite in all her life and figured Spirit must be around after all.

Duff's stepdaughter fixed two cups and put a steaming mug in front of Charlie. The aroma that drifted upward signaled it was freshly brewed. "Cream? Sugar?"

"Black is fine, thanks."

She sat down and took a deep breath. "Okay. First, what's your name?"

"Charlie. Charlie Welks."

The woman nodded in a deliberate way, as if tucking away information she might need later. "Apparently you already know mine. But you can call me Fern. What do you have to tell me about my stepfather, Charlie?"

Charlie hesitated, thinking back to yesterday and wondering if it had been her delivery that screwed things up. She flattened her palms against the table. "First, let me tell you I'm here to help. I don't want to upset you."

Fern took a sip of her coffee and then set the mug down. "Fair enough."

Charlie took a breath and then exhaled the words. "I died."

Fern didn't even flinch. Instead, she responded with the empty stare of someone accustomed to dealing with liars. "Okay…"

"The same day your stepfather did."

"But you—"

"I was given another chance. Grace, she—well, anyway…during the time I was dead I visited with Duff."

The words had the effect of a stray rock hitting a windshield, leaving a chink in the surface that stretched into a long, thin crack of vulnerability.

"You what?" Her voice was barely audible.

"I know it sounds crazy." If Spirit expected her to keep telling her story, Charlie wondered if he was ever going to make this part easier to explain. "I was dead, and I visited seven other people during that time."

"Seven dead people." The woman's blank stare returned.

"Well, mostly they weren't technically dead yet." Charlie began to roll her nose ring. "They were dying when I was there."

Fern took a dismissive sip of her coffee. "That doesn't sound possible."

"Lady, I know it sounds crazy." Charlie wrapped her hands around her mug for warmth and the courage to go on. "When I died, this guy, well, he's not really a guy but a spiritual being…he visited me."

"I'm lost."

"His name is Final Moment, and he visits everyone in the last sixty seconds before they die."

"And he visited my stepfather?"

Charlie nodded, encouraged by the flicker of interest she spotted in the woman's eyes.

"And you were with him?"

"Yeah, I had to go around and visit all these people with him."

"Why?"

The way she said it made Charlie think her answer was the password that would let her go on. She looked into her coffee. "I guess I had a lot to learn."

Fern leaned forward, as if Charlie had passed the test. "Tell me about my stepfather. What happened?"

"He ended up face down in his mashed potatoes."

A curtain of sadness dropped across the woman's face.

Charlie rapped her knuckle on the table in frustration. "I knew I'd screw this up."

"No. It's not you." Her eyes filled, and Charlie wondered why Spirit was making her do this. "I know the care there wasn't good, but it was all I had money for."

"Ma'am, I'm sure not trying to make you feel bad."

Fern grabbed a napkin from the holder and blew her nose. "I just wish…I wanted to take care of him here, but I just couldn't."

Charlie tiptoed into the question as if poking a bear. "Because he molested you?"

Fern's jaw went slack. "Who told you that?" she whispered.

Charlie hesitated. "Final knew it."

"That spirit thing?"

"Yeah."

Fern closed her eyes and just sat there. Charlie rolled her nose ring and wondered if there was something she should do. After a few minutes, Fern opened her eyes and looked at Charlie. "What did my stepfather say?"

"At first he said it never happened." As soon as the words came out, Charlie realized how matter-of-fact they sounded and longed for a do-over.

Fern's face dropped as if a sinker were attached to her nose. "Figures."

"But then he admitted it was true." Charlie was relieved to have this nugget of hope to offer, and that it wasn't something she had to make up.

Fern looked up. "He did?"

"Lady, I got to tell you I didn't like your stepdad at all."

The sad curtain dropped back over her face. "I've had to look long and hard to find something to like. Before my mom died, things were different. But after that…"

"There was a point where I kinda felt sorry for him." Charlie couldn't believe she said it. She hadn't even known she felt it until that very moment.

"You felt sorry for him?" Fern looked confused and hopeful all at the same time, as if there might be something that could explain her life after all.

"Yeah, 'cause I guess his dad molested him, too." Charlie was afraid the woman was going to fall over, and she'd have to admit to her mom this was a bad idea after all.

"What'd you just say?"

Charlie nodded. "That's what he said. Final knew it, too."

Fern propped her elbows on the table and rested her mouth in the angle of her folded hands. She closed her eyes and sat that way for so long Charlie thought maybe she'd dozed off. Finally, she opened her eyes and looked at Charlie. "What'd my stepfather say about it?"

Charlie rolled her nose ring, wondering if Spirit would be mad if she shared this part. "He said he hated God because he didn't protect him."

She sighed. "I know the feeling."

"I wanted to tell Final that God should do something about that." Charlie sat up straighter, as if the fact that she considered standing up to God on her behalf should win points with the woman.

"What did Final say about how Duff felt?"

"Something about the world being full of evil people and kids being innocent victims."

Fern nodded as if understanding but not buying it.

"But Final didn't cut him any slack. He said it was no excuse for what Duff did to you. That he could've broken the cycle of abuse." Charlie watched Fern's expression, hoping for a sign that knowing this somehow helped. When she didn't get one, she decided she might as well ask what had been bugging her since the encounter with Duff. "Why are you still here?"

Fern looked at her. "Here?"

"Why do you even care about him? Why didn't you just leave town?"

Fern looked out the window and sighed. "It never seemed as simple as that."

"What do you mean?"

When she turned back to Charlie, the woman's eyes were filled with such sadness that Charlie had to look away. Then she felt bad, since she was the one who brought it up. She gazed at Fern and waited.

"My real dad died when I was little. Then my mom. Duff was good to me before that happened. On some level I guess I hoped that part of him was still in there somewhere and I could find a way to forgive him. I was afraid if I ran off with my pain I'd never figure out how to do that and heal."

As the words drifted toward the windowpane, Charlie realized it could've easily been her sitting in that chair. There had been many men who'd crossed the threshold of her mother's life, but none had dared to even glance in Charlie's direction. It made her more grateful for clunky, loving, and reliable Dan.

"He said he was sorry." Charlie blurted it out. "For what he did to you."

Fern looked at Charlie as if she was afraid to believe it. "Do you think he was?"

Charlie nodded. "Yeah. When he found out you had a new therapist and were planning to come the next day…"

"My stepfather was told that?"

"Yeah. And he really wanted to see you." As the words tumbled out, Charlie kept discovering fragments of good stuff she'd forgotten were there.

"He did?"

"He really did. Especially…" Charlie paused, somehow knowing this one would be big.

Fern watched her, waiting. "Especially what, Charlie?"

No matter how many times Charlie had practiced the

conversation in her mind, it did her no good. The words just came tumbling out. "Final told Duff he was your son's father. That the bad things Duff said about you when you got pregnant at that age weren't true. That it was good you didn't have the abortion he wanted you to have. That your son was all that kept you going all these years."

Fern stood fast enough to topple her chair. She moved to the sink, her shoulders heaving, which made Charlie think maybe she was going to puke. Instead, she heard whimpering, then sobbing that grew so loud and so long Charlie wondered whether she should go get her mother.

She got up and went to the sink, then touched the woman's back as if testing a hot stove. "Fern, I'm so sorry. I just wanted to help." As Fern's sobbing gradually slowed to a sniffle, Charlie got caught off guard by her own well of tears and the sudden admission on her lips. "I…I had an abortion. But I wish I didn't. I wish I'd had the courage to walk out of that place like you did. I wish I had my little girl."

When Fern looked up, Charlie somehow knew the depth of compassion in her gaze was only possible from someone who truly did understand the predicament she'd been in. Then the woman turned on the faucet and leaned into the sink. She cupped her hands, splashed water on her face, tore off a paper towel, and patted it dry. Then she blew her nose and stood for several minutes, gazing out the window.

Finally, she turned, pulled Charlie into a sudden embrace, and whispered, "You've helped me more than you can possibly know."

Chapter 10

Ripple Creek Funeral Home
Wednesday

*H*er mother had given up on trying to change her mind. Charlie was five for six and hoped this final one would get Spirit to leave her alone.

"Are you sure you don't want me to come in with you?" Her mom put her right hand over the keys in the ignition, apparently eager to turn off the car and follow her daughter inside.

Charlie looked at her without saying a word.

Her mother held up her hands in surrender. "Just asking."

Charlie smiled. "Sorry you got all dressed up, but I need to do this alone." She stepped out onto the black pavement. The funeral home's lot had recently been scraped and salted, and the surface glistened with melted snow. The sun decided to appear for the first time in days, and its late afternoon rays bounced off the windshields of the cars that filled the lot.

Charlie watched the steady stream of visitors who entered through the front door and quickly moved to get into line. A solemn man was standing inside the door in a black suit, nodding silently and pointing to a sign-in book, which made Charlie wonder why they needed a head count. There were two viewing rooms in the funeral home, and they were both overflowing with murmuring bodies in various shades of black. She approached the man, since she didn't want to screw up the finale. "Excuse me, can you tell me which room Anna is in?"

The man answered by pointing to the room on the right. "She's in there, but we're using the other room for overflow."

Charlie looked at the huddled masses who crammed the doorways like a Black Friday sale. Every seat in both rooms was full, and the walls were lined with the standing. She turned back to the man, certain she must've heard wrong. "All these people are here for Anna?"

He nodded without speaking and turned back to greet more guests. Charlie took a deep breath and wondered how in the world she was going to find Patch.

"It's just awful, isn't it?"

Charlie looked sideways without turning her head. She saw a forty-something woman whose tears were slowly transforming her into a raccoon. Her perfume was thick enough to ward off insects, and Charlie tried to hold her breath. There was no one else around, and her heart sank as she realized she was going to have to respond. She turned to the woman, whose eyes were rimmed in red above scrawling paths that cut through her cake of makeup like dry riverbeds.

"Awful?" Charlie asked.

"Well, don't you think so?" The woman dabbed her eyes with a tissue. "We'll all miss her so much."

Charlie shrugged. "She said she was ready." She wasn't sure why she instantly disliked the woman and hoped Spirit was busy with other chores.

"Everybody says that, sweetie. It doesn't mean they are."

The clucking in her voice and the fact that she called Charlie *sweetie* were the final straws that pushed Charlie over the edge. "What would you know about it?"

The woman stepped back as if she'd been slapped. "I beg your pardon?"

Sighing, Charlie looked around the room. "Have you seen Patch?"

Fanning her face with her hand, the woman turned on a heel. Charlie watched her go, thinking she probably shouldn't have enjoyed that so much.

"Patch, I'm so sorry about your mom."

The words came from behind her, and Charlie turned to find the voice. Two women were embracing, and she recognized Patch from seeing her at Anna's side. "Thanks," she said to her friend.

Charlie was certain the room could hear the herd of horses pounding in her chest. When she saw an opening, she made her move. "Patch?"

Patch had started into the other room. She stopped and looked back, her face more peaceful than Charlie expected. "Yes?"

"Can I talk to you a minute?" Charlie stepped sideways when someone bumped into her. "Alone?"

Patch glanced at the crowd around them. "I hate to leave—"

"It won't take long, I promise."

She nodded and gestured toward a hallway. "Okay, just a few minutes. There's a family room down here."

As they walked, Charlie counted the ugly purple flowers beneath her feet, trying to step in the center of each bloom in the thick, musty carpet. *Purple, black, white, tan. Purple, black, white, tan.* The rhythm calmed her as she traced the patterns with her eyes and hoped Patch wouldn't think her story was crazy.

The room was dimly lit, with a pink daffodil lamp in the corner and fancy couches with dark wooden arms. The scent of flowers was heavy enough to snuff out a fire, and boxes of tissues were lined up like an army headed into battle. Despite the formality of her black dress, Patch folded herself onto the couch with the casual familiarity of an old friend. She looked at Charlie and smiled.

Charlie stood at the doorway, unsure of what to do next.

"Come in and sit down." Patch motioned to a chair across from her.

As she sank into the cushion, Charlie realized this visit didn't feel like any of the others. She looked at the woman on the couch. The salt and pepper hair that was disheveled enough to be approachable along with the bare necessities of makeup and flats instead of heels gave Charlie the impression this was someone she could talk to. Patch crossed her legs and then slipped her foot behind her ankle, a long thin vine wrapping around a tree. "I bet you met my mother," she said.

Charlie startled. "How did you know that?"

Patch smiled. "The nose ring and purple hair."

Charlie touched her nose ring and then her hair, which hadn't seemed nearly as purple these days. "Really?"

"Oh, yeah. You're the perfect candidate."

"Candidate?" Charlie wondered if this was some kind of dream.

"For a second chance." The tone in Patch's voice was a shrug. A given. A fact as simple and true as the air Charlie could no longer breathe. She opened her mouth to speak, but nothing came out.

Patch watched her with a tenderness Charlie didn't recognize. "What's your name?"

Her voice returned. "Charlie."

"Ah, yes. Of course."

Charlie's face felt numb. She wondered what in the world Spirit was doing. "I don't understand."

"I bet you've screwed up a lot."

She'd never heard an adult use that word. She nodded.

"And sometime in your life, you met Mom." Patch said it with such certainty Charlie began to wonder if her mother had already managed to talk to Patch. Or if Spirit was sharing her secrets.

"You could say that." Charlie began to roll her nose ring.

"So where? At church? At her group? At jail?"

"Jail?" Maybe she had the wrong Anna. Certainly, the Anna she saw in a shimmer of pink satin whose snow white hair looked like it had been recently rolled, teased, smoothed, and sprayed could not be the same woman Patch was referring to.

Patch pursed her lips, thinking. "Guess not."

Charlie put up a hand. "Wait. Anna was in jail?"

Patch paused, then smiled. "She ran a group for young women there.

"For what?" Charlie still couldn't believe this could be her Anna. A woman who goes to jail couldn't say things like, *Mercy sakes.*

Patch was watching her, and it was as if she knew what Charlie was thinking. "Mom was the most compassionate, loving person I've ever known. She had a heart for women who'd made mistakes. Who wanted to make it right. Who wanted another chance."

Charlie didn't move.

"Well, I can see that's not where—"

"I was dead," Charlie blurted.

Patch put her hands in her lap and laced her fingers together. "Go on."

"And so was your mom."

Patch uncrossed her legs and leaned forward, her face intense. "She was?"

Charlie hesitated. "Well, almost."

"Were you with Final?"

Charlie was sure her chin had to be inches from the carpet. "What'd you just say?"

Patch nodded slowly as she watched her response. "Yes…you were. And he took you to see my mother." Her dress flared a little when she jumped up from the couch and clapped her hands. "I knew it!"

Charlie stood with her, not sure if she should trust the jelly that was supposed to be her legs. She grabbed the back of the chair. "How do you know about Final?"

Patch stopped and looked at her. "He visited me too, kid."

"He…you—"

"Yep, I was dead too."

Charlie sat. "When?"

Patch sank back onto the couch. "During a dark time in my life. When I was a mess."

"How'd you die?"

"Just pulled my car into the garage, closed the door, and let it run. It wasn't long before Final showed up."

"How long were you dead?"

"Long enough. My neighbor found me and started CPR."

"Did you meet anyone else?"

"No, that part didn't happen to me."

Charlie began to wonder if she should go get her mother. "But you—"

Patch nodded. "I got another chance. Just like you. Bet you know Grace, too."

Charlie felt like her head was floating. She nodded.

"Pretty weird, huh?" Patch was watching her.

"I can't believe this." Charlie tried to ignore the nagging disappointment she felt. "Why didn't Anna say anything?"

"She didn't know." Sadness washed across Patch's expression. "I wanted to tell her about Final, but then I'd have to tell her the rest. I was afraid it'd break her heart."

Charlie stared at the pink glow of the daffodil and wondered why she didn't feel ecstatic. After all, here was someone who absolutely did not believe she was crazy. She looked at Patch. "I totally don't know what I'm supposed to do next."

"Tell me about Mom." Even in the muted lighting, Charlie could see the tears that welled in Patch's eyes. "Was she as ready as she seemed?"

Charlie nodded. "She said she was. And really peaceful. And really proud of you."

Patch smiled sadly, then reached for the tissue box on the table beside her and tugged one out. She blew her nose and looked back at Charlie. "Obviously, Spirit brought you here."

"You know Spirit, too?" With each new revelation, Charlie felt a little less special.

"Of course." Patch shrugged. "I'd be lost without him."

At that, Charlie realized she and Spirit would need to have a little chat, since she totally didn't feel as confident about their relationship as Patch apparently did. And maybe he'd been sharing her secrets after all. "So, did you know I was coming?"

"Oh no. Spirit doesn't work that way. At least in my life he doesn't."

At that tidbit, Charlie breathed a little sigh of relief.

Patch smiled. "I just had a feeling there was something special about you the moment I saw that purple hair in the middle of that crowd."

Charlie rubbed her hand over her scalp. "I might let it grow out."

Patch nodded as if she understood. "We all have to figure out who we are, Charlie."

"Have you?" Charlie realized she hadn't met anybody she really wanted to be friends with in a very long time.

"I don't know if anyone ever totally figures that out in this life. But I'm trying."

"Your mom said you were her prodigal." Even though she knew being a prodigal wasn't necessarily a good thing, Charlie said it as if she was presenting an award.

Patch smiled. "That would be me."

"She said she made mistakes, too." Charlie wondered what it would've been like to have had this kind of mom. Where things like that were said without the need to be dead.

"That's the beauty of knowing ourselves. It helps us forgive each other."

"I guess I messed up a lot before I died."

"But here you are, with another chance."

"Yeah, whatever I'm supposed to do with that."

"I'd say you're doing just fine, kid."

"Your mom really loved you." Charlie said it with both admiration and envy.

Patch's eyes filled with tears again, and she reached for another tissue. "She was my best friend. I'm going to miss her so much."

They were quiet for a few minutes, until Charlie finally spoke. "I think she's the reason I'm here."

Patch blew her nose, then wiped it a few times with the tissue to pat it dry. "What do you mean?"

"She asked God to give me another chance, like he did for you." She watched Patch, who seemed so together and calm, and wondered how it was that she was ever in need of another chance.

"Sounds like Mom." Patch's gaze drifted off. "She wore out her knees over me."

"Ian's mom was like that, too."

"Someone you met?"

Charlie nodded.

"They must've been powerful encounters." Patch stood and brushed her dress into place. "I should get back."

Charlie stood with her. She had to tip her head a little to look into the crystal blue of Patch's eyes.

"Do you know what happens when you get another chance, kid?"

Up close, she could see the lines on Patch's face, which added to her credibility. Charlie smiled a little. "I think I'm supposed to make the most of it."

Patch put a hand on her shoulder. "Of course Mom was right about you."

Chapter 11

Thursday

$\mathscr{B}$eing dead and brought back to life didn't change the fact that Charlie's blood alcohol content had been above the legal limit. Which, according to Vermont's zero tolerance law for minors, was a measly BAC of 0.02 percent. However, her dead-undead experience may have had something to do with the slap on the wrist she'd received in front of the judge that morning. When her lawyer called it a miracle, Charlie figured Spirit must've somehow been involved. The car heater blasted hot air onto her feet as she read the verdict she'd received and tried to figure out what her lawyer thought was so miraculous.

Charge: Driving Under the Influence
Sentencing: Loss of license for 90 days with restricted license eligibility after 30 days
Completion of the Impaired Driver Rehabilitation Program (IDRP)
8 sessions of counseling with a licensed clinician
Payment of a $650 fine, in addition to court costs
90 hours of community service in lieu of incarceration
Probation until all requirements are met.

101

Charlie sighed as she stared out the window at the slow-moving traffic. Her mother hadn't spoken since they'd left the courthouse. It felt like something had changed, but she wasn't sure what.

"Are you mad at me?" Charlie asked.

The tone in her mom's response sounded like she was sitting in a barrel. "No. I'm not mad."

"Then why does it feel like it?" When she glanced over, she saw a single tear roll down her mother's cheek. "Wait—are you crying?"

Her mom's chin began to tremble as she flipped on her turn signal and pulled to the curb. She put the car in park, her face into her hands, and began to sob.

Charlie panicked. "Mom? I'm sorry you have to pay all that money and I have to do all that stuff and I screwed everything up."

Her mother pulled a tissue from the console and blew her nose. Then she looked at her daughter. "It all hit me. In there. Listening to the accident report. To how you almost…"

Charlie sank back into her seat. "Died."

Her mom nodded. "I don't know how I would've gone on if that had happened, Charlie. Especially after—"

"Our fight."

Charlie watched her mother fold the tissue into a perfect little square.

"Yes."

"Mom, you know how bad I feel about that, right? I didn't mean the stuff I said. I was just…"

"Upset. Me too." Her mom waved the folded square as if sweeping away the memory. "It's water under the bridge."

Charlie watched a woman across the street who was getting her baby out of her car seat. An empty stroller sat on the pavement beside the open door. Before slipping her into it, the woman lifted the baby into the air and smiled at her. Charlie was too far away to hear the baby's response, so the giggle she heard had to be something she imagined. Or maybe it was how she thought

Rose would've laughed if she were here. When the woman held the baby close and brushed her cheek with her lips, Charlie figured she was savoring the aroma of her baby's skin and telling her how much she loved her. At least that's what Charlie would've done if that were her little Rose. Tears welled in her eyes as she swallowed and looked away, trying to ignore the empty longing for the baby she hadn't even given a chance to be born.

After a few minutes, she glanced at her mother out of the corner of her eye and realized she was watching the woman and her baby, too. Charlie didn't know if she was thinking the same kinds of things and had no desire to find out. "But the other…is it okay if we wait awhile to talk about it? It's too much right now."

When her mother looked over, Charlie was surprised to see relief. "Of course." Her mom patted her arm. "You can talk to the counselor about it if you want."

Charlie rolled her eyes.

"Well, you have to go. It's court-ordered."

"I read everything about the IDRP before we went. It said the program evaluator would decide if I had to go to counseling. Not the judge." Charlie crossed her arms in a pout.

"Maybe you'd rather have been sent to jail." Her mother said it so matter-of-factly Charlie wondered whose side she was on.

"Yeah, well, I don't want some shrink poking at me." The very thought of stretching out on a couch to have her every thought, every move, every word picked apart, examined, and judged like a piece of questionable produce made her stomach turn.

"I think you'll find it's a little different than that." Her mom flipped on her turn signal, looked into her side mirror, and pulled back out onto the street. "I've had it. It helped."

Traffic had let up, and Charlie was watching the accelerating brown landscape just outside of town when the words sunk in. "Wait." She turned so quickly the shoulder strap locked and pinned her to her seat. "You had a shrink? When?"

Her mother waved her hand as if they were talking about

shoes. "After your father died." She glanced at Charlie. "And she was a counselor, not a shrink."

"Why don't I remember that?" This mountain within a molehill made Charlie wonder what else she didn't know.

Her mom shrugged. "You were little. It's not something you share with your little kid."

"Why'd you go?" In that split second, between asking the question and her mother's response, Charlie ached for the smartphone that'd been destroyed in the wreck. If only she could slip her finger over the little red record button about now, she'd be able to play her mother's answer back indefinitely as part of her own defense. Then she felt bad about even thinking such a thing.

Her mother looked over her left shoulder, flipped on her signal, and changed lanes. "I was a mess."

"Is that why you—"

"Went through so many men?"

Charlie didn't say anything.

Her mother glanced over and then back at the road. "It's the truth. And yes, it was. I was lost and trying to fill a big hole in my life." She slowed behind the line of traffic that had stopped at a red light, tapping her fingers on the steering wheel as she stared straight ahead. "I know that was hard on you. I'm sorry. It must have been very confusing." She reached for the dash and turned on the radio.

Charlie stared at the panel of buttons where her mother's hand had just been, sweeping her momentary vulnerability under the rug of a used car commercial with the tap of a button. She looked out her window and wondered if feeling like her real mom had finally returned was something she'd made up. When she felt her mother's hand patting her knee, she looked down. The perfection of her recent manicure paused over the tear in Charlie's favorite jeans and then fingered the frayed edges. She gave Charlie's knee one final pat, then checked her lipstick in the rearview mirror and tapped the accelerator to rejoin the traffic. "We'll get you some new clothes before your first session."

Charlie folded her arms and glared at her mother, whose expression seemed to have locked into autopilot. "I don't need new clothes. I like the clothes I have."

"As I reminded you this morning, clothing with holes is not appropriate to wear out of the house. Perhaps if you'd worn the dress I suggested, you may have made a better impression on the judge."

Her mother's tone was nearly a dare, and the rush of emotion Charlie felt in response made her want to scream. Or cry. Or just open the door, roll onto the berm, and run. Anything to escape the woman beside her who seemed intent on making sure Charlie never knew what to expect from someone she was supposed to be able to count on.

But instead of doing any of those things, she just looked out the window as a single tear trickled down her cheek. She thought about what Anna had said about a mother's love and wished she could somehow know it was true. Not just the kind of love that shows up in extremes, like when someone returns from the dead, but the kind that sticks out in the midst of normal and doesn't disappear when you have to go to court or have an abortion you totally regret.

Then Charlie did something she would never have thought possible and which totally came out of the blue. *Spirit, help me.*

She watched the strip malls zip by as she waited for a response, her doubt growing with each block of dirty snow that passed. She wasn't sure she knew how to pray, so maybe this was something else she was messing up.

I'm right here, my child.

The voice was so clear that Charlie glanced at her mother to see if she'd heard it too. But since she seemed lost in her own little world, Charlie figured that wasn't the case. If she'd been alone, she would've started talking out loud. Instead, she tried to ignore the distraction of the commercial on the radio and the other person in the car so she could focus on this new experience that she was starting to think might be pretty cool after all.

I don't know what to do. I thought me and my mom were getting along better, but now she's being weird again. It makes me sad and mad, but I don't want to fight with her.

You did exactly the right thing, child. You waited and asked for my help.

Does that always work? I mean, do you always come when I call?

Yes. I'll always hear you and respond when you seek Me. However, my response may not always be quite as apparent as this seems.

Charlie was so engrossed in her conversation with Spirit that she barely noticed her mother patting her knee. Then she realized they had pulled into the drive and were sitting in front of their house. When she looked at her mom, she was staring at her.

"Where are you?"

Charlie gave her a dumbfounded look. "Huh?"

"I said we're home and asked if you planned to stay in the car."

"Oh. Uh, no. I was just, well…I guess I was praying."

Her mother turned off the car and leaned back in her seat. "Praying? Really?"

"You don't need to sound so surprised."

"Well, I mean, I'm glad, of course." Her mother patted her knee again. "That's good, honey. It's exactly what you need to do."

"I was mad and trying not to start a fight." As soon as she said it Charlie realized she was still upset and itching for a fight after all. The few seconds of peace she'd felt when she could hear Spirit's voice were gone and the condescending tone of her mother's voice had her steam rising all over again.

Her mother nodded as if she knew it was true but had no intention of joining in. She tugged the keys from the ignition and opened the door. "Wonderful. You can come with us to church this week, after all." Then she climbed out of the car, shut the door, and headed up the front steps.

Charlie sat in stunned silence as she watched her mother unlock the front door and go into the house without ever looking back. The tick of the engine's heat reminded Charlie of the overwhelming quiet when she was hanging upside down in Dan's car, wondering if help would ever arrive.

She knew that with everything she'd been through during and since that night, getting to go to church was something she should be grateful for. Grace would probably want her to do it, and Spirit, too.

But her mother's church? She'd tried that enough times to know it wasn't something she ever wanted to do again. The last time she'd been there she and her mom got in a big fight in the parking lot while her mother smiled sheepishly at everyone who walked by and stared.

But Charlie knew it wasn't their fight that all those perfect people were staring at as they tried so hard to seem they weren't doing exactly that. Instead, it was her. The purple hair her mother had wanted her to cover with a scarf. The nose ring she pleaded for her to leave at home. The tattered jeans she was wearing today, which were Charlie's favorites.

The very thought of stepping foot into that judgement hall made Charlie's hands sweat. She knew she should talk to Spirit about all this, but didn't feel like hearing what he might have to say. Then she thought about Esta and how she had turned down going to church with her friend.

But it wasn't the same. Charlie wasn't completely against going to church. Just her mother's church. She knew that the minute she walked through those doors, it would be like having a scarlet letter emblazoned across her forehead.

Somehow, they would all know exactly what she'd done.

Chapter 12

Friday
Bosko Counseling Services

Charlie rolled her nose ring between her fingers as she stared at the fake fur of the bear rug at her feet. Beneath it, the tight weave of industrial carpet extended in all directions, like a barren field waiting to be plowed. She was trying to ignore the big leather drum in the corner of the office, since she couldn't figure out what it was for. She heard people talking on the sidewalk outside, but the closed wooden blinds provided complete privacy. However, the blinds at the back of the office had been pulled neatly to the top of the window frame, allowing a view of the woods to pour into the room. The steady *tick, tick, tick* of a clock measured each second as it passed, occasionally interrupted by bursts of lavender air.

Across from her, the therapist's steady gaze felt like the pounding of the sun in July. Charlie had been under the interrogation lamp plenty of times in her young life, but never had she sat with someone so patient in the waiting. Finally, Charlie looked up. "Is someone else coming?"

The woman smiled without showing her teeth. She looked older than Charlie's mom, thicker around the middle, and free from the confines of makeup and the need for approval. The canary-yellow tone of her hair and emerging gray roots shouted a DIY dye job if Charlie had ever seen one. Stella Bosko had hazel eyes warm enough to bake a muffin, and Charlie was pretty sure she wasn't wearing a bra.

"No. It'll just be us," she said.

Charlie took a deep breath. "Okay. I don't know what I'm supposed to do."

"Well, you could start with answering the question I asked ten minutes ago."

"What question?" Charlie eyed the drum.

"I know you're nervous, Charlie. It's okay. Most girls your age would rather be lots of places other than spending an hour with me."

She looked back at Stella. "Yeah, this is pretty weird."

"I know. I asked where you'd like to start. What would you like to talk about today?"

Charlie sighed and looked out the back window into the spindly winter woods. The gray branches were still as stone, protruding from the granite trunks beneath them. "I have no idea."

"Okay, then I'll start."

Charlie nodded.

"Tell me about your relationship with your mom."

Charlie puffed her cheeks and blew out a stream of air. "Now, or before I was dead?"

"Take your pick."

"Well, now, things are better. I think. Though she's gotten a little weird again lately. But they were pretty bad before I died, so anything's an improvement." Charlie shrugged. "I guess I should've done that sooner."

Stella smiled. "Dying does have its benefits."

"Right? It changed everyone. Even my stepfather is nice to me now."

"I don't suppose that has anything to do with how it changed you."

Charlie watched the woman, wondering if she realized she'd have to work harder than that to get Charlie to spill her guts.

"So, let's back up to what led up to your car accident."

Charlie rolled her nose ring. "Do we have to?"

"Processing the pain is how we heal." Stella cocked her head. "I'm assuming there was some pain behind the fact that you were impaired when you hit that tree at that speed."

Charlie let her hand fall into her lap. "I don't know. Everything was a mess. It started getting worse after my dad died when I was little."

Stella nodded. "Tell me about that."

"Before he died, I thought everyone was so happy. Well, I found out recently that wasn't the case. But then, as a little kid, it all seemed pretty perfect to me. I guess I was in la-la land."

"Little kids shouldn't have to bear the burdens of the adults in their lives."

Charlie pushed the toe of her tennis shoe into the thick fur beneath it. "Well, I sure did after Daddy died. The mom I knew disappeared. She started bringing all these guys home. It was horrible. I lost my dad, and then I lost her, too."

Stella folded her hands and propped them on her belly. "Sounds pretty hard for a little kid."

Charlie shrugged. "Whatever. I decided if she was going to do her own thing, I was too."

"How old were you when you had sex for the first time?"

Charlie looked at Stella, whose expression was like the smooth side of a stone. "Cut right to the chase, don't you?"

Stella responded without missing a beat. "We only have eight sessions. Am I wrong?"

Charlie traced a pattern in the chair fabric with her finger. "Fifteen."

"So, last year?"

Charlie nodded.

"Did you care about the boy?"

"Not really."

"Did he care about you?"

"He said he did, but once he got what he wanted…I guess he got tired of me."

"Have you ever had a steady boyfriend?"

"Not really."

Then Stella was quiet. Charlie looked back out the window. "I guess you want me to talk about the other thing."

"The only information I have is what's on your arrest record. If you want to talk about *the other thing*, you'll have to fill me in."

Charlie was both relieved and disappointed by this news. Maybe she wouldn't have to talk about it after all, though she sensed a growing need to do just that. Just as she was thinking about tucking it away forever, she blurted it out as if it were a burp. "I had an abortion."

Although they were her own, the sudden words seemed like a knife to Charlie, slicing the peaceful lavender air and the pretenses she longed to protect. She bristled as she prepared to either defend herself or collapse with shame, but Stella just gazed at her as if she'd just been told there was a sale at the hardware store.

Unaccustomed to such calm, Charlie eyed her with suspicion. "Aren't you going to say something?"

Stella unfolded her hands and laid her palms on the tight polyester flowers covering her thighs. "What would you like me to say, Charlie?"

Charlie pushed out her lower lip and toed the rug. "I don't know. But I didn't have a choice."

"Okay."

She dug her toe deeper into the fur. "I mean, my mom would've kicked me out of the house."

"I see."

Charlie stood and started to pace in a tight circle, creating a whirl of fur in her wake. "Her and her fancy house and fancy church and fancy self. How was I supposed to tell her I was pregnant?"

Stella didn't move. "You were certainly faced with some difficult choices."

"You can say that again." As the last word floated into the air, Charlie spotted the mallet. Despite the siren inside her brain wailing that she'd just met this woman who might tell the judge Charlie was out-of-control crazy and should be thrown into jail, she took three long steps toward the drum, lifted the leather-covered stick from its holder, and slammed it against the tight cowhide. It cracked like a shotgun blast, bouncing off the walls, filling Charlie with the impulse to dive for cover. Instead, she gripped the wooden handle as if it were the edge of a cliff, desperately resisting the urge to swing it again and again until she had ripped clean through the leather. She stood as still as the granite trunks gracing the window to the woods and absorbed the reverberation of the drum as it ebbed into nothing. "And it sucked to be me," she whispered. Then she laid down the mallet as if it were an egg, walked to her chair, and dropped into it like a wet rag falling from a hook. "It seemed like the only choice."

Stella gazed at her as if having someone rage on her drum was nothing new. "And the baby's father?"

Charlie gave her a sideways look, but Stella held her gaze.

"I have no idea who the father was."

"Okay."

Charlie straightened in her chair. "Is that all you're going to say? Just, *Okay?* Aren't you going to give me some advice or something?"

Stella examined a broken fingernail, then lifted it to her lips to chew the unruly edge into submission. She straightened her fingers to assess the uniformity of her efforts, dropped her hand into her lap and looked at Charlie. "Not unless you want my advice. I'm here to help you process things. To figure yourself out. I can see in the brief time we've been together you're extraordinary for your age. Insightful. Intelligent. And the near-death experience you've been through has only sharpened those qualities."

Charlie was more accustomed to scrambling for crumbs than being served such generous helpings of praise. She shifted in her chair and rolled her nose ring. "I *was* dead. It wasn't near-death anything."

Stella shrugged. "Well, apparently it wasn't permanent."

"Apparently."

"How do you feel about your abortion now?"

"Final says the Father named her Rose." Another belch of words. Charlie silently cursed her verbal indigestion. Something about Stella was a magnet for everything she didn't want to talk about.

Stella cocked her head. "Final is…"

Charlie waved her hand. "It's a long story. But when I was dead, I met this spirit guy who told me my…baby…was already in heaven, and God had named her Rose."

Stella looked surprised to finally hear something original. "Well, now, that's something. How do you feel about that?"

Charlie watched the room blur through sudden tears. "I guess I didn't see her as real. As a baby. I just thought it—she—was a blob of tissue." The flow of tears came so fast that mucus began to drip from her nostrils and onto her upper lip. She tugged the collar of her t-shirt up to wipe it away. "I mean, that's what the abortion stuff says." Her tone was that of a deflated afterthought drifting unconvincingly into the air around her.

Charlie sniffed her composure back into place, took a deep breath, sat up straighter in her chair and looked at Stella with a half-hearted attempt at defiance. "And that you have the right to do what you want with your own body."

Stella smiled impassively as she held Charlie's gaze with an intensity so steady it seemed to penetrate her very soul; yet so gentle Charlie didn't even mind.

"Yes, that's the message women are often given," Stella said.

Charlie shook off the hypnotic effect of Stella's undivided attention and tried to pin her into taking a side. "But you don't agree with it?"

Stella shrugged. "My opinion on the issue isn't what matters here, Charlie. What matters is how you feel about yourself and your decision."

Realizing Stella didn't seem to be someone who would allow herself to be pinned into anything, Charlie gave up on defiance and looked out the window into the gray woods. "Now? I wish I could take it all back."

Stella crossed her hands and rested them on her belly. "Why is that?"

"Because I didn't know. I didn't know she was actually a baby. My baby." Charlie began to cry again, feeling stupid and helpless because it was one of the things she most hated to do, and here she was blubbering all over the place. Since the collar of her shirt was already damp with mucous, she tugged a tissue from the box on the table beside her, the whiff of its extraction synching with the next burst of lavender air. She blew her nose, cleared her throat, and crossed her legs ladylike as if it was something she normally did. "But Grace said the Father forgives me."

"Grace?"

"Someone else I met. Well, I mean, she's still around."

"And she said what?"

Charlie wondered if repeating herself was going to be an ongoing need with Stella. "That since I'm sorry and told God that, he forgives me. For the abortion."

"I bet that feels good to you."

"It does." When Charlie took a deep breath and blew it out, it was with the relief of having broken the water's surface to take a gulp of fresh air. "Plus, she backed Final up on saying the Father's taking care of her now. So at least I know she's okay."

Stella nodded and then yawned. As Charlie stared into the expanse of the woman's mouth—at the film on her tongue, the two gaps where rear molars used to be, and the pink uvula dangling in front of her throat—she longed for the intense and gentle gaze of only a few minutes before within which she'd felt cocooned and safe. Instead, she suddenly felt like her deepest revelations were old hat.

"You look like you've heard this before."

Stella closed her mouth and nodded. "I have."

Charlie sat up straighter. "You have? Did you have an abortion?"

"No, but I've worked with many women who have."

"Does it, like, mess with their heads?" Charlie eyed the drum, wondering if her outburst was something to worry about.

Stella shifted in her chair as if moving into new territory. "It's a difficult experience for many women to process. The amount and type of support they have matters a great deal."

Charlie looked back from the drum. "What do you mean?"

"It's a big decision, and some women regret it afterward. If the baby's father is involved, he may struggle, too. Abortion has a ripple effect across families, and emotions often run high. If a woman feels judged about her pregnancy instead of supported, it can be tough."

Charlie nearly snorted. "Tell me about it."

"Is that how you feel?" Stella's tone was more compassionate than clinical, which is why Charlie found her tongue unrolling like a red carpet. "Before my accident? Absolutely. My mom was really upset when she found out. We had a huge fight. She said I was a disgrace."

"Her exact words?"

Charlie rolled her nose ring as she stared at the floor. "Well… not technically."

"Not…*technically*."

"That's what she was thinking. I'm just the one who said it out loud."

"So…it sounds more like that may be how you see yourself."

Charlie looked up. "Seriously? Is that what this is going to be like?"

Stella gave a quizzical tilt of her head.

"Shrinky."

Stella smiled. "Ah. Is that what I'm doing? Being shrinky?"

Charlie sighed and rolled her vulnerability back into place. "Whatever. Then I wrecked and died and came back to life and we made up and everyone lives happily ever after." She listened to the methodical tick of the clock and wondered how much longer she'd have to sit there. Finally, she gave in to the tractor beam of Stella's gaze.

"It'll take time."

Charlie frowned. "What will?"

"For you to trust me."

"I don't know what you mean."

Stella smiled.

"Seriously. I don't know what that means. And I don't know how I ended up here."

"I think the judge had something to do with that."

Charlie shook her head. "No, I mean, I can't believe my mother picked you for me to see."

"It's a small town. Not like therapists are pouring out of the woodwork."

"Have you been here a long time?"

"In Ripple Creek?"

Charlie nodded.

"I was born here."

"So… Huh."

"Huh?"

"Well, me too. And I'm just remembering my mom said she saw a therapist after my daddy died."

Stella smiled without responding.

Slowly, the sun of realization grew on Charlie's horizon. "Were you my mother's therapist?"

Stella laced her fingers together and rested her hands in her lap. "Since she gave me permission…yes. I'm very fond of your mom."

"You are? But you're nothing like her. You're…"

"Frumpy?"

Charlie laughed. "I didn't say that."

Stella rose from her chair, placed her palms onto her lower back and leaned backward into them. Charlie had been right—no bra. "Well I am. And old. And proud of both. Coffee?" She headed toward the one-cup coffee maker with a rack of plastic containers beside it.

"Please. Black."

Stella rambled about at the counter, humming under her breath while she snapped one of the little containers into the machine. It chugged into life, and Charlie listened to the steady stream of liquid pelting the bottom of the ceramic mug. The thick scent of freshly brewed overpowered the lavender room freshener as if it never existed.

"Was my mom as much of a mess as me?"

Stella returned with two steaming mugs. She nodded toward a wooden coaster holder that looked like an old-fashioned radio. Charlie pulled out two coasters and set them on the side tables beside each of their chairs.

"If you think I'm going to give you the dirt on your mother, forget it. Client confidentiality. I only told you I was her therapist because she gave me permission to."

"Does that mean you won't tell her what I tell you?" Charlie eyed her hopefully.

"That's the way it works."

"Not that there's much to tell."

"Uh-huh." Stella murmured it into the mug as she took a sip of her coffee.

"So, are you a…I mean…do you believe in—"

"God?"

Charlie nodded.

"Yes. I have a very strong faith."

"The Jesus thing, too?"

Stella laughed. "Yes, Jesus and I are buds."

"Spirit?"

"He's part of the package."

"Grace?"

"I haven't met her in the same way you have, but I've certainly been showered with plenty of what she offers."

Unexpected tears sprang into Charlie's eyes. "I wish I could take it back." She felt a sob building within and then listened as it overflowed into the halting words she couldn't hold back. "I wish… Rose was here…with me…so I could…be her…mom."

Her breath came in short gasps as she gazed into the columns of gray trees outside and wondered what other option she could've possibly had. Somehow she suspected her mother's current level of support was more about being grateful to have her daughter back from the dead than an unconditional willingness to stand by her when she screwed up.

She took a cleansing breath, grabbed another tissue, and blew her nose. Then Charlie looked back at Stella and tried to keep her chin from quivering as she spoke. "Do you think I'm a horrible person because I had an abortion?"

Stella put her mug down, leaned forward, and propped her elbows on her knees as if ready to share a secret. "I think judging someone else is one of the most wasteful and damaging things we can do. And the glass house I live in is very fragile."

"So you're not going to throw stones."

Stella straightened. "Exactly. I don't think you're a bad person because you had an abortion, Charlie. What I think…what I know… is that you are a precious child of God who is deeply loved."

Chapter 13

One week later
Thursday

"It was Stella's idea. Well, and mine."

Charlie's mom cocked one eyebrow. "Stella has some pretty interesting ideas, that's for sure." She put the last cup into the dishwasher, closed the door, and punched a button to turn it on. The sound of trickling water drifted up from beneath the granite countertop. "How did you two come up with that?"

Charlie pushed against the counter and tipped her stool back on two legs. When her mother gave her a look, she dropped her hands and it clunked down onto all fours. "She said I should complete my community service hours someplace where I could help someone like me."

Her mom turned on the faucet, picked up a sponge, and held it underneath. "And that's an animal shelter…why?"

Charlie shrugged. "Lost animals no one else wants. Seems perfect."

She wasn't sure what she expected when her mother looked up and then turned off the water. But it wasn't that she would simply squeeze the excess from the sponge and begin wiping the surfaces surrounding her. "You know that's not true," she said to a stubborn patch of dried sauce as she leaned forward to examine and scrub it with determination.

Charlie watched her, feeling a familiar rush of unimportance and wondering if her mother had any idea how it felt to be trumped by a dirty countertop. "Anyway, I think those rescues need to know they matter. And I want to help them."

Her mother straightened, her gaze combing the rest of the counter as she spoke. "But you've never even liked animals, have you? I mean, you never wanted a dog. Or a cat. Or—"

"A hamster or a fish. I know. That was mostly because I didn't want to take care of anyone. I only cared about myself. Now it seems like Spirit wants me to be a little more helpful."

Charlie's mom finally stopped and looked directly at her. "Who are you and what have you done with my daughter?"

Charlie made a face. "Very funny. Anyway, Patch says I'm right."

"Patch?"

"Anna's daughter. She met Final, too."

Her mother dropped the sponge into the sink and looked at Charlie as if she had two heads. "Why am I just now hearing this?"

Charlie shrugged. "Guess I needed to chew on it for a while."

"When did she meet him?"

"I don't know exactly. She tried to kill herself."

Her mom moved around the counter, tugged out the other stool, and sat down. "Why?"

In light of the fact that she'd not only been dead and then undead like Charlie but had also met Final, Patch's *why* hadn't seemed important. Instead, Patch was a kindred spirit who didn't think she was crazy. The fact that her mother didn't latch onto this tidbit with the same amount of enthusiasm, but preferred to dig into Patch's pain instead, made the hair on the back of Charlie's neck stand on end. "Does it matter?"

Since her mother looked like she'd just been slapped, Charlie assumed the edge in her response was a little sharper than intended.

She figured Spirit was listening, so she tried again. "I think she told me something about it, but all I heard was she'd met Final, too. I couldn't believe it."

Her mother nodded, but the shadow in her expression meant she was still hurt. Charlie looked out the window, kicking herself, wondering if she'd ever be able to get the hang of this new way of doing things. But what she really wanted to do was plead her case. Certainly Spirit could see her point. It wasn't as if it was easy to have a mother who cared more about a dirty countertop than anything she might have to say.

"Charlie?"

When she looked back, her mom was watching her, waiting. Her features had softened, and Charlie felt instant regret for all the meanness that had just raced through her head. She stepped into the rollercoaster car that was headed back to the top of their relationship and turned on the stool to face her mom.

"What?"

"I asked how long."

"How long what?"

Her mother smiled. "Patch was—"

"Oh. Dead? I don't know exactly. She said it was long enough."

"So, did she meet other people like you did?"

Charlie shook her head. "No, apparently that just happened to me."

"But then she came back to life."

"She looked pretty alive when I talked to her."

Her mom smiled. "Ah, there's my sarcastic daughter."

Charlie savored the sense of relief between them, even if she wasn't sure how long it'd last. "Well, Mom. Dah."

"So anyway—Patch."

"Right. I told her that her mom asked God to give me a second chance, and then I came back to life."

Her mom's eyes filled with sudden tears. "You didn't tell me that."

"There's a lot I haven't told you."

Her mother was quiet for a moment, as if making a decision. "When you're ready. I want to hear it all. Anything you want to tell me."

Charlie knew her mother would never be able to handle everything she didn't know. Still, she wanted to hug the moment. Capture the attention in a jar so she could savor it later, when she again forgot what it was like to feel like she mattered. The only response she could manage was a thin smile.

Her mother nodded, and Charlie spotted her relief. "What did Patch say about her mom's prayer?"

"She asked me what I thought I was supposed to do with my second chance."

"And?"

"I told her I think I'm supposed to make the most of it. Then she said of course her mother was right about me."

Her mom smiled. "I like Patch."

Charlie slid off her stool and headed for the fridge. She opened the door and was greeted by a waft of cold air and the smell of the bleach solution her mother used to make the white shelves glisten. "So, I think I'm supposed to help somebody other than me. I don't know how, and I'm hoping Spirit's going to chime in. Since dealing with the families was kinda intense, I thought rescues might be a better place to start." She grabbed a cheese stick, peeled open the wrapper, and bit into one soft end. As she stood there, chewing with her back to her mother and cold air washing over her as if she were in a beer commercial, the door alarm began to chime.

"You weren't born in a barn." The familiar edge in her mother's tone had returned, and Charlie shut the door without turning. She gazed at the perfectly aligned magnets from places they'd vacationed, ordered in neat alphabetical rows, as she ignored the heat of her mother's stare on the back of her head.

"If you ask him, he will," her mother said. It was as if she were reading from a manufacturer's guide for a new appliance.

Charlie turned. "What?"

Her mother was watching her, sizing her up for some purpose Charlie couldn't place. Then she apparently spotted a crumb out of the corner of her eye. She reached over the counter, grabbed the sponge, and began to wipe the surface in front of her. "God. If you pray diligently, read the Bible faithfully, and go to church, then he will provide the direction you need."

As Charlie watched her mother lean down so she could see the surface of the counter at eye level, seeking errant substances she may have overlooked, it occurred to her that her experience with God so far was nothing like her mother's.

She sure hoped Spirit would keep it that way.

Ripple Creek Refuge
Friday afternoon

It looked more like a vacation cottage than a refuge for rescues. The sign by the road was a sturdy wooden affair, with RIPPLE CREEK REFUGE burned into the surface in neat block letters. Beside it, another sign directed visitors to park around the back. Gravel popped beneath the tires of a truck with ANIMAL CONTROL on the side as it eased past Charlie on the driveway as she walked up the hill. Barren sugar maples dotted the brown grass of the property, which stretched half the length of a football field from the front porch to the asphalt road behind her. As she neared the red brick structure, Charlie noticed several pet carriers stacked beneath leashes and collars that hung on the wall of the porch. Beside them, another sign read, LOANERS.

When she finally reached the corner of the building, she realized it was no cottage at all, but a sprawling structure with multiple additions. There were more buildings behind it and an array of fences and outdoor pens. As she turned the corner, the sound of barking dogs echoed across the property. In the distance, someone walked a dog on a leash in one of the pens. A couple emerged from the main building with a cat in a carrier. A young woman with puffy eyes and a Great Dane on a leash meandered toward the back door. The driver of the truck got out, opened a cubby from the side, and pulled out a small dog, who looked at Charlie with eyes sad as a melting candle.

Charlie sighed. "Spirit, what are you getting me into?"

Instead of waiting for an answer, she made her way up the walk. When she opened the back door, a bell jingled over her head and the aroma of lemon cleaning solution wafted from within. She'd braced herself for something much worse, but the tile floor in the waiting area sparkled. An orchestra played softly from a speaker near the ceiling. There was a long desk in the center of the room, with a sign on each end: SURRENDER and ADOPTION. A woman thin as a wire with a tight salt and pepper braid looked up and smiled. Her eyes were blue enough to swim in.

"Can I help you?" The words dripped with Scotland, and Charlie recognized the voice immediately.

"Yeah, I… I'm Charlie Welks. Well, Charlene is my real name. I spoke with someone on the phone about volunteering."

"That would be me." The wheels on the stool beneath her clattered as she stood and extended her hand. "It's nice to meet you, Charlie. I'm Lorna Darrow, the manager here. Let's go into my office." She opened a waist-level door and gestured toward a door behind the desk. When Charlie turned to follow, she caught the Great Dane in her peripheral vision. He sat quietly and stately beside the woman, who couldn't stop wiping her eyes.

"What's the deal there?" Charlie whispered.

Lorna turned. "Oh. Sad, but common. He got too big, and her landlord said they can't keep him."

"What will happen to him?"

"It's too soon to tell. Sometimes we'll strike it rich, and an adopter will walk in the door who's looking for a dog like that. But the big ones are hard to place. We try to work with breed-specific rescue organizations in such situations."

"What if you can't find him a home? Will he be…put down?"

Lorna turned so abruptly Charlie nearly ran into her. She pointed a long plain finger in Charlie's face. "Absolutely not. We are strictly a no-kill shelter. Every animal who comes in our door deserves love and a second chance."

Charlie put up her hands as if she were being robbed. "Sorry, I didn't mean to make you mad."

The woman waved her hand. "Nah. *You* didn't. It's the issue that makes me mad. People who discard animals as if they're objects. God created each of us for a purpose, including these wee ones."

Charlie followed her into the office and sat down. Each item on the small desk apparently had its place, including the five sticky notes lined up in a row along the right edge. On the walls, corkboards held an array of papers and clipboards, all arranged in categories that were labeled at the top.

"Wow."

Lorna nodded. "I run a tight ship, my dear. Which is something you need to know if we're to get along."

"Okay."

"And I understand you've gotten yourself into a bit of trouble."

"Yeah, but I'm different now. I think. I hope."

Lorna sat on the edge of the desk, leaned toward Charlie, and waved her finger like a windshield wiper. "Well, you'd better be. No alcohol. No drugs. No smoking. And no smartphones. When we work, we work. We love the animals who are right there in front of us instead of wasting the day watching them on social media."

Charlie swallowed and nodded.

The woman moved close enough for Charlie to smell the peppermint on her breath. "And if I ever catch you being anything but absolutely loving to the sweet creatures we are entrusted with here…" She shook her head as if imagining such a thing would be more than she could take. "The trouble you've been in so far will seem like a stroll in the park."

Charlie realized she'd been holding her breath. She exhaled and nodded. "Of course."

Lorna moved behind the desk, sat down, put on a pair of skinny black-framed reading glasses and poised a pen over the blank page of a notebook. She looked over her glasses and pinned Charlie to the chair with her crystal-blue gaze. "Now, tell me what this court order is all about. I need to know who I've got working under my roof with my babies."

Charlie rubbed her palms on her thighs in a useless attempt to dry them. "What do you want to know?"

"You could start with the reason you were arrested."

"Well, technically…"

Lorna lifted one eyebrow and gave Charlie a look she'd thought only her mother capable of.

"Okay. I got in a fight with my mom and had a wreck."

"Young women fight with their mothers all the time. Young drivers have car accidents. Neither necessarily leads to an arrest."

Charlie held up a hand. "Okay, I'd been drinking and smoking pot. I was charged with DUI."

"Now we're getting somewhere." Lorna made a note.

Charlie leaned forward to get a glimpse of the page. "What are you writing?"

Lorna looked up and held her gaze. "How do you feel about yourself right now, Charlene?"

"Well, it's Charlie, but—"

Lorna laid the pen across the pad, folded her hands, and gazed at Charlie without speaking.

"Uh…how do I feel about myself?" Charlie had no idea what Spirit must've been thinking.

"How does it feel to admit you made mistakes?"

Charlie's shoulders felt like someone was standing on them. First Stella, and now this. "Not very good."

"And that working for a grumpy Scot is part of your penance?"

"You don't seem very grumpy to me."

Lorna stared at her.

"Well, okay. You are kinda scary."

Lorna smiled. "Good."

"Good?"

She nodded.

"So you're trying to scare me?"

"I wouldn't put it that way."

"Then what?"

Lorna sighed and took off her glasses. "Charlene—well, we'll make it Charlie—do you think it's a coincidence you ended up in my shelter, with my rescues?"

"No. My therapist kinda told me to call you."

"Your therapist?"

Charlie sighed. "The other thing the judge is making me do."

Lorna watched her for a long moment.

"What?" Charlie adjusted her nose ring, thinking it might be crooked or something.

The woman put her glasses back on and made another note. "We'll see how you feel about that by the time you've completed your hours." She looked up. "And unless you want to see half your nose hanging from some pup's mouth, that thing must go."

Chapter 14

Friday evening

"Scary. That's what." Charlie sank into the couch beside her
mother, who was engrossed in the morning paper she never had
time to read before work. "Grouchy little Scottish thing who read
me the riot act before I hardly said a word. Plus, she won't let me
wear my nose ring."

The newspaper crinkled when her mom turned the page. "I
like her already."

Charlie crossed her arms in a pout. "Why does everyone think
I need to be taught a lesson? Isn't dying good enough?"

Her mother didn't look up but continued to scan the obituaries, of all things. "I didn't mean you needed to be taught a lesson.
I just think it's good for you to have strong women in your life."

"But I don't need all these other people. I've got you." The
words were laced with more hopefulness than Charlie intended.

Her mother licked her right index finger, teased the corner of
the next page toward her thumb, and leaned in to examine the fine
print of a sale. "I'm not strong, Charlie. I should've stood up for you
long ago, and I didn't." The admission should've been something
for Charlie to celebrate. A milestone of honesty, delivered eye to

eye with a pinky-swear pact. Instead, her mother's words felt like more of a shrug than a hug, which was less than Charlie hoped for—but typical of what she'd come to expect.

"You did the best you could at the time." Charlie murmured it more to herself than her mother, surprised she'd said it at all.

Her mom folded the paper, tucked it into a stack, and picked up a magazine. "Now that…is something Stella told you to say."

"No, seriously."

Her mother finally looked at Charlie. "I am being serious. How'd you come up with that one?"

Charlie shrugged. "Just starting to understand how hard things were for you, too. After Daddy died."

Her mother flipped open the magazine. "They were. But you shouldn't have had to pay for that. A mother is supposed to take care of her children."

Charlie suppressed the urge to jump up from the couch and pump her fist in satisfaction. Instead, she just smiled a little and hoped Spirit was keeping track of her brownie points.

Her mother sighed, closed the magazine, and looked at her watch. "Which is something I need to do more work on." She patted Charlie's knee and started to get up. "Time to make dinner. It'll be just us girls. Dan's working late."

Charlie put her hand over her mother's. "Wait. What is something you need to do more work on?"

Her mom pulled her hand away as a wave of sadness rolled across her face. "Nothing."

Charlie shook her head in disgust. "I see. I'm supposed to spill my guts, and you're allowed to get away with that?"

Her mother raised one eyebrow. "There are some benefits to being the mother."

Charlie slumped back against the couch. "It's still not fair." Then she sat up. "Does that mean you're going to start seeing Stella again?"

"No, I don't think that's a good idea."

"Why not?"

Her mom stood from the couch and walked toward the kitchen, her words drifting along behind her like a tail. "Not while you're seeing her. One of us is enough."

Charlie scampered after the disappearing figure of her mother as if she were about to miss the bus. "What's that supposed to mean?"

By the time she got to the kitchen, her mother's head was already in a cupboard under a cabinet, fishing out a pot. The clatter from below meant that when Charlie had last unloaded the dishwasher, she'd put the dishes away in her usual haphazard manner. Her mother finally emerged, a soup pot in hand, her thin face flushed with the effort and one strand of hair dangling unusually out of place. "Don't get defensive. I mean I want you to feel free to talk about anything you need without wondering if I'm her next appointment."

Despite all of her perfections, her mother wasn't much of a cook, so the grind of the can opener was like the ring of the dinner bell at their house. She deposited the contents of the first can of soup into the pot on the counter, flipped a switch on the front of the stove, and stared into the flames that emerged from the gas ring in front of her as if huddled up to a campfire. She stood there for so long, Charlie began to wonder if she forgot about dinner.

"Mom."

Her mother startled from her trance and looked at Charlie. "What?"

Charlie pointed at the lonely pan full of soup. "You planning to cook that?"

Her mom followed Charlie's finger to the pot as if they were linked by a string. "Oh. Yes. Of course."

For any other mother and daughter, Charlie thought, it could've been a great moment. A chance for Charlie to tease and her mother to laugh at herself. But Charlie knew her mother rarely did so. She didn't think it was funny when she got distracted or made a mistake. Instead, in her mother's home, mistakes were something to be corrected—and sometimes punished—for the errors in judgment they were deemed to be. Charlie had mistakenly thought maybe being dead and then undead might have changed things, but increasingly, that didn't seem to be the case.

Which is why, when her mother blushed and reached for the next can of soup instead of letting her guard down to bond with her daughter, Charlie walked to the doorway leading into the hall, then stopped to gaze at the woman at the stove. "Stella says I might want to do some kind of memorial thing for Rose."

"Rose?" Her mother said it absently as she pulled a spoon through the soup.

Then Charlie turned toward the hall, depositing the words over her shoulder as if they were carefully placed bombs. "My baby. That's what the Father named her."

One week later
Saturday morning

Charlie pulled on a fresh pair of latex gloves and adjusted her paper mask. It was the fifth litter box she'd cleaned that morning, and she was ready for her break.

"But you guys don't care, do you?"

She looked down at the five gray kittens who wound themselves around her ankles, a chorus of high-pitched meows with brief intermissions to mow each other over and roll around, transforming into one giant ball of fur. She reached down and gently tugged one from her jeans, which were apparently being mistaken for a tree.

"You'll be much happier over here. Well, I'll be much happier with you over here." She lifted the kitten by the scruff of her neck and placed her on the cat tree in the corner of the enclosure. Five carpeted platforms jutted out from the trunk, which was also covered in carpet. She placed her on the highest one, hoping it would take some time for her to make her way back down. As soon as her paws touched the surface, she ran for the trunk and began to scramble toward the bottom.

Charlie felt a tug from below and looked down to see two more kittens climbing, one on each of her legs. "You guys. I'm not the tree." When she grasped the scruff of each neck, the kittens went limp. They dangled in the air like wet rags as she deposited them on the top of the platform. By then, the first kitten had nearly made it to the bottom, and two more were already ascending her legs like determined climbers about to reach the peak. Charlie leaned down and the two kittens stared at her with their gray-blue eyes as they shrieked a unified meow. "If you don't stop, I'm never going to get my work done."

"It helps if you put them in a carrier while you're cleaning the boxes."

Charlie turned to see Lorna watching from outside the enclosure. "Now you tell me."

"Well, my dear, if you would've asked, I would've told you."

Charlie steamed in silence. She leaned back down to address the climbers who were now on her thighs. Their sharp little talons occasionally broke through the fabric of her jeans and discovered the sturdy foundation of her flesh. "Ow." Charlie resisted the urge to yank the kitten from her thigh. She heard the latch of the enclosure door click behind her.

"Here, let me help."

That would be nice.

Lorna lifted each one by the scruff of its neck, walked to the corner, and sat down in a single, seamless, cross-legged motion. As soon as the other three kittens realized what was happening, they charged toward her and began to climb up the fabric of her sweatshirt, a meowing chorus of delight. Lorna smiled as she stroked them firmly, undoubtedly half with love, half with trying to keep them from climbing onto her face. "Okay, okay. I know." She looked up at Charlie. "They love to be loved. Just like the rest of us."

Charlie didn't say anything and returned to cleaning out the litter box.

"You don't like it much here, do you?" Lorna's brogue seemed thicker than usual.

Charlie shrugged without looking up. "It's okay, I guess."

"Maybe it's me you don't like."

Charlie didn't say a word as she tied up the old liner and replaced it with a new one.

"I suppose it's a good sign, you not liking me."

Spirit, I'm trying here.

"It doesn't matter, you know. Whether you do or not."

I didn't say I didn't like you, lady.

"What matters is that you learn from these wee ones. They always have lessons to teach us, if we'll only listen."

Finally, Charlie stopped and looked at her. "What have they taught you?"

Lorna's petting stopped, her hand in midair. She dropped it to her lap. "Well, now, that's a good question, lass."

Charlie picked up the bag of litter and poured it over the new liner. A cloud of dust rose from the pan.

"They've taught me that everyone matters. That everyone is important. That everyone needs love."

Charlie stopped mid-pour and looked up. "Then why are you…"

Lorna gave her a stony glare. "Then why am I *what*, my dear?"

Charlie sighed. "Never mind."

"No, I'd like to hear it."

Charlie set the litter bag on the floor and straightened, planting a steady gaze on her new boss. "You're kinda mean."

Lorna raised her eyebrows. "Mean?"

"Yeah."

She looked down into her lap and stroked her sleeping brood. "How am I mean?"

"Not to them. To me."

"Oh. To you?"

Charlie nodded.

"And how am I mean to you, my dear?"

"You harp on me if I'm a minute late. You go behind me, checking everything. And you won't let me wear my nose ring." At that, Charlie started to reach for her nose, but the gloves reminded her she'd just been digging in cat poop.

Lorna sighed. She pulled a cushion onto the floor next to her and gently poured the ball of fur onto it. Then she stood so she and Charlie were eye to eye.

"The wee creatures who arrive at my door have been through enough. They don't need to have one more person reject them or treat them poorly. What they need is love and acceptance, no matter what." She took a step forward, and Charlie took a step back. "I must tell you my track record with teenagers has not been a good one. Too often, they come in here for some school project or to get out of trouble—just like you. They are not here because they want to be. They are here because they have to be."

Lorna moved toward the door and put her hand on the latch. She turned and looked back at Charlie. "I'm still figuring out which you are."

Chapter 15

Saturday afternoon
Bosko Counseling Services

"Yeah, well, I don't like her either." Charlie sat in Stella's office, listening to the occasional squish of the lavender-scented aromatherapy contraption and the tick of the clock on the desk.

"Just because she's protective of her rescues doesn't mean she doesn't like you, Charlie." Although Stella was adorned in her usual state of disarray, Charlie hoped the image before her meant Saturday sessions were even more casual than during the week. It was more for Stella's sake than hers that she cared, since sitting in a therapy session with someone who looked like they'd just rolled out of bed made her more willing to loosen her tongue than what her mother's precise persona ever allowed.

"I felt it the day I walked in there. The first thing she did was glare at my nose ring." Charlie lifted her hand and rolled her nose ring as if protecting a pet.

Stella took a sip of her coffee, pausing with her lip on the rim to give Charlie a look through the rising steam. "And…"

"And she decided before I even opened my mouth that she didn't like me." Charlie crossed her arms into a pout.

135

Stella placed her cup on the coaster beside her, laced her fingers together, and propped her hands on her belly. "You're certain it's your boss who doesn't like you?"

Charlie sighed. "Not you, too."

Stella tapped her thumbs together as she gazed at Charlie. "Me too?"

"Yeah. Don't get weird and shrinky on me."

Stella smiled. "Okay, if that feels weird and shrinky, then let's talk about something else."

Charlie squinted a little, as if she didn't trust the tone of Stella's suggestion. "Like what?"

"Like why you smell like pot."

Charlie felt the flash of heat that rose in her face. She rolled her nose ring as she studied the fabric of her chair. "I don't know what you're talking about."

Stella didn't respond.

A burst of lavender filled the air.

The clock counted out ten more seconds.

When Charlie looked up, Stella was gazing at her with an expression that indicated she could wait forever.

"It was just a few hits."

Stella nodded. "Okay."

Charlie assumed the lack of expression and monotone response couldn't be good. "So? What's wrong with that?" She heard the rising pitch of her voice but had no desire to tame it. She stood from her chair, put her hands on her hips, and leaned toward Stella as if she were the one doing the interrogating. "Isn't a person allowed to relax a little?"

Stella calmly looked up from her spot. "Did I say anything was wrong with that?"

Charlie held her ground as if she'd just planted a flag. "Well, you're staring at me like my mother does."

Stella shrugged. "I'm simply waiting for you to expound."

Charlie dropped her arms to her sides and slumped back

into her chair. "Well, there you go. I smoked some pot. It's legal here, you know."

Stella cleared her throat and repositioned herself in her chair. "Yes, it is. But not for a 16-year-old."

Charlie waved her hand. "As if anyone cares."

"I'm pretty sure a judge would care about a 16-year-old on probation for DUI smoking pot illegally."

Charlie leaned forward and nearly sneered. "Who says any judge is going to find out?"

Stella folded her hands in her lap. "What's going on, Charlie?"

"Nothing."

"You're pretty hostile today."

"Now that's funny. You think this is hostile? You haven't seen—"

"I've seen plenty." Stella put her hand over her mouth to suppress a yawn. "Plenty of young women sitting in my chair giving me the same little tough-girl act."

The fact that Stella looked like she was about to nod off infuriated Charlie even more. She clenched her jaw and stared into the woods outside the window.

"What happened to the new leaf you were planning to turn over?"

Another burst of lavender.

The clock counted ten more seconds.

"Someone stepped on it."

"How so?"

Charlie sighed. "Do we have to talk about this?"

Stella shrugged. "If you were an adult paying your own way, I'd say no. And you'd be free to leave anytime you'd like."

"But I'm a prisoner instead." Charlie longed to follow the sentence with a dry spit but figured that'd only make things worse.

"Hardly. But it's up to you to decide how much you want to get out of our time, Charlie. And I'm not about to let you off that easy."

"I'd rather be left alone." Charlie glared at Stella. "And then you could go take your nap."

Stella shrugged. "I'm old, Charlie. I may not seem like I'm hanging on your every word, but I am. Even if I need to indulge in a yawn every once in a while." Then she rested her elbows on her knees and pinned Charlie to her seat with the gaze of a wizard looking through a window into Charlie's soul at things Charlie didn't even know were there. "You may pretend to see some tough chick when you look in the mirror, but I see a hurting little girl who needs my help."

Her words were so warm Charlie wanted to reach out and wrap herself in them like a blanket. Instead, she cocked her head and smirked. "Chick?"

Stella waved her hand. "Hey, chick's still a great word. I'm an old chick. You're a young chick."

"What happened to the old hens?"

Stella laughed. "That…is a whole other group of women I don't care to be associated with." She took another sip of her coffee. "*Blech*. Let it get cold." She set the cup back down on the table beside her. "How are you and your mom doing?"

"Okay, I guess."

"You guess?"

"Seriously?"

"I'm your therapist. It's my job to dig. And we only have an hour."

Charlie rolled her nose ring. "I thought things were getting better—until I went to court. Since then, up and down. One minute, I have hope. The next minute, she's so busy in her own little world she hardly notices I'm there. Except when I'm somehow disrupting her perfection. Especially…"

Stella watched her. "Especially…"

"Especially when I told her about Rose. I mean, of course she knew about my abortion, but not the rest. That now I know she was a girl and God named her and she's with him. All that. And that you said I should have a memorial for her." Charlie shook her head. "Then she got even weirder."

Stella cocked her head. "In what way?"

"I don't know. Crying and stuff. Right after I returned from the dead, things were really good. But now she's like…pulling away or something."

"How do you feel about that?"

"Stella—"

Stella held up her palms. "It's just a question. That's what I do. I ask questions."

"Yeah, well, I'm tired of answering them. Just tell me what you want me to say."

"You know it doesn't work that way. My job is to help you look inside to discover your own answers."

Charlie snorted. "Believe me, I don't have any answers hiding in there."

Stella smiled. "You'd be surprised."

"It's just what she did before."

"We're back to your mom?"

"Yeah." Charlie stood from her chair and walked to the drum. She eyed the mallet but settled for placing both hands on the cowhide stretched across its surface, finding comfort in the fact that it was so different from anything in her mother's house. "She said everything was behind us. But I guess not. I guess she's mad at me after all."

"Maybe you should talk to her about it."

Charlie ran the tips of her fingers over the smooth surface, savoring the imperfections in the leather that were allowed to remain. She shook her head.

"Why not?"

She could tell from the angle of Stella's voice and the grunt that preceded it that she'd stood from her chair. Charlie turned to face her. "And have her start pointing the finger of judgment at me all over again? No thank you."

Stella clasped her hands in front of her like a schoolteacher. "Maybe that won't happen."

Tears welled in Charlie's eyes, and a single tear rolled down her cheek. She wiped it hastily and headed for her chair. "I ain't takin' the chance."

Stella watched her. "Is this why you started smoking pot again?"

"I guess."

Stella nodded and sat back down. She tugged a tissue from the box beside her and blew her nose. She held the box out to Charlie as if offering a cigar. "Have you talked to Spirit lately?"

Charlie yanked out a tissue. "Spirit who."

"He doesn't usually just drop in without an invitation."

"I ain't seen him do me much good so far."

"So coming back to life is old hat now, is it?"

Charlie stood and paced about the room, rolling her nose ring. "I don't know what I'm supposed to do. Grace said Spirit was going to tell me what to do all the time, and at first that sounded terrible because I hate to be told what to do, but then I thought it might be nice, but I haven't heard a word from him in over a week, so I'm starting to wonder if the whole thing was some kind of dream."

Charlie collapsed back into her chair and began to cry.

Stella nodded. "Now we're getting somewhere."

"Is this what it's like?"

"What what's like?"

"The God thing. The being-a-good-person thing. I was so sure Final and Grace and Spirit were all being straight with me, but…"

Charlie blew her nose and stared at the floor.

"Charlie, look at me." Stella's voice was smooth as butter. Charlie met the warm hazel gaze.

"But what?"

Charlie's words sounded as if they were falling down a well. "I feel more alone now than ever."

Chapter 16

Ripple Creek Refuge
Monday afternoon

Charlie was sitting at the front desk manning the phones when she heard the jingle of the front door. His black nose was the first thing she saw. It inched around the edge of the door, a sniffing scout, testing the air ahead for safety. As the man holding the leash entered behind him, the dog spotted the little beagle sitting at a woman's feet in the corner. He began to whimper and strained so hard against his collar he started to hack.

"Dog, no." The man tugged on the leash and pulled him toward the counter. The starched white edge of a priest's collar was visible under his coat.

Charlie eyed the man's neck. She'd come to expect the unexpected in this place, but this was something new. "Can I help you?"

"Yes, I'm from Ripple Creek Hospice, and I have this little guy who's going to need a home."

When Charlie stood and looked over the counter, the dog looked up at her. The knowing sadness in his brown eyes startled her, and she quickly averted her gaze to the long-haired white coat with irregular black spots. The patches of black around his paws

141

resembled boots, and his floppy ears sagged like withered spinach. Charlie was getting good at estimating weight, and she guessed him to be about forty pounds. He began to pace in a circle at the man's feet, his long tail tucked between his legs and panting as if he'd just chased a rabbit into its den.

"It's not exactly hot in here."

"He's nervous. His owner said he hates these places."

"So you're not the owner?"

"No. I'm his owner's chaplain."

Charlie stared at the collar and wondered what that meant.

The man followed her gaze. "I don't usually wear it to work. Just finished a memorial service for a patient."

Charlie gestured toward the dog. "Did he go?"

The chaplain smiled. "No, my team was in a jam and asked me to swing by and pick him up and bring him over after the service."

"Was the service for his owner?"

"No, another patient. His owner is sick, and there's no one to take care of Dog."

"Dog?"

"I know. Not very creative. His owner is…an interesting man."

Charlie heard the faint sound of an alarm bell going off in her head. "So…hospice. That means the guy's dying?"

"I really can't say."

"Where does he live?"

The chaplain looked around. "Is there someone…"

Charlie felt the beat of her heart pulsing in her ears. "Mister, is the guy dying?"

"Well…let's just say most patients who are in hospice die eventually."

She surprised both of them when she reached across the desk and put her hand on the chaplain's arm. "Can I talk to him?"

He took a step back. "I don't know that—"

Charlie removed her hand. "Sorry. It's just…I have some important stuff to tell him."

The chaplain smiled. "Me, too. But that doesn't mean he wants to hear it."

"But I—"

"Miss…what's your name?"

"Charlie."

"Charlie, I'm due at a patient's house." He gestured toward Dog. "I really need to get him checked in."

Charlie sighed, feeling like she'd just screwed something up. "Okay. Let me get the manager."

She went in search of Lorna, her mind straining for some word from Spirit. "I could use a little help here, you know."

Nothing.

"Look. Grace promised you'd help me. She and Patch both said you have work for me to do. How am I supposed to know what I'm supposed to do if you're gonna clam up?"

"Who are you talking to?"

Distracted by her prodding of Spirit, Charlie hadn't noticed how quickly she was moving through the building. Lorna stood next to Stuart's open cage. She'd been cleaning it out, but she presently was staring at Charlie as if she had three heads. The white rat sat on Lorna's shoulder, tucked against her neck. He peered at Charlie from behind Lorna's braid as he strained his snout toward her, wiggling his tiny pink nose in a frantic search for her scent. She stared back at the beady black eyes.

"Huh? Oh. No one who's listening. There's a guy out front from hospice with a dog. He said the owner's sick and can't take care of him anymore."

Lorna returned to her task, wiping down the inside of Stuart's cage and putting down a fresh layer of newspaper. "That's common. I'm done here. Let me wash up, and I'll be right there."

Charlie watched as she tugged Stuart from her shoulder, cradled him in her palms, and looked into his eyes. "There you go, my little lad." Then she gave him a kiss on the tip of his pink nose and placed him in his cage as if handling an egg. After washing her hands at the utility sink in the corner, she eyed Charlie as she was drying them. "Did you need something else?"

"Huh? Oh, no. Well, I just thought I'd wait for you."

"My dear. You are apparently forgetting there is a wee one in the waiting area who is likely scared to death about now. Perhaps you should go and see if some love is needed."

Charlie took a deep breath and nodded. "Right."

"But since you've dawdled here for so long, I'm ready as well." Lorna took the lead, her short, thin legs propelling her like a rocket through the multiple additions linking the back of the shelter to the waiting room. Charlie nearly had to jog to keep up.

When they entered the waiting room, the chaplain was sitting in the corner, trying to talk on the phone and hang onto the leash while the dog jumped up and down from the bench to the floor in a ping-pong of nervous energy.

"Aww, a little pit bull."

Charlie looked at Dog. "A pit bull?!"

Lorna walked toward the pair and sat on the floor cross-legged about three feet away from him. Dog watched her warily as he pushed his torso against the chaplain's leg.

"Yes, you can see it in his face. He's a mix, but that thin white line running along his nose and between his eyes is classic for the breed. He's beautiful."

Charlie looked at him, wondering if her initial reaction of pity was yet another of her hasty moves. "But aren't they dangerous?"

Lorna shook her head in resignation.

"What? I've heard they bite people."

"Dogs who bite usually have owners who bite," Lorna said. "It's not the dog's fault the owners don't know what they're doing. And don't care to learn any better. This wee lad's breed is very misunderstood." She sat with her hands on her thighs, palms up. Dog watched her, content to be molded into the chaplain's shin.

"Right, okay," the chaplain said. "I'll call them as soon as I'm done here. Thanks." He tapped a button on his smartphone and tucked it inside his coat. He smiled at Lorna and watched as she performed her magic.

Apparently aware something was up, Dog straightened his baby-deer front legs and pushed his paws against the floor, determined to keep the chaplain in place with the full weight of his body.

Lorna nodded in response. Remaining on the floor, she shifted her position so her back was toward Dog. Then she stuck her hand into the pocket of her jeans and fished out several small biscuits. She laid one on the floor next to her.

Dog quietly assessed this new development. After watching Lorna's unmoving form for several minutes, he finally stood on all fours and crept toward the treat as if it might bite. His long pink tongue snatched his prey. Then he immediately returned to the chaplain's feet, chomping as he watched Lorna's back.

Without turning around, she replaced it with another treat. After retrieving it, Dog didn't return to the chaplain. Instead, he stood next to Lorna, waiting with expectation. She tried to pet his head, but he ducked from her touch and backed away. "Okay, too soon. But, progress."

She stood and shook the chaplain's hand. "Lorna Darrow. I'm the manager."

"Tom Englewood. From hospice."

"Nice to meet you, Tom. Charlie says this little guy's owner needs to surrender?"

The chaplain smiled. "That's one way to put it."

Lorna laughed. "I mean his pet."

"Yes. He was moved to the hospice house today, and there's no one to take care of Dog."

"Dog?"

"Like I told Charlie, his owner's a little different."

Lorna nodded. "Familiar with the type. If he named this sweet boy, Dog, I bet he's a crusty old curmudgeon."

The chaplain folded his arms and laughed. "No comment."

"What's a curmudgeon?" Charlie leaned down and reached

out her hand to Dog. He stretched his neck for a distant whiff without budging from the chaplain's safety.

"A curmudgeon is what people will call me when I'm old," Lorna said.

Charlie dropped her hand to her side and got down onto her knees so she was nearly eye level with Dog. She relaxed back on her heels, and he cocked his head, watching her. "Doesn't his owner have any family?"

"Let's just say this is the only option we have."

Lorna nodded. "You know I'm going to need some paperwork, right?"

"Sure, I have everything."

Charlie repositioned herself like Lorna had, so her back was facing Dog. She put her hands behind her back, palms up, and rested them against the floor. It wasn't long before she heard the hesitant tap of his nails against the tile, moving toward her. Then she felt the sniffing heat of his breath against her right palm. She wanted to swing around and greet him but made herself sit still. Her discipline was rewarded by a tentative lap of his tongue against her fingers, which was followed by a thorough cleansing of her hand.

"Well, I'll be. It looks like you've made a new friend, my dear."

Charlie sat still as a stone as Dog sniffed at her ear. When a long lap of his tongue cut a path along her right cheek, she couldn't help but giggle—which was something she hadn't done in a very long time. She turned to face him and held out her hands. "He is kinda cute."

She scratched Dog's right ear, which resulted in a little moan of pleasure. He moved in for more, stepping into her lap to embark on a determined bathing of her face.

"Okay, okay, I give up." Charlie gently pushed him away and rubbed his head. "He's sweet."

"Don't sound so surprised, my dear. As I said, we have to open our eyes to the potential in all of God's creatures."

When Charlie stroked the length of Dog's back, his tail

wound into a tentative curl, like a piece of ribbon responding to the edge of a blade.

"Well, I'll be," Lorna said. "A curly tail on a pit. I wonder who else is in those genes."

"It's awesome." Charlie gently wrapped her fingers around Dog's tail and followed its furry curve, which rolled into a confident, near-perfect circle.

"Yeah, he seems to be a good dog. Never left his owner's side."

The statement made Charlie stop mid-stroke. She gazed into the pool of his brown eyes, wondering what he must be thinking. "Won't he be sad without him?"

The chaplain squatted beside her and rubbed Dog's ear. "Yes. Animals experience grief just as people do." Then he stood and smiled at Charlie and her new friend. "You're welcome to bring him by the hospice house anytime you'd like. It'd be good for both of them. But I've got to warn you, his owner can be a handful."

~

Monday evening

"Sounds like an interesting day." Charlie's mother sat at her desk in her home office, typing while she talked, the glow of the monitor screen casting shadows into the lines of her face which had emerged during the day's erosion of the foundation she'd applied that morning. Television sounds drifted from above, which meant Dan was probably in his man-cave with his feet propped up in his favorite recliner.

Absorbed with thoughts of Dog, Charlie barely noticed either one. She kicked off her shoes, stretched out on the couch, and stared at the brown railing holding the white panels of the drop ceiling in place, savoring the moment when Dog rolled his tail into a circle at her touch, as if he'd been stashing a present meant for her alone. "Since his tail is curly, Lorna says he must have another breed in him."

"I bet." Her mother's words floated toward the clatter of her keyboard, which stopped when she leaned to look over her reading glasses at the screen, hit the backspace key twice, and then resumed.

"The chaplain says his owner is a curmudgeon."

"That's nice."

"Well, Lorna called him that. Says that's what people will say about her when she's old."

"Uh-huh."

"If she keeps up the rat thing, they'll probably say a lot more."

"I bet."

"Dog's owner's in bad shape. I guess he's going to die."

"Sounds good."

"But the chaplain says I can take Dog to visit him."

"Uh-huh."

"And that once he dies, he'll end up a zombie."

"That's nice."

Charlie sat up. "Mom."

The clatter of the keyboard nearly drowned out the word.

"Mom." Charlie said it more forcefully.

Her mother stopped typing and looked at her. "What?"

"What did I just say?"

Confusion washed across her mother's face. Charlie watched her grope for an answer as if under the gun of a game show. Finally, her face lit up. "A new pit bull came in, and you think you have rats?"

Charlie slumped back onto the couch. "What's wrong with you?"

Her mother took off her reading glasses. "That's a loaded question."

"You've been a million miles away lately."

"I could say the same about you."

"Lately?"

"Well, no. Not lately. Before."

"Before is right. Lately, I'm the one who's trying, and you're not." The sudden tears in her eyes took Charlie by surprise. One spilled onto her cheek, and she quickly wiped it away.

"Oh, honey. Are you crying?" Her mother swiveled in her chair to face her.

"It's nothing."

"It's not nothing. What?"

Charlie looked at the unpredictable and complicated woman who was her mother and had the fleeting wish that bonding with her could be as easy as it'd been with a dog she'd just met. "I just… it feels like you're gone again."

Her mom gave a sigh which could've been filled with either impatience or regret. Typically, Charlie had no idea which it was and felt a surge of heat pulse up her neck. "When I first rose from the dead—"

"Don't—"

"When I first rose from the dead…" Charlie felt like a locomotive that had suddenly lost its brakes. "I thought everything had changed between us. At least I hoped it had. But after I went to court, you got weird again. Pulling away. Being your old perfect, cold self. Crying when you didn't think I could hear you." She took a breath and exhaled the rest. "And things have been even worse since I told you Stella wants me to have a memorial for Rose."

Her mother's only response was to stare at the block wall behind Charlie's head, which had been painted a muted shade of melon because it apparently made the basement office feel more professional.

"I mean, I know it's hard for you. She would've been your granddaughter and all. But it's hard for me, too." Charlie started to cry again. "I wouldn't have done it if I knew then what I know now."

When her mother dropped her gaze to look at Charlie, there was a sheen in them that, if unleashed, could've been tears. "What do you know now?"

Charlie's words came out in halting sobs. "That. She. Was. A. Baby."

Her mother didn't budge except to lace her fingers together and rest her hands in her lap.

Charlie stared at the floor, letting the snot drip from her nose and onto her shirt. "I didn't know what else to do. I knew you'd hate me for getting pregnant. And now you hate me for having an abortion."

Finally, her mother stood from her chair and sat down on the other end of the couch. Although Charlie took some comfort in this, she also realized it meant her mother didn't have to look at her when she spoke. "I don't hate you. I'm sorry you haven't felt supported."

When Charlie pulled the collar of her t-shirt up to wipe her nose, her mother reached for the box of tissues on the table beside her and held them in the air in front of Charlie. Wishing the apology had sounded more sincere, Charlie wrapped her shirt around her nose and blew into it.

Her mother sighed and placed the tissues back on the table. They sat in silence for several moments, until the furnace kicked on in the next room.

"I can't be supportive if you won't let me, Charlie."

Charlie listened to the soft whoosh of air coming from the vent overhead and wondered what Dog was doing. "I guess everything's my fault, then. As usual."

"I didn't say that."

"That's what it sounds like."

Her mother stood from the couch and looked down at her, pausing as if making a decision.

Charlie eyed the length of her height, thinking she should stand too. "What?"

"You were right. How could you have possibly come to me? I would've been as upset about your pregnancy as I was about your abortion."

Charlie licked her lips, ready to pounce.

Don't do it, Charlie.

Spirit?

Just listen to your mother.

Now you show up? When I finally have the chance to prove her wrong?

Just listen, child.

Charlie gritted her teeth and took a deep breath.

After a moment, her mother shook her head and turned toward the door. "I need to start dinner."

Chapter 17

Ripple Creek Refuge
Tuesday afternoon

"*R*eady for a walk, buddy?" Charlie stood outside of Dog's cage, dangling a leash like a carrot on a stick. His ears stood at attention as his curly tail wagged back and forth in a sideways circle. The latch on the door gave a metallic *clunk* when Charlie lifted it. When she stepped inside his enclosure, Dog backed toward the corner.

"It's okay, I'm not going to hurt you." Charlie got down on both knees and held out her right hand. He watched her for a moment, tentatively sniffing the air without budging.

"I see how this is going to go." Charlie fished a treat out of the pocket of her jeans and laid it between them on the floor. Dog watched her as he took a step forward and snagged it with his tongue. With three crunches he had it devoured and eyed Charlie's pocket for more.

"Ah, are you hungry, buddy?" Charlie glanced at the bowl in the corner that was full of food, but hadn't been touched. "Not your brand?"

"He's probably too nervous to eat."

As usual, Charlie hadn't heard Lorna's approach. But she was starting to get used to the brisk brogue that seemed to appear out of thin air. She glanced over her shoulder to see her boss standing in her usual posture of observation: hands on her hips and a disapproving scowl.

"Apparently that doesn't apply to treats." Charlie turned back around and laid another on the floor. This time, Dog didn't hesitate but moved in right away. He stood his ground as he chomped, and Charlie reached out to gently run her hand over his silky black and white fur.

"His appetite will pick up. This is all new to him, and he misses his owner. A little exercise will help."

Charlie turned. "Can I take him to see his owner?"

Lorna looked at her doubtfully.

"Please? The chaplain said I could."

"I don't know if that's a good idea. It may be better for him to start learning to adjust to life without him."

"But he said it would be good for both of them."

"Charlie, we have rules here—"

"And rules are meant to be—"

Lorna's right index finger popped up like a sudden sword. She slowly waved it at Charlie in a gesture of warning. "No, they are not."

Charlie gave a sigh of resignation as she turned back to Dog. "Okay."

"But I will let you do this."

Charlie turned back around. "Do what?"

"Usually, walks are restricted to our grounds. But if you want to take him a little farther, you can go around the block."

"Awesome!" Charlie stood, pulled the pin on the leash with her thumb and slid the hook through the metal ring on Dog's collar. It clinked when she let go to secure it into place.

Dog seemed aware something good was about to happen, since the sideways wag of his curly tail picked up speed.

"But only around the block. And put a coat on him. It's freezing out there today."

"A coat?"

Lorna sighed. "Yes, a coat. I just washed some. They're in the cabinet by the back door, organized by size."

First the rat, now coats for the dogs. "I suppose you have boots and a hat for him, too?"

"Don't get wise with me, young lady. These wee creatures—"

"I know. They need all the love they can get."

Lorna nodded with satisfaction. "Perhaps there's hope for you yet."

~

Charlie pulled the collar of her coat up around her ears and wiggled her nose to try to loosen the hairs inside that were frozen into a clump. Her breath came out in a frosty plume in front of her face, and she was sure her toes were black with frostbite inside her boots, even though they'd been outside less than ten minutes.

At her side, Dog trotted along in his royal blue coat as if he were in paradise. His tail was looped in a tight circle over his back, and he stopped every few feet to sniff and mark each tuft of dead vegetation that held any sort of apparent scent. A perpetual cloud of steam rose from his nostrils as his paws crunched against the day-old snow on the sidewalk.

"If I'd known it was this cold, I'd have worn your coat under mine."

Dog ignored her, picking up the pace and tugging Charlie along behind him as he strained at the leash. He pulled so hard he hacked when the collar pressed against his throat.

"Whoa. What are you doing?" Charlie had to hold the leash with both hands to keep him from running free. He was much stronger than he looked, and she had no choice but to stumble along behind him. "Dog!"

The snow crunched beneath them, and frosty air bellowed from their bodies as Dog tugged her along like he was pulling a sled. When he stopped, it was so abrupt Charlie nearly ran into him.

She'd been so focused on trying to keep her footing she'd paid no attention to their route. She looked up to see a weathered No Trespassing sign on a rusty metal gate that held a padlock with rust to match. Beyond it, tufts of weeds protruded from the snow, as did the skeletons of two old cars and a truck. A tattered American flag hung from a silver flagpole in the middle of the yard and flapped gently in the breeze, the clasp of the rope tinkling against the metal. A dilapidated trailer sat behind them, with a wooden front porch that looked suspiciously close to crumbling. Facing the property, Dog sat down in the snow and whimpered.

Charlie looked down at him. "What, buddy? Is this where you used to live?"

As if sensing her momentary distraction, Dog wound himself into a spring and jumped over the fence, yanking the leash from her hand.

"Dog! Wait!" Charlie was so stunned by his burst of agility that by the time she got her words out, he'd turned the corner of the trailer and disappeared.

"Oh, great." She yanked on the padlock, which only resulted in a palmful of rusty debris. Charlie looked up and down the empty street, planted her hands on the top of the gate, pushed the toe of her right shoe through the chain link, and hoisted herself over. The snow crunched beneath her feet when she landed. Aware of the sign's warning and the fact that she was still on probation, she didn't waste any time hustling toward the back of the house.

When she turned the corner, she could see it was merely a continuation of the front yard's litter of rusted car skeletons and humps of snow that hid the objects beneath them. There was a light blue deck attached to the back of the trailer, with peeling paint, rotting steps, and the naked body of an apple tree growing up through the middle. Where the deck attached to the structure, there was a sliding glass door with windows covered with so much dirt she could've written a novel in it. Charlie could see movement within the trailer, barely visible through the filth. As she moved closer, she realized it was the wag of Dog's tail as he smiled at her with satisfaction.

"How'd you get in there?" Charlie traced his paw prints up the steps and across the deck to a doggy door that was attached to the slider. Everything was so dirty it blended in with all the rest.

"Think you're pretty smart, don't you?" At her words, his tail wagged even faster.

"Well, how am I going to get you out of there?" Charlie eyed the doggy door, wondering if she would fit. Fortunately, it was oversized for Dog's needs. She shook her head and sighed. "You're gonna get me so arrested."

The cold of the snow burned her knees through her jeans when she knelt in front of the flap. She pushed her hand in first, which was greeted by a wet welcome on the other side. "I know, yes. I'm coming through your door."

When she stuck her head inside, Dog was waiting to smother her face with long laps of his tongue. Charlie giggled. "Okay, okay, I love you, too. Now stop so I can get in there."

Dog backed away as Charlie squeezed one shoulder through and then the other, finally thankful for all the times she'd been teased about being so skinny. Once her torso was in, the rest was a piece of cake. She took one whiff of the house and decided not to breathe through her nose. Charlie stood just inside the door, ignoring the little voice in her head that told her she should just pick up the end of Dog's leash, unlock the door, and leave. "If that's you, Spirit, this isn't the time."

Dog watched her expectantly. Charlie moved through the tiny trailer, eyeing empty whiskey bottles and ashtrays overflowing with cigarette butts. What used to be a white tiled floor in the kitchen had aged to a dingy gray. The once-white metal cabinets were now dirty yellow, which Charlie assumed was from being saturated with years of cigarette smoke. But on the floor in the corner of the kitchen sat two shiny metal bowls on a clean linen placemat. Charlie looked around and spotted a new pet bed on the floor beside a dilapidated recliner in the middle of the living room. "Well, looks like somebody loves you."

Dog wagged his tail and headed down the narrow hallway.

"Dog—" When Charlie ran after him, the flooring creaked beneath her feet. She poked her head into a tiny bedroom on the way. A large table saw took up an entire corner, and there was a workbench in the other, with a variety of tools arranged neatly on the wall above it. Metal shelves full of plastic bins occupied the rest of the room.

Charlie stood with her hands on her hips, puzzled by how neat the room was, and that someone would have a workshop inside such a tiny trailer. From down the hall, Dog's whimper pulled her back to the moment.

"Dog?"

She found him lying on a double bed in the second bedroom. It wasn't made, and he'd curled himself into a ball against the pillow. Despite her first instinct, Charlie sat down on the dingy sheets. She put a gentle hand on his head and then ran it the length of his back. This time, his tail remained flat. "I know you miss him."

Dog gave a sigh and stared straight ahead.

"Well, I'll let you in on a little secret."

He lifted his head and looked at Charlie, cocking it as if he understood exactly what she was saying.

"We…" She pointed at him and then back at herself. "You and me. We're going to go see him. Whether Lorna likes it or not."

Dog tipped his head to the opposite side, apparently not sure how he should respond.

"Do you want to go see your daddy?"

As soon as he heard the word, he jumped up, gave her cheek a quick lap of his tongue, and headed out of the room in search of his owner.

Charlie stood to go after him. "Dog! He's not here. I meant—"

She froze at the sound of a car door slamming outside. Charlie took a quick peek through the dusty miniblinds that covered a single square window. Her heart sank as she watched a woman sorting through a ring of keys and heading toward the front porch.

Charlie raced down the hall, envisioning the look on her probation officer's face when she tried to explain the charges: breaking and entering, trespassing…

By the time she got to the living room, she heard the woman's footsteps crunching across the front porch. Charlie started to open the sliding door for a quick escape but realized she'd have to leave it unlocked on her way out, and the woman would know someone had been there. She knelt and pushed her right shoulder into the flap of the doggy door. Dog was waiting for her on the back porch. When her head joined him in the cold, he covered her face with kisses of delight.

"Okay, okay. Not now," Charlie whispered. She shimmied her hips through the opening and was just about to breathe a sigh of relief when she felt the grip of a hand on the foot that was still inside the house.

So much for staying out of jail.

Dog gave a low growl as he stared through the window, the fur on the back of his neck standing on end. Charlie heard the click of the door lock and the scuff of the metal track as the door was opened. She leaned into her hands on the deck and hung her head, one leg folded beneath her and the other jutting into the house like a piece of impaling debris. She felt the accusing silence behind her and the weight of the woman's glare. Dog moved into position between the two, his throat rumbling in warning.

"And you are…"

Charlie sighed. She pulled her foot through the door and stood, absorbing the shock of the cold air through the wet knees of her jeans. The woman was taller than her, with shoulder-length blonde hair and brown eyes that could probably be kind under different circumstances.

"I know this doesn't look good."

"And you would be correct."

"I just…Dog. He got loose and ran in here after his owner. I didn't know what else to do except come in after him."

The woman looked down at Dog, who had quit growling but remained planted between the two of them.

"And crawling through doggy doors is a habit of yours?"

"I didn't want to leave the house unlocked."

"You're quick on your feet."

Charlie gave her a sheepish smile. "And I heard you coming."

The woman nodded. "I thought maybe."

"I'm sorry. I didn't want to get into trouble. I didn't touch anything, honest."

"Do you work at the shelter?"

"How'd you know that?"

She gestured toward dog. "I'm from hospice. His daddy's social worker. I know our chaplain took Dog to the shelter." The spine of fur on dog's neck relaxed into his coat when the woman said his name.

"Yeah, I met the chaplain when he brought him in. He said I could bring Dog to see his owner."

The woman nodded. "Sure. His owner is a crusty character, but he sure had a soft spot for Dog. He really misses him."

Charlie leaned down and ran her hand along Dog's back. "He does, too. He bolted for the bedroom and curled up on his pillow."

"I'm not surprised. Pets deeply grieve the loss of loved ones. Do you want to take something familiar for him?"

"What, like his bed?"

"Sure. And maybe something that smells like his owner."

Charlie made a face, wrinkling her nose.

The woman smiled. "In my line of work, you get used to it. When people are sick and alone, they have a hard time keeping up."

"I guess that makes sense."

"Listen, I have to get going. I have more visits to finish today. I just stopped by to get a few things Quinn asked me to bring him. Get what you want for Dog, and then I can lock up before I leave."

Quinn. Charlie nodded and tucked this new information away.

The woman headed back into the house, and Charlie followed. Dog was close on her heels, apparently anticipating something good was about to happen. She leaned down and picked up his bed.

"This? You want your bed, buddy?" Dog sniffed it and wagged his tail. "Looks like that's a yes." She eyed a stained naked bed pillow jammed against the bend of the ragged recliner. When she tugged on it, a microburst of fur and dust filled the air. Charlie coughed and then let out a sneeze. Dog cocked his head as he watched her lay it on his bed. He moved closer and sniffed, then curled up against it.

"Looks like another yes. And maybe a blanket, too?" Charlie spotted a red and black checkered blanket on the couch under a pile of scattered newspapers. When she moved the papers, a congregation of roaches ran for cover. Charlie let out a startled scream.

The social worker came running from the back of the house. "What's wrong?"

"Roaches," Charlie moaned.

"Ah, yes. Lots of those guys around. Quinn kept it so hot in here they didn't know it was winter and forgot to die. You about done?"

Charlie nodded. "Definitely." She gestured toward Dog, curled tight against the pillow, making it clear he had no intention of leaving his familiar spot.

"Is it okay if I take his bed and that pillow?" She glanced toward the couch and made a face. "The critters can have the blanket."

The woman looked doubtfully at the couch. "Wise decision. Yes, it's fine to take the other things. I know Quinn would want him to be comfortable. Are you going to visit him now? Because I've got to warn you—"

"No." Charlie looked at Dog. "My boss is going to be mad enough as it is."

∽

Ripple Creek Refuge

"Absolutely not."

"But look at him, he loves them."

Lorna eyed Dog, who was curled up on his bed against Quinn's ratty pillow—both of which were lying on the covered front porch of the shelter. It's as far as Lorna let them go.

"First, those linens are filled with who knows what. Second, you completely disregarded my instructions when you left. I told you not to go far and to come right back. Instead, here you are, hours later after having broken the law and trespassed inside someone's home."

Charlie waved her arms in exasperation. "I told you, I was chasing Dog. He's the one that ran into the house."

Lorna crossed her arms. "Who."

"What?"

"Dog is a who. Not a that."

Charlie shook her head. "Whatever."

"What I should do is call your probation officer."

Charlie glared at her with saucer-eyes. "What? Why? I told you, the social worker was there. She didn't care."

"I doubt that was her initial reaction."

"Well, she didn't care once I told her why I was in there."

"And this poor creature is counting on us to care for him and keep him safe."

"He was safe! He just misses Quinn."

"Oh, Quinn, is it now?" Lorna's brogue thickened with sarcasm.

Charlie sniffed in defiance. "The social worker told me his name. She said he loves Dog."

"And Dog will be better off if he learns to live without him."

Charlie got on her knees to run her hand across Dog's head and down his back. His tail didn't curl as it usually did to her touch. Instead, it seemed limp with sadness. "I can't believe you can be so cold."

Lorna gave the pair a steady gaze. "It's not a matter of being cold, lass. It's a matter of being realistic. I've seen this play out over and over again. These wee creatures all love their owners and don't understand why they have been left here without them. I'm glad Quinn was good to this wee boy, because that's not always the case. But Quinn is going to die, and Dog needs to begin to adjust to that."

As if he understood what Lorna was saying, Dog whimpered a little and tucked himself tighter into the pillow.

"What if I wash them?"

"They're filthy—"

"But he loves them."

"We have a policy that—"

"And he needs them."

"I—"

"Please, Lorna. Just this one time."

Lorna sighed. "You will be the reason I decide to retire early."

Charlie looked at her hopefully. "Does that mean yes?"

"I should still call your probation officer."

"Oh, c'mon, Lorna."

Lorna shook her head in resignation, then pointed her right index finger at Charlie. "If you wash them. Thoroughly. But they do not come into my shelter before."

Chapter 18

Ripple Creek Hospice House
Thursday afternoon

It wasn't at all what she'd expected. When Charlie walked through the sliding doors of the hospice house, she felt like she was entering a bed and breakfast instead of a medical facility.

The building was old, but it had been well maintained, and the front desk looked like it belonged in a hotel. It rose to the level of Charlie's chest and was covered with deep brown buttoned leather. On the floor beneath it, cracked-tile colors flowed like a river in a warm mix of yellow, red, brown, gray, green, and white. The waiting area contained a cozy gathering of white linen couches and chairs that encircled a big square structure in the middle that was more of a bench than a coffee table. The ceilings were made of old wood that had been stained to match the deep brown paneling on the walls. A palm tree in the corner seemed out of place in the dead of winter in Vermont.

Dog's nails clicked with hesitation along the surface of the floor. The automatic door had spooked him, and his tail was flat with wariness as he gingerly sniffed the air around him. It was as if he knew Lorna was going to be mad when she found out what they'd done.

A sign perched on top of the desk indicated the volunteer would be right back, so Charlie moved to the waiting area. Apparently, Dog was afraid she was going to leave him there, since he started to pant and salivate a little. His brow was laced with worry as he glanced around with his tail nearly tucked between his legs.

Charlie put a gentle hand under his chin and tried to get him to look at her. "What is it, buddy?" But he resisted, intent on maintaining his nervous surveillance, his gaze fixed on something down the hall.

Charlie looked up to see a tall, thin woman walking in their direction. She had her head down, as if studying the cracked tiles as they passed beneath her feet. Her dress slacks and top were fairly casual, but not as casual as the fluorescent green running shoes. Something about her looked familiar.

"Patch?" The thought was so forceful Charlie said it out loud.

The woman looked up, slowing to a stop as she neared. "Charlie?"

Charlie nodded eagerly. She was so relieved to see a familiar face she wanted to hug her. Patch beat her to it.

"It's so good to see you. How are you?"

"I'm good. Really good."

Patch nodded. "You have a sparkle in your eyes that wasn't there the last time I saw you."

"Really?"

"Really. So…do you have family here?"

Charlie shook her head. "No, I work at the animal shelter."

"Good for you. And I see you've made a friend."

Charlie smiled at Dog. "Yeah. We're kinda glued at the hip these days." She eyed the tag hanging around Patch's neck. Patricia Linnak, MSW, LCSW. "So you work here?"

Patch nodded.

Charlie leaned closer to read her tag. "What's an L-C-S-W?"

"Licensed Clinical Social Worker."

"That sounds important."

"Just part of the team."

Charlie nodded. "Cool."

"So…if you work at the shelter, and you're here…I'm betting he belongs to one of our patients."

"Uh-huh, Quinn."

"Quinn…"

Charlie sensed it was a test. She shrugged sheepishly.

"I don't mean to be hard on you, Charlie, but we're really strict about maintaining the privacy of our patients. It seems a little odd that you're allowed to see Quinn but you don't know his full name. Certainly, the shelter has it."

"Well…my boss kind of doesn't know I'm here."

Patch raised an eyebrow. "Is that so." It wasn't a question.

"Yeah. I told her I wanted to bring him to see Quinn—I mean, the chaplain and the social worker both said I could—but she was too mad about the other day and said no."

"The other day?"

"Let's just say Dog remembers where he used to live, and I found out I can fit through a doggy door."

Patch let out a belly laugh. "A doggy door?" She shook her head in a mixture of admiration and disbelief. "Sounds like you're committed."

"Or should be."

"And quick, too."

Patch put her arm around Charlie and lowered her head in commiseration. "Let me go confirm a few things. I'll be right back."

Charlie nodded, then watched Patch head down the hall. Her sneakers squeaked against the tile when she stopped mid-stride and turned around. "We have a cat. Maggie. So hang onto him."

"A cat? Okay."

Then Patch pulled a phone from her pocket and resumed her mission.

Dog looked up at Charlie and start tugging her toward the front door.

"No, not yet." She sat down in the waiting area again. Dog

wound himself into a circle twice, settled at Charlie's feet, and let out a sigh. She rubbed his head. "I think you'll be glad we stayed."

It wasn't long before Patch returned. "I talked to the social worker on the home team, and she thinks it'll help Quinn. Then I checked with Quinn to get his permission, and he said it was okay. But you're going to be in hot water with your boss."

"I know."

"And you don't care?"

"I think I'm growing on her."

"I can understand why." Patch smiled and then lowered her voice. "But a word of warning, because I don't want you to get your feelings hurt."

"What do you mean?"

"Well, Quinn can be kind of—"

"Crusty?"

Patch nodded. "Something like that."

"It's okay. I can handle crusty."

~

Charlie had never been around anyone who was dying before. She guessed the visits with Final probably counted, but it wasn't like being there in real life. As she walked down the hall beside Patch, her heart raced, and her mouth was dry as cotton. She expected Dog to be scared, too, but his nails clicked with confidence against the tile, and his tail was looped into a full circle as he walked beside her. As they neared a room at the end of the hall, he started pulling on his leash with such determination Charlie could barely hang on.

"Wow, that's impressive," Patch said.

"Dog?" Charlie said it in a loud whisper as she tried to hold him in check. "I don't see what's so impressive."

Patch stopped outside the closed door and looked at Dog, who was sniffing at the crack under the door, whimpering. "He knew exactly where to go."

Charlie looked at the nameplate on the wall beside the

doorframe. There were flowers carved into the wood, and a tan strip of paper behind a clear plastic sleeve with QUINN M. written with fancy calligraphy letters.

Patch nodded and lifted her hand to knock.

Charlie grabbed her arm.

"Final?" She mouthed the word.

Patch leaned closer. "What?"

Charlie whispered into her ear, "Did you tell him about Final?"

Patch stood up straight, her expression changing as abruptly as the drop of a curtain on a show. She shook her head.

"Why not?" Charlie whispered.

"Long story." Then she tipped her chin and gave Charlie a conspiring look. "You ready?"

Charlie swallowed hard and nodded.

Patch glanced at Dog, who was starting to scratch at the door. "He's definitely ready. You'd better hang tight to his leash. We don't want him to jump on the bed on top of Quinn. He's pretty fragile."

Charlie put both hands on the leash. "Okay."

Patch rapped on the door.

"Yeah?" The voice on the other side was faint.

Patch cracked the door, keeping Dog at bay with her shin. "Quinn? It's Patch. I have your visitors. You ready?"

"Whatever."

Patch winked at Charlie, put one hand on Dog's leash to help her, and then opened the door. Dog immediately began dragging the women into the room like a sled dog hauling cargo. Charlie planted her feet and held him in check.

The man in the bed was watching television. Instead of looking at them, he dropped his arm over the side of the bed and opened his hand. At the gesture, Dog pulled so hard on the leash the hook unsnapped.

"Dog, wa—"

He sprinted to the bed, pushed his head into Quinn's hand, and wagged his tail fast enough to support flight. Quinn didn't look down but continued to watch the television as Dog covered the battered skin with kisses.

"Looks like he's glad to see you, Quinn," Patch said.

"Hm-hm."

"And this is Charlie."

Quinn nodded, still staring straight ahead.

"How are you feeling today?"

"How do you think? I'm dying, ain't I?"

Patch looked at Charlie and gave her a reassuring smile.

"Do you need anything, Quinn?"

He didn't respond. Dog was making his way up Quinn's arm with his tongue.

"Well, okay, then I'm going to let the three of you visit."

Charlie gave her a glare that could've fried an egg.

Patch shrugged, aiming her words at Charlie. "I've got work to do, Quinn, but if you need anything, just ring the bell."

Charlie gritted her teeth and shook her head in disgust. Then Patch patted her on the shoulder and headed for the door. Charlie turned to watch her go, her heart sinking as she realized she was going to be left there all alone. She turned back to the bed. Quinn still didn't acknowledge her, so she just stood there and stared.

An oxygen machine hummed in the corner. The way the room was arranged, she could only see the right side of his body. A single vine of green plastic tubing curled over the bed, onto the bony terrain of his face and around his ear, which was a blotchy pink and blue. It led to a little green knob that poked into the gray tufts of hair that sprouted from his right nostril. The dim lighting in the room highlighted the valley beneath his cheekbone. Charlie wondered if being in hospice meant you didn't get to eat.

"Why don't ya take a picture?" He was still staring at the television, and his words startled her.

"Huh?"

Finally, he turned and looked at her, which gave her the full picture of the oxygen tubing's path. His eyes were so blue they probably sparkled once and the cleft in his chin so deep it was like looking into a whirlpool.

"Ain't never seen a dying person before?"

"Well…technically, no."

Quinn shook his head and turned back to the television.

Charlie braced herself for another assault, but he silently stared straight ahead. During the interaction, Dog had jumped onto the foot of the bed and was now pacing in a tight circle within the covers, building a nest with his paws. He made one more loop and then settled into a roll of black and white fur against Quinn's lower leg. He took a deep breath and let out a contented sigh.

"Is he bothering you? Patch said I shouldn't let him get on the bed."

Quinn didn't answer.

"I can make him get down, if you want."

He continued to stare at the television.

"Mister?"

"You always talk so much?" He didn't look at her when he said it.

Charlie bit her lip as she watched Dog. She longed to curl up next to him to get a little comfort of her own.

"Sorry. I don't mean to bother you, I just thought you'd like to see Dog." Charlie lowered herself onto the overstuffed recliner positioned next to the bed. She waited for him to respond, but several minutes passed before he did.

"Thanks." His tone sounded more accusing than grateful, but Charlie decided she'd take whatever she could get.

"Do you like it here?"

"What a stupid question."

She took a deep breath and tried to ignore the racing of her heart and the single bead of sweat slowly making its way down the middle of her back.

"I didn't think so."

Quinn gave her a brief glance and then returned to his show.

"Who cares what you think?"

Charlie felt her steam rising. "Do you want me to leave?"

Quinn didn't respond.

"Because I can, you know. I'm going to get in a lot of trouble for being here. But I thought it'd be worth it."

Charlie watched the old man for some sign he was listening to a single word she'd said. Nothing. She stood from the recliner. "Come on, Dog."

Dog was so entrenched in his spot he might as well have been a thread in the spread. His chin was resting on Quinn's lower leg, and he eyed her without budging. Charlie watched with irritation as the shadow of a smirk teased at the corners of Quinn's mouth.

"Good luck with that."

"You could help, you know."

"Seems to me he's exactly where he wants to be."

"Well, if you want me to leave, he's coming with me."

Quinn shook his head. "Nope."

Charlie gave an exasperated sigh. "He can't stay here. You know that."

"I know they stole my dog."

"No one stole him."

Quinn turned his head toward her, his blue eyes narrowing into a crevice. "If yer dog's there one minute and not there the next, then he got stole." His cracked lips retracted across crooked yellow teeth, emphasizing each word in a deliberate and accusing march. "And whoever shows up with him musta been the one that done the stealin'."

Charlie's jaw went slack. "Me? I didn't steal your dog."

"Well, he got stole, and now he's with you. You do the math, missy."

"No. I work at the animal shelter. You surrendered him when you had to come here."

"Surrendered? Ha! I ain't never surrendered in my life. And I sure as shootin' didn't surrender my dog." Quinn glared at her, daring her to try to take his dog from him again. Dog watched them like a ping-pong match, his gaze bouncing back and forth each time he heard his name. But he never lifted his chin from its perch on Quinn's left shin.

"Why are you such a curmudgeon?"

He looked at her, startled. "A what?"

"Curmudgeon."

He shook his head and returned to his show. "Whatever that is."

"It's a mean and miserable person."

Quinn didn't respond, and Charlie immediately felt bad. She hoped Spirit was busy with someone else.

"Look, I'm sorry. I shouldn't have said that." She willed Quinn to look at her, but he wouldn't do it. "It's just—"

Without warning, he whipped his head around and gave her a hard glare. "It's just what? Spit it out."

Charlie's steam fluttered away like a punctured balloon. "Dog misses you."

"Of course he does."

"And I—"

"You what?"

"I know stuff you should know."

"What could a kid possibly know that an old man doesn't know?"

"About the dying thing."

"How could you know anything about dying?"

"Well, I died, and there was this guy—"

Charlie felt the squeeze of a hand on her shoulder that was more a warning than a greeting. She hadn't even heard Patch come in. "You two about ready? Quinn probably needs some rest."

"Well, I was just about to tell him—"

"—that it's time for you to go."

Charlie looked at Patch, unsure why she sounded so insistent.

"But Dog just got comfortable."

"I see that."

Quinn was watching the television as if there was no one else in his room. Dog shifted a little, deepening his cover in the foxhole he'd created within Quinn's blanket.

"So maybe we could stay just a little longer?" Charlie surprised herself with the pleading she heard in her voice. Just a few minutes ago she was ready to give the old man a piece of her mind.

"You leaving suits me just fine." Quinn didn't look at her when he said it. "But he's staying."

"Now, Quinn, you know we've been over this. We can't take care of the patients' pets here," Patch said.

"You got that stupid cat running the place."

"Maggie is a different story."

"Right."

"She belongs to the house. And there's only one of her. If we took every pet a patient wanted to bring here, we'd never have time to take care of the patients."

"Sounds like a rule that needs changed."

Charlie finally found a place to chime in. "He's right."

She felt Quinn glance in her direction and then return to staring at the television.

Patch put her hands on her hips. "Not you, too."

"Well, look at Dog. He's so happy. He doesn't want to leave Quinn."

"I know he doesn't. But he has to. And so do you. The shelter called. Your manager is looking for you."

Chapter 19

$\mathcal{I}$t was one of the longest walks of her life. With each step that took her closer to the shelter, Charlie could hear Lorna's voice more clearly, her thick brogue dripping with fury. She'd probably lose her job. Go to jail. Never get to see Dog again. She looked down. He was slogging along beside her, tail hanging low, his eyes fixed on the ground.

"I know, buddy. But somehow, I'll take you back to see him. I don't know how, but I'll figure something out."

When she turned the corner from the sidewalk onto the shelter property, she saw Lorna standing on the porch. The front yard was big and the drive long, so at that distance she couldn't see the expression on her face. She wasn't wearing a coat, even though it was in the high 20s. Her arms were crossed over her chest and her feet planted in a stance that created an equilateral triangle between her legs. Her posture held all the welcome of a drill sergeant dealing with a new recruit.

Charlie paused, and Dog did, too. His tail lifted, and he gave her a hopeful look, as if she might've changed her mind about leaving his daddy.

She reached down and cupped the top of his head the way Quinn had done. She'd forgotten her gloves, and her hand was raw and red from holding his leash in the cold. When he leaned into her touch, she wanted to pick him up and take him home.

Home.

Charlie ignored Lorna and squatted to meet Dog's gaze. A slow smile spread across her lips as the idea emerged from within her like a vase on a potter's wheel. She leaned in so the wind couldn't catch her words and carry them to the porch. "That's it. I need to take you home. With me. I'm going to adopt you."

Dog seemed to know something exciting was happening. He gave Charlie's cheek a quick lap with his tongue and lifted his tail into a full curl before wagging it back and forth in his crooked way.

Charlie gave him a conspiring look. "But we can't let her know yet. I have to get Mom on board."

He wagged his tail in a nod.

"So get ready. This one's gonna be mad at us. But Mom, you'll love her." She kissed the thin white line that ran between his eyes. "I just hope she feels the same about you."

The sound of crunching snow startled her. She'd been so delighted by her idea and letting Dog in on her secret she hadn't noticed Lorna marching down the driveway in their direction. She stopped a few feet away and held out her hand. "Give me the leash."

Charlie stood and looped the leash around her hand. "What?"

"I said give me the leash."

She took a step toward the shelter. "It's okay, I'll bring him in."

Lorna moved to block her path. "No, you will not. Your time here is finished."

Despite the cold, Charlie felt the flash of heat in her face and the throb of her pulse in her ears. "But, Lorna, I—"

"You completely disobeyed my orders."

Her words were more biting than the cold wind cutting through Charlie's jeans.

"Your orders?"

Lorna planted her hands on her hips. "I told you not to take him to see his former owner."

Charlie dug deep into her arsenal of sentiments that had rescued her from previous tight spots. "But Dog wanted to see him. And Quinn—"

"I told you he needs to get used to a life without him."

"But he's not dead yet!"

"He will be soon enough."

Charlie stooped to put her hands over Dog's ears. "What a terrible thing to say."

Lorna sighed. "That's ridiculous. He doesn't understand what I'm saying."

Charlie cupped his face in her hands. When she did, the pleading sadness in Dog's eyes confirmed the fact that she couldn't possibly leave him at the shelter. "He's very sensitive and smart. You should've seen him find Quinn's room."

Lorna held out her hand again.

Charlie took a step back and shook her head.

"No? I think not, young lady. I've not yet called your probation officer but will be happy to do exactly that."

"I'm going to adopt him." Charlie blurted the words and then looked at Dog to see if he realized she'd just raced way ahead of their plan.

Lorna gave a bitter laugh. "You? Oh sure, you are."

Charlie took a step toward Lorna, shielding Dog behind her. "Yes, I am."

Lorna's eyes narrowed into a crevice. "You're a teenager who is nothing but trouble. I will not permit you to adopt one of my wee precious creatures."

"First of all, he's not yours. He's Quinn's. And second of all, he likes me. More than he likes you. He hates it here. He needs to be part of a family."

Charlie savored the wisp of hurt that hovered over Lorna's expression. Then, as if discovering a diamond in the rough, Lorna's face lit up. "Minors are not permitted to adopt our animals."

Charlie felt her hopes drop as if stepping on a trap door. But she took a deep breath and put her shoulders back anyway. "Well, my mom will let me. And she'll sign whatever's needed."

Lorna eyed her as a smirk played at the corner of her mouth. "Oh, will she now? With all the trouble you've been in, my dear, I wouldn't be so sure about that."

Charlie kneeled on the icy ground and pulled Dog against her, hoping he didn't realize she was thinking the same thing.

It took ten more minutes of standing in the arctic air and pleading to the point of embarrassment before Lorna agreed to let Charlie walk Dog back into the shelter and suspend her plans to call the probation officer. But Lorna still refused to let Dog see Quinn again, an absurd restriction which would be history if Charlie could adopt him.

~

"Mom, please." A cloud of frosty air formed around her words. Charlie gripped the shelter's portable phone with one hand and a leash with the other. Wanting to make sure she was out of Lorna's earshot, she'd volunteered to walk Goliath, the Great Dane who had come in two days earlier. This time, she wasn't allowed to leave the property but agreed to stay inside the fenced exercise area. Charlie was grateful it was such a gentle breed since Goliath's back was level with her waist.

"Dog is so good. He won't be any trouble."

Her mother's response was, unfortunately, predictable. "You know how I feel about pets in the house."

"Mom, I died. I thought you wanted things to be different between us this time around." Charlie felt bad about stooping to such a level, but desperate times call for desperate measures. The phone line was silent for so long Charlie thought maybe they'd lost the connection. "Mom?"

When her mother spoke, her words were barely audible. "That's not fair, Charlie."

Charlie ignored the hurt in her mother's voice. "C'mon, Mom. I won't let him mess up your white carpet."

"It's not—"

"Or leave poop in the yard."

"I know that—"

"And I'll use my allowance to pay for his food."

"Charlie, I don't—"

"Stella says pet therapy would be good for me."

She felt the leash go taut and turned to the splattering behind her, where Goliath stood with his leg lifted, spraying an arc of steaming urine onto the gray metal of a fence pole as if it were a building on fire. A yellow pond spread onto the ground at its base as the liquid streamed down the pole, leaving a sheen of frost in its wake like a thin layer of icing. She followed Goliath as he walked a few steps, sniffed the remnants of another dog's deposit that hadn't been fully removed, then hunched his pony-sized frame into a crouch.

"Mom? You there?"

"Really? The Stella card? And just when did you talk to her?"

Charlie held the phone between her shoulder and her ear as she folded a plastic bag over her left hand and bent over to pick up the generous brown pile Goliath deposited at her feet. It took two warm and gooey passes to get it all. She suppressed a gag as she folded the bag shut and tied it in a knot.

"Well, technically, not since my last session."

"So—"

Having completed all his tasks, Goliath began to tug her toward the back door. Charlie stumbled along behind him, trying to stay upright while she finished her conversation. When she almost dropped the phone, she stopped and planted her heels. "Wait!"

"Wait?"

"Not you. Hang on."

She put the phone in the pocket of her jacket and then grasped the leash with both hands. "Goliath, wait a minute." At the sound of his name, the dog stopped and stood as still as a statue. "Well, if I knew it was that easy…" Charlie pulled the phone from her pocket. "Sorry. I'm walking a little horse."

"A horse?"

"Never mind. Anyway, Stella said before that other stuff could help me, and pet therapy was one of the things she recommended."

"Is that so?" The tone of suspicion in her mother's voice was a familiar one.

"Yep, it was on the list."

"Pretty clever pulling that one out of thin air."

"And I know Dan won't mind."

"Dan's a pushover, and you know it."

"Does that mean yes?"

The sigh from the other end of the phone held the weight of weariness Charlie often felt from her mother. "No. It means I'll stop by after work. I need to meet this hound who has stolen my daughter's heart. You know, the daughter who never liked animals?"

Chapter 20

Later that evening

$\mathcal{D}$og's sopping tail was limp and hanging so low it might as well have been lying on the black rubber mat covering the shower floor. Since Charlie had zero experience in washing a dog, she was as soaked as he was. He looked up at her with eyes that pleaded for her to stop. His steaming body began to tremble with a shiver, as if to emphasize his point.

"I'm sorry, buddy. I know. But you have to smell better than you did if we're going to have a shot at this."

As if he understood the stakes, he sighed, lifted his right front paw, and held it in the air for her to wash.

Charlie laughed. "That's my boy."

"That poor creature had a bath on intake."

Charlie glanced over her shoulder to see Lorna watching them in her usual cross-armed stance of disapproval. Then she turned back, pulled the handheld shower head from a hook and aimed the gentle stream of warm water over Dog's back. Shampoo poured from his fur in rivers of foamy white bubbles.

"You haven't seen my mother's white carpet."

"It sounds like you shouldn't get your hopes up."

Charlie put her hand over Dog's right ear to protect it from the stream of water as she rinsed that side of his head. Although she'd never bathed a baby in her life either, the tenderness with which she did it gave her a thought of out nowhere that she might've done the same with Rose. How she would've protected her little eyes and ears from the bathwater and held her close in a thick warm towel as she dried her off. Charlie shook the image from her mind and returned to earth. "I don't understand why you don't want me to adopt him."

"Don't you, now?" From the tone of Lorna's response, Charlie might've been asking for a pot of gold. "Dogs take commitment. Dedication. An extreme amount of love and patience."

Charlie ignored the sarcasm behind her and continued to rinse the black and white of Dog's fur until the rivers ran clear. Then she reached up and turned off the faucet. Sensing an end to his torment, Dog popped his tail into a curl and gave a shake that started with his floppy-eared head and rippled across his body.

"Dog!" Charlie held up a hand to block the incoming tide, but it didn't do any good. Whatever inch of her body that hadn't already been soaked was now good and wet. She could feel Lorna's smirk of satisfaction.

"A perfect example," she said.

Charlie didn't respond. Instead, she stood, grabbed a towel from the cupboard next to the stall, wiped her face, and then draped it over Dog. He immediately buried his snout in the fabric and began to snort and wiggle with delight.

"We'll do just fine together." Charlie said it as if the adoption papers had already been signed.

"Even if your mother agrees, I'll still need to evaluate the home."

Charlie shook her head. "Whatever."

"I mean, not every home is suited for a dog. One with white carpet certainly may not be."

"Whatever."

Refusing to take Lorna's bait, Charlie pushed the towel over every inch of Dog's body, capturing the water in the fabric until his fur was damp-dry enough to brush. She ran the soft bristles through his fur. By the time she finished with the last stroke, his coat nearly shimmered in the light from the fixture overhead. Dog gave Charlie a look of such innocent gratitude that if hearts could melt, hers was now a puddle. She'd always thought it stupid when people said dogs could smile. She'd been so wrong.

She heard the familiar click of her mother's heels on the tiled floor in the hall and looked up to see her standing in the doorway. Her tailored wool coat made her all business.

"Well, it looks like you two are getting along famously."

"Of course we are."

Her mom's thin frame made her look even taller than she was, but when she was standing next to someone short, Jack's beanstalk always came to mind. Since she'd come straight from work, her heels gave her another inch or so. Lorna looked up and gave her a smile as thin and straight as the skinny side of a ruler. Charlie sensed from the look on her face that her mother's height and the fact that she hadn't heard the bell on the front door had put her at a disadvantage.

"Ah, you must be Charlie's mother." She stuck out a muscle-roped hand.

Her mother politely grasped it and quickly let go. "Beth."

Lorna nodded. "It's nice to meet you, Beth. Lorna Darrow, the manager here."

"Yes, I've heard a lot about you."

Lorna gave Charlie a stern look. "I imagine you have."

Her mother laughed and shook her head. "Actually, it's been good. You've been good for my girl."

Charlie was stunned by the blush that washed over Lorna's face.

"I believe she would differ with you on that point."

"Which is one reason I know you've been good for her."

Charlie watched the exchange with a growing knot in the pit of her stomach. Although it might be good for her if they got along, she didn't want to be the brunt of their mutual admiration. She squatted beside Dog and wrapped an arm around her sole ally. He responded by leaning into her so hard she nearly fell over.

"It's okay, buddy. It's just Mom."

"*Just* Mom? Thanks." Her mother gazed at them with one eyebrow raised.

Charlie smiled. "As in, someone he can trust."

Her mother nodded with the knowingness of having just been fed a line. "So, what's this I hear about an adoption?"

Lorna shook her head. "I don't think it's a good idea."

"Why not?"

Charlie breathed a sigh of relief to hear the defensive tone in her mother's voice as she stepped across the line toward Team Charlie.

Lorna shrugged. "She's not ready. She's too young. She's too irresponsible. She's too troubled."

Her mother turned to face Lorna, crossing her arms and making the most of her height. "That would be my daughter you're referring to."

Lorna had to crane her neck to make eye contact. "And I mean no disrespect. It is my responsibility to guard the best interests of the wee creatures I'm entrusted with."

"I see. Well, if you have concerns about my daughter's ability to care for this dog, whom she has quickly come to love, then I will take full responsibility for the adoption."

Charlie stood up so fast she got dizzy. A cloud of grayness zigged across her vision like a sudden downpour. She put her hands on her knees and tipped her head toward the floor, which delighted Dog. He immediately smothered her face with kisses.

"Honey?" She heard the quick click of her mother's heels and then felt the warmth of her hand on her back. "Are you okay?"

Charlie straightened with the caution of someone moving through fog. "Yeah. Stood up too fast." Then she looked at her mom. "You will?"

Her mother frowned. "I will what?"

"Dog? You'll let me adopt him?"

"Oh." She dropped her hand from Charlie's back. "Sorry. I was still envisioning you crumpling to the floor." Then she took a deep breath, as if convincing herself. "Yes. If he's good for you, I want you to have him."

Charlie wrapped her arms around her mother and squeezed. "Thank you," she whispered. Since it wasn't something either of them normally did, her mother seemed startled by the affection, but Charlie didn't care. She squatted beside Dog, whose tail was in overdrive. He licked her face as if it were covered in peanut butter.

"A-hem."

Charlie looked up to see Lorna watching them with that familiar and tiresome look of disapproval. "You seem to be forgetting the home must be evaluated first, and I must approve the adoption."

Her mother's wince was visible. "I can assure you we have a beautiful home for this dog."

Lorna sniffed. "I'll see."

Charlie's mom took a step in Lorna's direction. "*You'll* see?"

"Yes. *I'll* see. This dog isn't going anywhere without my approval."

Her mother crossed her arms and stood a little straighter. "I'd be more understanding about your policies if I was convinced you were applying them fairly."

Lorna frowned as if the statement were nonsense. "Of course I am."

"And that you didn't have it out for my daughter."

"I have no ill feelings toward Charlene."

"That wasn't what I heard a few minutes ago."

Lorna shrugged. "I speak my mind."

"I see. Then I suppose I must, as well."

Charlie and Dog watched the two like a tennis match.

Her mother cocked her head to the side as she looked at Lorna, who was glaring at her silently. "Do you know what I do for a living, Ms. Darrow?"

"I don't see what—"

"I work in a legal office."

Lorna watched her with the wariness of a new rescue. "So?"

"For a very powerful group of attorneys."

Lorna raised her eyebrows. "If you think you can intimidate me into approving an adoption I don't agree is good for the animal, you are quite wrong."

Charlie's mom pulled a tube of lipstick from her purse, slid the column of color from within, flipped open the attached mirror, and applied a fresh layer which perfectly matched her nails. "Of course not," she murmured into the tiny mirror. "I certainly wouldn't want that. For the sake of the animal."

Lorna nodded with satisfaction.

Then her mother rolled her lips together to spread the cream evenly, flicked the mirror shut with her right index finger, and replaced the cap with the slow precision of someone threading a needle. When it clicked into place, she looked at Lorna. "But in this case, it appears your negative feelings for my daughter may be a barrier to sound judgment."

"I don't have—"

"Save it." She pointed the tube of lipstick at Lorna as if it were a sword. "I already heard how you feel about Charlie. And I don't appreciate it one bit."

When Charlie had to suppress the urge to tackle her mother and smother her with kisses, she realized Dog must be rubbing off on her.

"Part of my job is research," her mother continued as she slipped the lipstick back into her purse.

"Good for you." Lorna turned and began to walk toward the door. "If we're through here, I have work—"

"And in that research, I found the grant which is providing the majority of the funding for this shelter."

Lorna stopped as suddenly as if she'd grabbed a live wire. She slowly turned, a line of muscle standing from her jaw. She looked up at Charlie's mother.

"So?"

"Well, I just thought it was such a coincidence that the grant manager is friends with my boss." Her mom crossed her arms and gazed at Lorna. "In fact, they went skiing together a few weeks ago."

Lorna's eyes narrowed into two crevices of rage. "Are you threatening me?"

Charlie's mother smiled evenly. "Of course not. I just think it's such an ordained coincidence. I mean, consider the odds? I have this wonderful daughter who works at the shelter which is receiving funding from my boss's friend. At said shelter, there is a sweet and intelligent dog who needs a home. It's a perfect match, and the two fall in love. The only reasonable and logical outcome is for a smooth adoption to be arranged."

Lorna looked like she wanted to spit. Without a word, she turned and marched down the hall.

Charlie stood with her mouth hanging open as if she were gazing at someone from another world.

Her mom smiled. "You're going to catch flies."

"I can't believe you just did that."

Then something happened that Charlie had wanted for so long. Her mom put an arm around her shoulder and pulled her close.

"Nobody messes with my girl," she said.

Chapter 21

Ripple Creek Refuge
Friday afternoon

Dog apparently sensed something was up. He'd been on Charlie's heels all afternoon as she worked through her list of chores at the shelter. When she turned to put the dirty paper from Stuart's cage into the garbage, she nearly tripped over him. "Dog. I know you're excited. But we'll never get out of here if you don't let me get my work done."

She looked at Stuart, who was sitting on his hind legs on the floor, his pink nose twitching in an effort to make sense of the energy around him. Charlie knew he was waiting for Dog to lie down so he could climb onto his usual perch in the middle of his back. But today, his canine companion wasn't having it.

Charlie picked up Stuart, then cupped him in her hands and looked into the two black beads of his eyes. "I know, buddy, but change is a fact of life. And he needs somebody to love him. She already loves you." Charlie deposited him on her shoulder and winced when his tiny talons dug through her shirt as he scampered to the angle at her neck and settled in. Dog whimpered and pawed at her foot.

Charlie felt bad about the worried look in his eyes and bent to cup his head. "Believe me, you're still my favorite." When Stuart deepened his grip on her skin to hang on, she winced and used her other hand to cup him, too—which resulted in the whisk of his sandpaper tongue against her neck. "Thank you, Stuart. But like I said, she already loves you."

"That I do."

Charlie looked up to see Lorna standing in the doorway. If she hadn't known who it was, she may not have recognized her at first glance. The difference wasn't in anything she'd added, like a new haircut or a clothing style she'd never worn—but in what she lacked. The disapproving scowl. The drill-sergeant stance. The never-ending list of things Charlie couldn't do right. Instead, it was as if she'd decided to swap personalities for the day with someone more generous and peaceful. Maybe a little melancholy, too. "That's certainly not a sight I thought I'd ever see," she said.

Still unsure about the transformation before her, Charlie didn't respond for a minute. Then she ran her hand across the silk of Stuart's back. "He kinda grows on you."

Lorna smiled. "That he does."

Feeling like an intruder who'd been caught in the act, Charlie began to tug Stuart from her shoulder. "Do you want to hold him?"

Lorna shook her head. "No. He looks quite happy where he is."

"You look different. Sad or something." Charlie blurted it out and then thought better of it. The tight ship Lorna ran included rigid personal boundaries.

Lorna raised an eyebrow.

"Sorry, I just—"

"No. You're right. I am."

First her mother, and now Lorna. Spirit must be up to something big. "You are?"

"Yes. I…" Lorna pressed her hands together and looked at the floor, appearing to search for words which didn't normally roll off her tongue. Charlie gazed at the tent of Lorna's fingers. She'd never noticed how big her hands were in contrast to her size, or that her knuckles stuck out like knots on a tree. "I regret how I've treated you."

"You do?"

Lorna nodded. "And I'm…"

"Lorna, it's—"

"Sorry."

Charlie felt the sudden weight of Dog's rump on her foot and the whisk of Stuart's tongue on the lobe of her right ear. She didn't know what to say.

"I mean, look at you. The animals love you."

"I guess."

"No, they do. They take to you immediately. And I think I've been jealous."

Charlie's jaw went slack. "You have?"

Lorna nodded and gestured toward Dog. "He's never warmed to me, and that has never happened. I've always been able to relate to every creature who has come in here, no matter what their circumstances have been. I considered it a gift." She sighed. "But you. He immediately bonded with you. Apparently your gift is greater than mine."

Charlie frowned. "I don't think that's true. He likes you."

Lorna waved her hand. "It's okay. I was being immature, and I'm sorry. I just…these animals mean a lot to me. I want them to love me as much as I love them."

"I think that's true for everybody."

Lorna cocked her head. "Now that's insightful for someone your age."

Charlie smiled. "Blame my therapist. She's always spewing that stuff at me, hoping something will stick."

"Well, it appears to be working."

"So, you're not mad at me anymore?"

Lorna shook her head. "No. I know your intentions were good."

Charlie sighed. "Thanks."

"And your mother. I owe her an apology as well."

"Are you sick or something?"

Lorna put her hands on her hips. "An apology from me is that unexpected, is it?"

Since Lorna had decided to be nice, Charlie decided on tact rather than honesty. "Well, I mean, it's so sudden. This change of heart."

"It would appear so, wouldn't it? No, I'm not sick. Just re-evaluating some things."

"Okay, good." The unmoving warmth against Charlie's neck probably meant Stuart had fallen asleep. Dog, on the other hand, was lying with his chin planted on her other foot with his eyes wide open. Apparently, he was going to make sure Charlie didn't go anywhere without him. "Well, I guess if I can get these two unwrapped, I'll finish my work."

"And take Dog to his new forever home." Lorna looked at him and smiled.

At that, he sat up, wagged his tail, and looked at Charlie expectantly. Lorna watched them for a moment, then stepped forward and gently lifted Stuart from her shoulder. "I'll finish your chores. Your boy needs to go home."

Charlie's house
One hour later

Charlie's mother watched nervously as Dog walked gingerly from room to room, sniffing furniture and trying to find a familiar scent in the thick pile of white beneath his feet. His tail and ears were down as if he knew this wasn't a home created for his kind.

"He'll be fine, Mom. I promise."

"I just don't want any stains on my carpet." A parade of second thoughts marched across her mother's face.

"That won't happen. He's totally house trained."

"How do you know? The shelter isn't a house."

"Because he never went in his cage. He always waited until we went outside."

As if on cue, Dog stepped back from sniffing the leg of her mother's antique side table, lifted his leg, and baptized it with a golden stream of urine. The sound of it pulsed against the wood, splattering a shower of yellow droplets onto everything within reach.

"Charlie!"

"Dog!"

He dropped his leg, looked up in stunned surprise, and took off into the house.

Charlie ran to the table, dropped to her knees, yanked up her shirt, and tried to catch the yellow river before it hit the white valley below. She didn't make it. She sopped the carpet with her shirt. "I'm so sorry, Mom. I'll clean it up. He didn't mean it. He's just nervous. He's really a good dog. You're going to love him once you get to know him. I promise, it'll be okay."

The silence behind her was so thick Charlie was afraid to turn around. When she did, her mother was gone.

She jumped up and raced through the house in search of the pair. "Mom? Dog?"

She found them in the front hall. He was tucked under the linen bench, his shoulders hunched, his chin on the ground, and his tail nowhere to be seen. Her mother was standing over him with her hands on her hips.

"This isn't going to work."

"No, Mom. Please. He'll be okay." Charlie knelt beside Dog and cupped his trembling head in her palm. "He's just scared and nervous. He doesn't know what's going on."

"He just ruined my antique table, the couch, the carpet…"

"I'll pay for everything."

Her mother raised an eyebrow. "With what? The allowance you already allocated to pay for his food, which won't begin to cover it?"

Charlie slumped against the bench. "I don't know. I just know he belongs here. With me."

"Just because you like each other doesn't mean he belongs here."

"But, Mom—"

"No buts, Charlie. I've worked hard to have nice things. I'm not going to let some mutt ruin them."

Charlie reflexively covered Dog's ears. "Don't say that."

"Well, he is. Maybe if he was a purebred it would be different."

Charlie felt the steam rising up her neck. She stood and faced her mother. "That's the difference for you? The fact that he doesn't have some fancy bloodline?"

Her mother shrugged. "I doubt he'd act like that if he did."

"You have no idea what you're talking about."

"Oh, and you're suddenly a dog expert?"

"Obviously, I know more than you."

Her mother crossed her arms and shook her head.

"So you're not even going to give him a second chance?"

"I've seen enough."

"And I should've known better."

"What's that supposed to mean?"

"Just more of the same."

"I have no idea what you're talking about."

Charlie gave her a bitter smile. "Don't you? Dog and I are the same. We're not fancy enough for you." She lowered herself back to the floor and ran her hand along Dog's head. He looked at her with the sadness of knowing it had all been too good to be true.

"Honey." Charlie's mother touched her shoulder, which felt like the singe of a branding iron. She jerked away and heard her mother sigh. "Look at me."

Charlie shook her head.

"I know we don't see eye to eye on some things, but I love you."

When Charlie rubbed Dog's ear, he leaned into her touch as if absorbing the last drop of love he'd ever know.

She felt the bench shift and heard the whiff of the cushion

when her mother sat down. "And I know I've made a lot of mistakes."

"So you've said." Charlie gave a dry spit.

"Don't…" She heard the restraint in her mother's voice and then the words that tumbled into a sigh. "I just want what's best for you."

Charlie stood from the floor and looked at her mother. "No, Beth. You want what's best for you. You always have, and you always will. I should've known better than to fall for your fake show with Lorna." Then she lifted her shoes from their proper place on the rack, set them on the floor, and slipped them on. When she opened the hall closet and pulled out her coat and Dog's leash, he crawled out from beneath the bench and stood at her feet.

"Where are you going?"

Charlie gave her mother a stony look. "Any place where we're more welcome than here."

Chapter 22

Bosko Counseling Services
One hour later

"He is awfully cute." Dog had taken to Stella right away, and he was currently resting his chin on her knee, a low moan of pleasure humming within him as she rubbed his ears with the knowing touch of someone who loved animals.

Charlie was at the drum, resting her palms on the surface as she contemplated skipping the mallet and just railing on it with her fists. "Tell my mother that."

"But her antique table? You can't really blame her for being upset, Charlie."

"Yeah, well, she didn't even give him a second chance. One mistake and it was over."

"Have you ever considered that your expectations may be unrealistic?"

Charlie hated the reasonable tone in Stella's voice that sounded too much like her mother. She turned from the drum to glare at the woman who never seemed phased by the world around her. "I'll tell you what's realistic. She never intended for it to work."

"What do you mean?" Although the question was directed at Charlie, it was Dog's chin she lifted. Stella smiled into his gaze and leaned to plant a kiss on the top of his head. Then she stood for a stretch, reaching for the ceiling as if it were a ladder hanging from above. Charlie watched in awe as her body unfolded with the ease of someone who didn't care about the sag of breasts too-visible through her top, the balloons of fabric that stretched from her buttons and exposed white puckers of flesh, the shadow beneath the mound at her waist, or the fringes of black hair that peeked from the edges of her shirt sleeves, which now only partially covered her armpits. When Stella had completed her stretch, she lowered her arms in a single, exhaling sweep that generated a gentle breeze of stale coffee and honeysuckle perfume.

Charlie shook her head to clear the image from her mind. "It was all show. The only reason she let Dog in the door was because she didn't want Lorna to have the upper hand."

Stella sat back down.

"And to make me think she's something she's not."

"Come over here." Stella patted the chair beside her. "Tell me more about that."

Charlie sighed and slumped into the chair.

"It's my job. Tell me what you'd hoped for from your mother." Dog nudged Stella's hand to remind her he was still there. She smiled at him. "What's wrong, boy, think I forgot about you?" She ran her palm down his back and patted his rump. Then he curled into a ball at her feet.

Charlie felt a poke of jealousy. "I can't believe he took to you like that."

Stella shrugged. "You did, didn't you?"

Charlie rolled her nose ring and stared at the floor. "Eventually."

"The truth is, you've both felt like you didn't belong. But I try to remind you that you do." She gestured toward Dog. "Never underestimate the sensitivity of God's creatures. They know who they can trust."

"Now you sound like Lorna. Minus the accent and the obnoxious *wee* she puts before everything."

Stella smiled. "Well, in this case, Lorna's right. Animals help us every bit and more than we help them. I think that's especially true with rescues."

Charlie got on the floor beside Dog and cupped his head in her hand. He leaned into her touch, apparently savoring the renewed attention.

"Why?"

"Why rescues?"

Charlie nodded.

"I don't know. Maybe it's just me that's partial because they remind me of me."

"Because…"

"Because I'm a rescue, too. We all are, in one way or another."

Charlie sighed. "Lorna said that, too."

Stella smiled. "Maybe if you hung out with Lorna more, you could save your mom some money on these sessions."

"Well, I have to admit she was nice to me today. But I could care less about saving my prissy mother any of her precious money."

"Speaking of your mother. You didn't answer my question."

"What question?"

Stella raised an eyebrow and cocked her head. "We only have an hour."

"But since this was an emergency, I thought—"

"The question, Charlie."

Charlie rolled the soft flesh of Dog's floppy ear around her finger like a ponytail, then ran her hand down his back, relishing the one place where she'd finally felt she belonged. After a few minutes, she looked up at Stella. "What do I hope for from my mother? That she'd quit judging my every breath. That she'd admit she's made mistakes, too. That she'd finally be real with me. Not just when it's convenient. Not just when it's a show. Not just when I'm upset with her. But really real. Once and for all."

~

Ripple Creek Hospice House
Friday evening

Quinn already looked worse than he had during their last visit. Dog had wasted no time in jumping onto the bed and curling up at his feet. He seemed to sense his master didn't have the energy for much else.

Charlie sat in the overstuffed chair next to the bed, hoping the feeling in her toes would eventually return after their walk in the cold. As she listened to the hum of the oxygen machine and gazed at Quinn, she wondered how long she and Dog could hide out in the shadows of a dying man. When she shifted her weight to cross her legs, the material beneath her crinkled.

"Shouldn't sit on that." Quinn had his eyes closed, and his words were barely audible, drifting from his lips like a curl of smoke.

Charlie glanced at the seat of the chair. The white paper beneath her had a green border that resembled plastic. "I shouldn't?'

"It's in case I crap myself."

She jumped up as if someone had lit a flame beneath her butt. She glanced at the chair and then back at Quinn. His eyelids were still closed, but Charlie saw the hint of a smile at the corners of his mouth. She gazed at the bony ridge above his eyes, the two gray unruly eyebrow forests, and the deep hollows beneath them that resembled caves cut into a cliff. Grateful to discover that a sense of humor was part of the curmudgeon package, she leaned over to examine the glistening paper more closely.

"Doesn't look like you've crapped on it recently."

With as much flair as she could muster, she lowered herself onto the crinkling pad, wiggling her rear for extra sound effects. This time, Quinn didn't try to hide the slow smile that emerged from his lips.

Charlie sighed and crossed her arms. "You'll have to work harder than that to get rid of me."

Quinn replied with a single grunt, which Charlie interpreted as her admission to the club.

The volume of the television was turned to low, where Skipper was trying to tell Gilligan why his coconut conveyor belt was a bad idea and Ginger was smelling flowers, trying to decide which should be picked to adorn her new hat. As Charlie watched her lean into the fragrance of one plant after another, it occurred to her that Quinn's room didn't smell. Not that it was absent of odors—like the cleaning solution that wafted from the bathroom in the corner, the antiseptic air that hovered in his sheets, or the lingering aroma of steamed cauliflower that filled the halls. But it didn't smell *bad* and it certainly didn't smell like death, as if everyone who used the term knew what that particular aroma was supposed to be.

The thought of cauliflower reminded her to ask about the card. On her way down the hall, Charlie had noticed many of the patients' rooms were filled with flowers and balloons and armies of cards lined up on the shelves like soldiers at attention. But Quinn's room was empty except for a single card, which had been tacked to the corkboard on the wall at the foot of his bed.

"Who's the card from?" she asked.

When Quinn didn't respond, Charlie glanced over, watching for the rise and fall of his chest to make sure he was still alive. Dog looked at her and then put his chin on Quinn's lower leg.

"You have any family?"

It was as if the question itself were a piece of steak abruptly lodging in Quinn's airway. He tried to sit up, his breathing ragged, sucking oxygen from the prongs in his nose like a drowning person gulping for air. His chest heaved, and the blue tinge of his lips grew purple.

Charlie stood in a panic. "You want me to get the nurse?"

He nodded with the desperation of a man clinging to the ledge of a cliff. He fumbled with the call button that was pinned to his sheet, but Charlie bolted for the door. She yanked open the door and stepped into the hall.

"Nurse!"

The light over the doorway to Quinn's room was flashing in rhythm to a soft bell. At the far end of the corridor, a woman in street clothes looked up from a medication cart, then began to run toward Charlie. When she got to the room, she took one look at Quinn's heaving chest and pushed a button on the siderail. She held it down while the head of his bed chugged to nearly ninety degrees.

"It's okay, Quinn. I've got you." She reached for the small fan by his bed and flipped it on. "Here, let this blow in your face. I'll get you some medicine."

Quinn nodded as he tried to wrap his trembling fingers around the fan's stem, but he was too weak to lift his arm. When he looked at the nurse, his head tipping back with the effort of each breath, his lips pursed with each exhale, and the breeze of relief fluttering against the sheet instead of his face, all Charlie could think was she'd never seen someone in real life who was so completely helpless. The nurse gently pulled the fan from his hand and aimed a steady stream of air toward his cheeks. She glanced over her shoulder at Charlie. "Can you hold this for him?"

Charlie felt like there was glue on the soles of her shoes. "Me?"

The woman shot her a look over her reading glasses. "I'm not talking to the dog. Get over here and help him. I need to go get him some meds."

Charlie swallowed hard and stepped closer to Quinn's bed. The nurse sighed and reached for Charlie's hand, tugged her forward, then placed it on the stem of the fan above hers as if they were climbing the handle of a baseball bat.

"That's it. Aim it at his cheeks."

Charlie watched as Quinn closed his eyes, apparently savoring the flow of air and the ability to breathe again.

"It's simple, but it works. Right, Quinn?"

He gave a single nod.

"I'm going to go get you some medicine to help you relax, okay?"

He nodded once more, and she patted his arm. "I'll be right back."

Charlie gripped the fan like it was a life raft in a storm. She looked over her shoulder longingly at the nurse's back as she walked out of the room. Then she looked at Dog, hoping for some kind of support. But he was curled into a ball on the bed, his chin on Quinn's shin, his gaze fixed on Quinn's face. Finally, she looked back at Quinn. The heaving of his chest had stopped, and he was back to breathing in his usual rhythm. The breeze on his face made the few eyelashes he had left flutter like leaves in the wind.

Charlie cleared her throat, and Quinn gave a weak wave of his hand.

"What?" she asked.

"Enough."

"But don't you need it? The nurse said—"

"Enough." Quinn seemed to push all the energy he had left into that single word.

Charlie turned off the fan and put it back on the side table. Then she stood there with her hands at her sides, unsure of what to do next.

Quinn kept his eyes closed, focusing on his breathing. "Sit." It was more of an exhale than a command.

She looked at Dog.

"He's already—"

"You. Sit." The words were wispy fragments that seemed to hang there, floating above the bed.

Charlie immediately lowered herself onto the edge of the recliner beside him, and the pad crinkled beneath her.

"Here we go." The nurse walked back into the room, and Charlie resisted the urge to tackle her in relief.

Quinn opened his trembling lips like a little bird eager for a worm. They were as cracked and dry as a riverbed, but less purple than a few minutes earlier. The nurse inserted a small syringe with no needle into Quinn's mouth. He lifted his tongue without being told and she squirted the clear liquid into the space beneath it. Quinn closed his mouth.

"You know the drill. That'll start to kick in pretty quickly."

Quinn nodded. His eyes were closed, his bed was still cranked up at a 90-degree angle, and his skin was gray. To Charlie, he looked like the sitting dead. She looked at the nurse doubtfully, wondering if she was about to see someone die for the first time in her life.

"Is he okay?"

The nurse nodded. "Yes, I gave him a small dose of morphine. It helps relax the pulmonary vasculature."

"The what?"

"Blood vessels in the lungs." Quinn said it so clearly, Charlie thought there was someone else in the room. He opened his eyes and looked at her with such steel blue clarity it startled her. "Ain't dead yet, kid."

The nurse smiled and patted his arm. "No, Quinn, you certainly aren't. You okay now?"

He nodded.

"Need anything else?"

He shook his head.

The nurse looked at Dog and then at Charlie. "And how about you two? Are you staying?"

"Staying?"

She shrugged. "You can if you want."

"We can?"

"Well, that is, if Quinn wants you to."

Charlie looked at him hopefully. His eyes were closed and his breathing was even.

"I know you're listening," she said.

As if he understood that staying right where he was through the night was a possibility, Dog did a low crawl toward Quinn's right hand, stretched his neck, and licked it.

The tight line of Quinn's lips surrendered the slightest of

smiles. He opened his hand, and Dog greeted the invitation with an eager and thorough bath of his palm.

"Just him."

The nurse bent closer.

"What's that, Quinn?"

"Just Dog." His words were a soft wheeze. The effort made him cough, and Charlie could hear the mucous rattling in his chest.

Her heart sank. The nurse's sympathetic look made it worse.

"I'm afraid he can't stay here by himself, Quinn. Somebody has to be with him."

When the coughing stopped, Quinn responded by cupping his hand over Dog's head. His expression was so peaceful Charlie thought this time he might actually be dead.

Finally, he gave a nod so brief it would've disappeared into the hum of his oxygen machine had they not been looking.

The nurse gently laid her palm against his chest. "What does that mean, Quinn?"

He lifted a bony gray finger and pointed it at Charlie. "She can stay."

That's when Charlie realized she'd been holding her breath. She let out a sigh, and Dog followed with one of his own.

"Okay, then." The nurse turned to her. "If Quinn says you can stay, it's okay with me." She put a hand on Dog and ran it down his back, which triggered a curling response of his tail. "It's good for him to be here. They're good for each other."

"Awesome."

The nurse turned to go.

"What time are visiting hours over?" Charlie asked.

"Oh, we don't have any. Families are welcome to be here as much as they want. As long as it's okay with the patient."

"Well, I'm not exactly…"

"Family? Here, family is whoever the patient says it is." She nodded at Dog. "Like him."

She looked back at Charlie. "Maybe you, too."

Charlie thought that might be going a bit far, but at this point, she'd take it. She looked at Dog, curled against his master, and realized he hadn't eaten since morning. The clock on the wall read nearly eight. The nurse put her hand on her hip. "Now what?"

"Well, I was wondering if you have anything he could eat. Breakfast was a long time ago."

"I suppose that goes for both of you."

Charlie hesitated, then nodded.

"Let me finish my med rounds, and I'll see what I can come up with."

"Thanks."

The woman waved an index finger in the air. "But he'll probably get cat food. Which Maggie will not be the least bit happy about sharing."

"We'll take whatever we can get."

She smiled. "Don't worry, you can have people food." She turned to go, then stopped and looked back at Charlie. "How old are you?"

"Sixteen."

"I assume this is okay with your parents. Staying, I mean. They know where you are?"

Charlie held the woman's gaze, then nodded, somehow surprised it was still so easy to lie.

Chapter 23

The first thought that came to Charlie's mind when she opened her eyes was that she had no idea where she was. She licked her dry lips and tried to get her bearings. Dim light from the television danced through the shadows. The only sound was a hum from the corner of the room and a hissing from somewhere near.

There was a digital clock on the wall. The orange numbers read 10:45.

Charlie sat up, and something crinkled beneath her. She looked at the bed beside her.

Quinn.

She realized the hissing was coming from the two green prongs that jutted into his nostrils. The attached vine of tubing traveled across the bony rim of Quinn's jaw, around his ear, and onto his chest, where it disappeared into the darkness. His breathing was even, and he seemed to be sound asleep.

Dog was curled into a ball of black and white fur on the bed at Quinn's feet, his chin propped on his lower leg. He heard Charlie move and opened his eyes to gaze at her without moving his head. Two metal bowls were on the floor. One was full of water, and one held food that hadn't been touched.

Someone squeezed her shoulder, and Charlie jumped. She

looked up to see Patch glaring at her from the shadows. She leaned and whispered into Charlie's ear. "What are you doing here?"

Charlie sat up straighter. "I—"

Patch put her index finger over Charlie's lips and then jammed it in the air toward the hall. Charlie got up to follow with the enthusiasm of a sheep going to slaughter. She'd known she'd have to deal with her mother when she found out where she was. She hadn't been counting on dealing with Patch, too.

When she got to the hall, Patch was waiting for her, hands on her hips. Charlie figured the jeans covering the long thin lines of Patch's legs and the sweatshirt beneath the lanyard of her ID tag meant being here at this hour wasn't something she'd been planning to do.

"Well?"

"I didn't know you were working." Since she'd never seen Patch mad, it was the first time she noticed the twitch of her left eye. Charlie gave her a nervous smile and pointed to the lettering on Patch's sweatshirt that confirmed her survival of Ripple Creek's 10K Adventure Run. "Did you actually do that? That's—"

"Don't change the subject."

Charlie sighed. "He said I could stay."

Patch crossed her arms and glared. "Apparently your mother didn't say you could stay. Since she's standing at the front desk. Furious."

The pace of Charlie's pulse picked up. "She is?"

"Of course she is, Charlie. What'd you think? She had no idea where you were."

"Apparently she did." Charlie said it with a shrug, hoping Patch wasn't as durable as either Lorna or her mother.

But Patch leaned in, and Charlie took a step back. "Don't get smart. The evening nurse is furious with you, too. Since you lied to her."

"Technically—"

"Save it."

"But, Patch, Mom kicked Dog out, and we didn't have any-where to go." Charlie knew the desperation in her voice sounded fake and pathetic, but she had no choice.

Patch pointed an index finger at her. "You have a home." Then she pointed it toward Quinn's room. "He has the shelter. You could've taken him back there."

Charlie shook her head. "I'm not doing that to him."

"You don't have a choice."

"So say you."

"What?" Patch planted her hands on her hips as her eye began to twitch again.

Charlie sighed. "Patch, this is important to me."

"And honesty is important to me."

Charlie felt the steam rising up her neck. "Really? Then why haven't you told Quinn about Final?"

Patch looked like she'd been slapped. "What?"

"Final. Remember? The guy we both met when we were dead? The guy who's waiting around the corner for Quinn?"

Patch sighed. "Charlie, it's complicated."

Charlie shook her head. "Yeah, well, being a big chicken isn't."

Patch put a hand on her elbow and steered her into the empty patient room next door to Quinn's. It was inky black until she flipped on the overhead light. Charlie winced against the brightness.

"So, what, now I'm in trouble because I have guts and you don't?"

Patch closed the door behind them. There was only one chair in the room. She motioned toward the bed.

"What?"

"Sit."

The corners of the spread were tucked neatly into the foot of the bed, and the pillowcase on the pillow was so crisp it looked like it had been ironed. The aroma of candle wax filled the air. When Charlie sat down, the bed creaked beneath her, and she caught a whiff of bleach from below. Patch lowered herself into a spot beside her.

"I can't talk about Final Moment here."

"Why not?"

Patch crossed her legs and propped her folded hands on top of her knee. "Because I like my job."

Charlie turned to look at her and noticed the twitching of her eye had stopped. "You mean you're not allowed to talk about him?"

"I mean people have the right to die the way they want to. We don't get to impose our personal beliefs on anyone."

Charlie paused, considering the response as if tasting a new dish. "So, let me get this straight. You just let people head into death without telling them anything?"

"Well, not *anything*. I support whatever faith system they embrace."

Charlie crossed her arms and stared into the white gleam of the tile floor. "That's a party line if I ever heard one."

"You don't understand, Charlie."

The bed creaked when Charlie stood, and the mattress where Patch sat dropped briefly as if Charlie had stepped off a seesaw. She turned and looked down at Patch. "No, I think I understand perfectly, Patch. There's a bunch of people in this place headed for heaven or hell, and you have the power to help them change things before it's too late. But you won't."

Patch held Charlie's gaze. "I'm doing what's best for the patients. To respect and honor their beliefs. That's what they deserve. That's my job."

Charlie shook her head and started for the door. "Whatever."

"And you should follow suit."

Patch's words held such a shift in tone, Charlie stopped in her tracks and turned. "What's that supposed to mean?"

When Patch stood from the bed, she looked taller somehow. "It means I don't want you to start any trouble here, Charlie."

"Like what? Telling Quinn the truth?"

"Like imposing your beliefs on him."

Charlie eyed the woman before her, feeling foolish for having thought they could be friends. "You know, Patch, I'm new to this Spirit thing, but I bet he's not very happy with you."

The twitch returned to Patch's eye, accompanied by a stony stare. "That's none of your business."

The words stung, but Charlie bit her lip and willed away the tears that threatened. Then Patch's expression softened. "It's just…I need you to listen to me, Charlie."

Charlie gave a slow and bitter nod. "Oh, I'm listening, Patch. Believe me, I hear you loud and clear. If my lecture is over, I need to go deal with my mother."

~

Somehow, the hallway seemed to have gotten longer since she arrived. Charlie's heart pounded harder with each step that drew her closer to her mother. When she got to the end, she stopped and eyed the woman sitting in the waiting area. Sweatpants. Tennis shoes. Ski coat. And no makeup. Charlie didn't think she'd ever seen her mother out in public in such a state. She cleared her throat, and her mother looked over.

"Hi, Mom." Then it occurred to her that pushover Dan might be outside and could help plead her case. "Is Dad with you?"

Unfortunately for Charlie, her mother could spot manipulation from a mile away. "Dan is in bed. Which is something people who have to work in the morning normally do at this hour instead of chasing their children around town." The car keys in her right hand jangled when she rose from the couch. "I'm disappointed, Charlie."

"But, Mom—"

"You couldn't even have the courtesy of letting me know where you were."

Charlie opened her hands and held them out as if exposing the linings of empty pockets. "I don't have a phone."

Her mother lifted one eyebrow. Then she pointed at the telephone sitting prominently on the front desk with a plastic sign propped beside it: Guest Courtesy Phone.

"That wasn't there when I came in."

"And I've offered to get you another phone many times."

"I told you I don't want a phone."

Her mother waved her hand as if erasing a chalkboard. "None of that's the point. The point is, you ran out and have been gone for hours, and I had no idea where you were or if you were…" Her mother's voice faltered as tears glistened in her eyes.

Charlie took a step toward her. "Mom?"

Her mother sank back onto the couch. At first, she sat silently, giving her eyes a delicate sweep of her hand when the pebble of a tear threatened to spill onto her cheeks. But it wasn't long before she was pressing her fingers against her eyelids to hold off the impending flood, which suddenly broke free into a string of sobs so intense Charlie thought maybe she should go get Patch. She stepped forward and lowered herself onto the couch as if it—or her mother—might break.

Her mom's sobs slowed to a trickle. She pulled a tissue from her pocket and blew her nose. Then she dabbed her eyes, took a deep breath, and looked at Charlie. "The last time you disappeared, you almost died."

Charlie looked at her shoes. "Actually, I did—"

"Don't."

Charlie looked up.

"A mother can't bear to keep hearing that."

Charlie gazed at the red rims and dark shadows that adorned her mother's normally beautiful and perfect eyes. "Okay."

"I am so tired, Charlie. To the bone. Tired of fighting with you. Tired of fighting with myself…" Her voice broke, and she pinched her lips together to control the trembling of her chin.

Charlie watched her mother, feeling both bad and exhausted herself. For this was the roller coaster of their relationship—hot and cold with nothing in between. "Mom, I'm sorry. I'm not trying to make things harder. I just…I thought things were going to be easier than this after I came back from the—"

"When you were revived."

"Right, when I was revived. I mean, Grace made it sound like it would be a piece of cake the second time around." The thought of Grace made her think of Spirit, which made her wonder what in the world he thought of all of this—or if he was even still around.

"Or that's what you wanted to hear."

"Maybe." Charlie looked at her hands and then back at her mom. "So, what now?"

Her mom stood from the couch and picked up her keys. "You're coming home, is what now."

Charlie's heart leapt with hope. "So Dog can stay with us?"

Her mother shook her head. "I didn't say that."

If Charlie looked confused, it's because she was. "But what's he supposed to do? They won't let him stay here with Quinn if I'm not here."

Her mother shrugged. "Then I guess he'll have to go back to the shelter."

Charlie stood so fast the fake palm leaves waved in her breeze. "No."

Her mother's gaze held such stern steadiness that all Charlie's just-recent warmth toward her disappeared like water down a drain.

"Yes," she said.

Charlie sat back down in a huff and crossed her arms. "Then I'm not leaving."

Her mother sighed. "You can't just stay here, Charlie."

She shrugged. "Why not? The nurse said families could stay as long as they wanted. Including dogs who are family."

"Well, you're not his family."

The words were so matter-of-fact and concluding Charlie wanted to give a dry spit right then and there. She looked up at her mother, thinking she'd rather be family with a dying curmudgeon who barely spoke to her and his sweet dog destined to be hers than the cold woman before her who happened to be present at her birth. "Family is whoever the patient says it is. And Quinn said I could stay."

The car keys dangling from her mother's right hand jangled with each jab of her forefinger into the tension between them. "Young lady, you are not staying here."

Charlie felt the heat rising in her face as she stood. "Just watch me."

Then she turned and walked back down the hall toward Quinn's room.

~

When she finally stopped outside of Quinn's door, Charlie realized she'd been holding her breath. Each step had compounded her growing anticipation that her mother was likely close behind, about to tackle her like a linebacker. She exhaled and turned, looking back down the empty hall with disappointment. When she put her hand on the doorknob, it disappeared from her grasp as if repulsed by her touch. But it was Patch on the other side of the door, opening it and then easing it closed behind her as she stepped into the hall. "Well?"

Charlie bit her lip and looked away. "She said we could stay."

"Are you sure?"

Charlie nodded and rolled her nose ring.

"Then why are you looking at your shoes?"

She looked at Patch and sighed. "Well, I said we were staying and she didn't chase me down the hall, so…"

Patch eyed her. "Were you like this before you were dead?"

"Worse."

"Hmm. Well, me too."

Charlie leaned forward and lowered her voice. "So, speaking of dead. You'll talk to Quinn with me about Final Moment? I didn't tell my mother this, but it's the other reason I need to stay. Besides the fact that I'm not taking Dog back to the shelter."

Patch shook her head. "No, I told you. I won't."

"But if you tell him too, then maybe he'll believe both of us."

"No."

Charlie took a step back and put her hands on her hips. "That's why you got a second chance, Patch. To help people get ready for what's ahead. From what you said at the funeral home, I thought you knew that."

Patch sighed. "That's all good in theory, Charlie."

"I don't see what the problem is."

"I told you. I'll get in trouble for sharing my faith."

"Do you believe it? The whole Jesus thing? The heaven and hell and make a choice and all?"

Patch nodded. "Yes, I do."

Charlie slumped against the wall. "Then I really don't get it, Patch. How can you work with people who are dying and not tell them that?"

Patch's attempt at a whisper may as well have been a shout. "Because it's disrespectful. Because everyone gets to choose how they want to die, Charlie. Because I don't get to claim I have all the answers. Because they've heard it all before and have already made a choice. Because I can't proselytize and expect to keep my job."

Charlie watched her for a moment, then shrugged. "Well, I don't work here."

Patch sighed. "No, you don't."

"So I can say whatever I want."

"Technically."

"Technically?"

Patch lifted her index finger and waved it in a deliberate, threatening way that reminded Charlie of Lorna. And of her mother. "If you upset one of our patients, both you and Dog will be asked to leave."

Charlie stood from the wall. "You'd just kick us out into the street?"

Patch rolled her eyes. "Save the drama for someone it'll work on."

"Seriously."

"Charlie, you will seriously be asked to leave if you upset one of our patients. That includes Quinn."

"So, I can choose between having somewhere for us to stay tonight and Quinn going to hell."

"Like I said, save it for someone it'll work on. I have to work tomorrow and my bed is calling." Patch turned to go.

"Stella. I bet she'll let us stay with her." Charlie said it more to herself than Patch.

"No, she won't." Patch didn't turn around but just kept walking.

Charlie jogged a few steps to catch up to her. "You know Stella?"

Patch stopped. "It's a small town, Charlie."

Charlie moved in front of Patch. "How do you know her?"

"How do you think? She's my therapist."

Charlie chewed on this news, wondering why she hadn't thought of this possibility before. "Mine, too."

Patch tipped her chin and gave Charlie a look that made her think twice about running back to Quinn's room and telling him everything. "I would hope so."

"What, you think I need a shrink?"

Patch sighed as if Charlie were a ball and chain around her leg. "I just know you've been having a rough time."

"Did Stella tell you that?"

"Of course not. Stella might know everybody's secrets in this town, but she has lips like a vault door."

Patch started walking again. Charlie tried to match her stride, but she had to do double-time to keep up with Patch's long legs. She bobbed along beside her like a toy on a string. "So why'd you say she won't let us stay with her? She's nice and knows how mean my mom is. She's her therapist, too. Well, she was. Mom said it was a long time ago."

"Then Stella knows that's just your perspective. And her professional boundaries are much too healthy to let you invade them." Patch stopped and looked at her. "As are mine."

Charlie took a step back. "What's that supposed to mean?"

"It means if you do something for which you need to be kicked out of this house, don't expect me to come to your rescue."

Chapter 24

$\mathcal{D}$og lifted his head from the mattress when Charlie eased her way into the cool darkness of Quinn's room. Even though she'd previously thought there was no such thing as the smell of death, she was starting to wonder. Maybe the strange odor she couldn't quite place had something to do with Quinn sleeping with his mouth hanging open. His upper dentures drooped from his gum line like a garage door that wouldn't quite close, and with every breath she could hear the sound of mucous rattling like marbles in the back of his throat.

But he looked peaceful.

Maybe too peaceful. Which made Charlie wonder if she should wake him up to tell him about Final before it was too late.

She glanced at the clock. It was almost midnight. Patch's words rang in her head. If she got herself kicked out, she'd have a hard time finding a place for her and Dog to stay at this time of night. She lowered herself onto the chair, trying not to rattle the paper liner beneath her. Dog watched her for a moment and then lowered his chin back down to Quinn's shin.

She eased her shoes off and tucked her feet beneath her. When she had herself rolled into a tight ball in the corner of Quinn's chair, she decided to close her eyes and rest. The sounds were

213

sharper then, and for the first time she realized that in addition to the hum of Quinn's oxygen machine and the hiss coming out of his nose tubes, there was a bubbling somewhere in the room. She opened her eyes and located the source: a bottle of water between the machine and the tubing. Satisfied, she closed her eyes again and listened to the seesaw of Quinn's snoring, like wind whistling through the narrow passages of a cave. Every once in a while, there was a pause, and then he would start up again.

But once, he didn't.

Charlie opened her eyes and looked at him. His chest was heaving up and down, but no air was moving. She sat up straight and the paper crinkled. "Quinn?"

Dog looked at her and then at his master.

Charlie stood and moved to his side, wondering if she should call someone. She shook his shoulder. "Quinn?"

He inhaled sharply. It was as if the breath caught the knob of a partially closed door and scraped it wide open. Startled, he clamped his mouth shut and the dentures popped back into place. He took a deep breath and looked around as if he didn't know where he was.

Charlie let out the breath she'd been holding and sank back into the chair. "You scared me."

He looked at her. Then at Dog. "Who are you?"

She glanced over her shoulder as if someone must be standing there. Then she looked back at him, caught in his stare like a moth in a web.

"Me?" She put her hand on her chest.

"I ain't talkin' to Dog."

"You don't remember?"

"Remember what?"

"I'm Charlie. I brought Dog to see you. You said I could stay."

He waved his hand. "Oh, yeah."

Charlie settled back into the chair. When Quinn closed his eyes, she figured he'd drift back to sleep. But clear as a bell, he asked, "So who's Final?"

Charlie sat up as if someone had pulled a fire alarm. "Final?"

Quinn still had his eyes closed when he spoke again. "You two might as well have been sitting on the bed with Dog."

"Oh, you…heard us?"

"Every word. So what's all the fuss about whether to tell me about some guy named Final?"

Charlie took a deep breath, not sure how to proceed now that her opportunity was presented on a silver platter. "If you get mad at me, we'll get kicked out."

Quinn opened his eyes and looked at her. "Doubt you'll make me any madder than you already have. And unfortunately, you're still here."

For some reason, that gave Charlie some comfort. And courage. "I died." She blurted it like a burp and waited.

"You on somethin', kid?" When Quinn looked at her and frowned, the two unruly patches of gray hair on his brow stitched together like two pieces of shag carpet.

"I'm serious. I was in a car wreck a month ago, and my heart stopped for a long time."

Quinn reached a bony hand into the air and adjusted the prongs in the forest of his nose. "So, you were dead and came back to life. Heard of that before."

"But that's not all. When I was dead, I met this guy named Final Moment."

"That's a dumb name." Quinn looked at Dog briefly, then closed his eyes and folded his skeletal hands across his chest as if he were already dead.

Charlie turned in the chair and leaned toward him. "It's what he is. The last sixty seconds before we die."

"And what, he just appears and announces that?"

"Kind of." Charlie's heart was throbbing in her ears.

"I think you'd better get some sleep." Quinn's tone was as ho-hum as sitting on a bench sucking on a toothpick.

"No, I'm serious."

Quinn sighed. "Okay, I'll play along. And then what?"

Charlie took a deep breath and plunged ahead. "Well, he says he administers the Regrets Evaluation and Pliability Assessment."

"I have no idea what you're talking about, kid."

"The first is to see if you have any regrets before you die. The other one is to see if you're open to a relationship with God."

"With God?" Quinn opened his eyes, turned his head on the pillow, and looked at her as if she had three heads.

Charlie nodded. "Yeah, but he's very specific about that one."

"What do you mean?"

She rolled her nose ring. "It's Jesus or bust."

When Quinn frowned, the overwhelming presence of his brow made the crystal blue of his eyes appear to sink into the deep hollows behind them. "Jesus or bust?"

"Yeah, he said it's a relationship with Jesus that gets us into heaven."

Quinn sat up. "That's a buncha crap. You been smokin' something," he wheezed.

Charlie shook her head. "Not lately."

Quinn began to cough, then hack, and then he spit a glob of brown mucous into a tissue. His hand trembled as he wiped his blue-tinged lips. "Whenever it was, it fried your brain," he mumbled.

"No, wait. Let me tell you what else. I met people."

Even though she could see his chest tugging for air, Quinn pulled the two prongs of tubing from his nose and honked into the tissue. Then he pushed them back in and flopped his head against the pillow with the exhaustion of someone who'd just crawled across the finish line of a marathon. He closed his eyes and didn't respond while his chest heaved in an effort to catch his breath. After a few minutes, his breathing eased and he murmured into the air above him. "What people?"

Charlie wondered if she should go on, but it didn't seem like Spirit was stopping her. "Seven other people, during their last sixty seconds. I was with Final. I thought I was a goner because I pretty much told him the same thing you just said about it being a bunch of crap. Then, when I realized he was serious, I got scared and wanted another chance. Before I knew it, he said things had changed and I was supposed to make the rest of his visits with him. It was weird, but they all happened here in Ripple Creek."

Quinn pushed his cheek against his pillow and looked at her. "They did?"

Charlie nodded. "Yeah. I met seven other people."

"When was this?"

"A month ago. Today, actually. It was a month ago today."

Quinn turned back to the silent flicker of the television and stared. After a few minutes, he spoke again. "Who were they?"

"All different kinds of people. A 14-year-old kid. Ian. He had cancer."

Quinn looked over. "Yeah? A kid with cancer. I have cancer."

"Do you? It was sad. His family was sad, but he was ready. He and Final got along really good. Ian said he and Jesus were tight."

Quinn shook his head. "Tight with Jesus. That's a new one."

"Was for me, too. But it's what Ian said. Final said it was true."

"And you saw his family?"

"Yeah, it was weird. I could see and hear everything that was going on as he was dying.

"And then what?"

"Then it's over."

"Over?"

"Well, wherever they go next. Final said deciding that wasn't part of his job. He was just there to administer the RE and PA."

"RE and PA?"

Charlie sighed with frustration. She had a lot of ground to cover and she was afraid she wasn't going to have time to get it all in. She got up, turned her chair toward Quinn's bed, and sat back down. "What I said before. The Regrets Evaluation and Pliability Assessment."

"Oh." Quinn was quiet for a moment, then asked, "Who else did you meet?"

She clicked through the list as though she were reviewing a ship's manifest. "Anna, Duff, Galen, Esta, Ruby, and Shane."

Charlie watched in déjà vu as Quinn's breathing changed as suddenly as if he'd inhaled a coin. He started to gasp and even in the darkened room she could see his coloring turn from grey to blue. This time, she knew what to do. She hit the nurse's light, cranked up his head, grabbed the fan, switched it on, and let it blow on his face. She grabbed his hand and wrapped his cold bony fingers around its stem. "Let me get a nurse."

The fan clattered onto his lap when he dropped it to grab her hand. Charlie winced, surprised at his strength. With pursed lips and heaving chest, he shook his head.

Charlie grabbed the fan and held it up to his face. "Okay. It's okay. I'll stay right here." She couldn't believe how calm her voice sounded. She hoped he didn't notice the tremble of the fan or the white of her knuckles that seemed to glow in the dark. Her heart thumped in her ears as she kept her eyes locked onto his. "Take it easy. It's okay, Quinn."

She felt Dog lick her arm. She glanced down at him. He had squirmed his way up the bed until he was almost in Quinn's lap. Quinn's breathing began to ease a bit, and he stretched his fingers out in search for his companion. Dog rewarded him with a thorough bath of his hand. Charlie watched in amazement as the fan and Dog did all that was needed to ease Quinn's labored breathing.

She heard the click of the doorlatch behind her.

"You need something, Quinn?"

"He was having trouble breathing, but he seems a little better with the fan. And Dog."

The nurse went to the other side of the bed, pulled the stethoscope from around her neck, and listened to Quinn's chest. She frowned and then gave him a look of concern. "You want me to get you some medicine for your breathing, Quinn?"

He nodded.

She patted his hand. "I'll be right back."

The struggle to breathe had Quinn's shoulders around his ears like they'd been pinned to a clothesline. With the news of medicine on the way, they suddenly relaxed as if freed to float to the ground.

Charlie remembered that after his last episode, he'd waved off the fan after he was feeling better. "You want me to stop with the fan?"

He nodded.

She flipped it off and set it on his bedside stand. The nurse returned with a syringe in hand. "Here you go, Quinn. A little morphine. You can have the lorazepam too, if you want."

He shook his head, opened his mouth, and lifted his tongue. The nurse squirted a small amount of fluid into the space, and Quinn closed his lips over it. Satisfied he was okay, she turned her gaze on Charlie. "So what brought that on?"

Charlie felt a twinge of anxiety creep up her spine. "What do you mean?"

"He was sleeping peacefully the last time I checked on him."

She shrugged, hoping her ears weren't as red as they felt. "I don't know. All the sudden he couldn't breathe."

"Just out of the blue."

Charlie nodded.

"The evening nurse told me your very unhappy mother was here. And that if your presence was upsetting to Quinn, you should be asked to leave."

Charlie swallowed and looked at Quinn, who was judge and jury. The nurse followed her gaze.

"Quinn? Did your visitor upset you? Is that what brought on your episode?"

When he didn't respond, Charlie's heart sank. She looked at Dog and began to visualize the two of them walking in the cold, dark street with nowhere to go.

Finally, Quinn looked at the nurse. "Ain't nobody told you people with lung cancer can't breathe right? The kid stays."

Chapter 25

Saturday morning

Charlie woke to the aroma of bacon. Coffee. Toast. The sound of vacuuming in the hall. A tinkling noise coming from the metal bowl. She opened her eyes and looked at Dog, who had finally decided it was time to eat.

He was right. She was starving. She looked over at Quinn, who appeared to be sound asleep.

Charlie eased out of the chair, wincing against the stiffness that had taken up residence overnight in her lower back and neck. Dog finished his meal by loudly emptying half of the water bowl, splashing puddles onto the floor with each lap of his tongue. When he was done, he walked to the door and looked back at Charlie expectantly.

"He has to take a crap."

She spun back around to see Quinn eyeing them both.

"I thought you were asleep."

"I was. Until you two decided I shouldn't be."

"Sorry."

He responded by reaching for the remote and turning up the television. Charlie decided that was her cue to use a bathroom other than the one in his room, let Dog relieve himself, and find herself something to eat. She hooked the leash onto his collar and opened the door.

Maggie the cat was sitting in the hallway outside Quinn's room. She jumped straight into the air like an animated stepstool and bolted down the hall.

Dog jerked the leash from Charlie's hand and raced after her, barking as loudly as possible, the great hunter in pursuit of the bobbing calico prey ahead of him.

"Dog!"

Charlie bolted past the housekeeper, a metal cart of breakfast trays, and a nurse who stood in the center of the hall, slack-jawed and frozen mid-step as she watched the stream of chaos pouring through the hall around her.

"Sorry!" Charlie dodged the woman to keep from mowing her over. Dog's tail was flat as a nail in front of her, stretched out for speed as he gained ground on the terrified cat. "Dog!" He might as well have been deaf. Charlie was sick with visions of how much damage he might do if he caught her.

When Patch stepped into the run of the animals from a room somewhere down the hall, Dog tried to evade her, but she was too quick. She stomped on his trailing leash, which caught his collar like a clothesline and landed him on his rump. Charlie raced toward him, afraid he might be hurt. But he was immediately back to his feet, pulling so hard against the collar to resume the chase he started to hack.

Patch wrapped the leash around her hand and glared at Charlie. She shook her head, apparently too furious to speak. Instead, she handed Charlie the leash, raised her arm, and jammed her index finger in the air toward the exit. "Out."

"Patch, I'm so sorry, he—"

"Now."

Charlie sighed. She gathered Dog's leash and started for the door. Then she remembered her coat. She turned back around, and Patch stepped into the center of the hall, blocking her way.

"But I have to get my coat."

"I'll get your coat."

"And say goodbye to Quinn."

"I'll tell him."

"But Patch, he wants to know about Final. I didn't get to finish telling him."

Patch glared at her. "I'm sure you've told him enough."

"And he'll want to say goodbye to Dog."

Patch looked down at Dog, who had his tail tucked between his legs. Charlie sensed her crumbling resolve.

"Please, Patch?"

"What's going on here? I heard barking."

Charlie watched Patch visibly straighten and her hesitation flick away like a dead dandelion in the wind. She looked up to see a tall, thin woman walking toward them. Her red hair was perfectly sculpted back from her face into a tight bun, accentuating emerald eyes.

Tree frog.

It was all Charlie could think, and she came dangerously close to a completely inappropriate giggle. She glanced at the name tag on her perfectly cut suit. Erica Miller, RN, MSN, Clinical Director.

"Good morning, Erica. I was just helping our guests to find their way to the exit. Dog was visiting his previous owner and then met Maggie."

"Ah. I see. Which is why we must supervise our canine visitors so closely, right, Patricia?"

Patch nodded. "As I was just explaining to Charlie."

The woman's gaze felt like an ice cube sliding slowly from the tip of Charlie's purple hair to the souls of her beat-up shoes. Finally, she nodded. "Charlie. I'm sure you understand."

"But lady, Quinn is going to be so disappointed when Dog doesn't come back, and I have to tell him—"

"Charlie." Patch cut her off with a glare.

Charlie shook her head in frustration. "I'll wait in the lobby for my coat."

~

The gurgling in Charlie's stomach was so loud Dog looked up at her. "Well, if you hadn't decided to take a morning run, I could've had some of that bacon by now."

At the word, Dog tipped his nose into the air and sniffed. He stood and pulled on the leash toward the door.

"No. You can hold it. This is your fault, and I'm waiting for my coat. It's freezing out there."

A blast of cold air confirmed her weather forecast when a young woman pushed open the door. A small boy was on her heels, and Charlie recognized them immediately. After seeing Charlie in her wild-eyed, bare-butt state in her hospital gown, Shane's wife and little boy probably wouldn't want to talk to her again. The woman looked at her and stopped. "You're…"

"Charlie. Yeah."

The little boy tucked himself behind his mother's leg, just as before. His red curls looped along the edges of his blue knit hat like a child's cursive. Her jeans were too big, and he used the sturdy seam that ran along her outer leg as a handle for his shield.

Charlie smiled at him. "It's Shane, right?"

His mother looked down at him and tugged the hat from his head, freeing the curls to spring into action. She ran her fingers through them, both to smooth and to comfort. He bit his lip and watched Charlie.

"Yes. You have a good memory."

Charlie nodded. "But I don't think I know your name."

"Amber. Amber McDonough." She extended her hand and Charlie rose to take it. When she did, Dog pulled at his leash, not for the door, but for the boy. Charlie held him back.

"Dog. No."

But he was persistent, and it took everything she had to

restrain him. "Dog. No." She looked at Amber. "Sorry, I've never seen him do that. Guess he likes kids."

Amber smiled. "It's okay. Is he friendly?"

Charlie nodded. "Yeah. He's a really nice dog. His previous owner is here. We came to visit and…"

Little Shane moved from behind his mother's leg and leaned against her knee. His eyes were glued to Dog, except for a quick glance up at his mother.

She put her hand on his head. "How about if I meet him first?"

The little boy nodded.

Amber tucked him behind her and took a step toward Dog. He wagged his tail and lowered his ears into a smile. She placed her hand on his head and then gently stroked his back. Charlie watched as Dog indulged her but continued to stretch his neck toward the boy, sniffing the air.

"Guess you're the one he wants, Shane," Amber said.

Shane gave a shy smile and took a step toward Dog, whose tail went into curly overdrive. He whimpered with apparent delight at the prospect of contact. Charlie kept him on a short leash, so when Shane extended his hand, Dog had to extend his tongue to give it a single lick.

The little boy giggled.

"He doesn't usually warm up to people like that." Charlie squatted so she was at eye level with Shane. "You must be pretty special, buddy."

He took another step toward Dog, who sniffed his ear and lapped his tongue once across the cleft in the little boy's chin. The giggle that erupted egged him on, and he gave him another. And another.

"Okay, that's enough. You're going to drown him." Charlie put her arms around Dog's neck and gently pulled him back.

Amber knelt with them. "You like him, huh, Shane?"

The little boy was smiling. He nodded.

"That's the happiest he's been since…"

Charlie looked at her. "The hospital?"

"Yeah. That's hit him really hard. I didn't expect it to, but he's been droopy ever since."

"Well, if he wants a dog, there are more at the shelter. That's where this guy came from. I work there. I adopted him." She tried to hold Dog close, but he wiggled free and laid down at Shane's feet. The little boy knelt and put a hand on his head. Then he looked up at his mom.

"Can I have him?"

Charlie reached for Dog, but he didn't budge. "Well, no. He's mine." She stood up and wrapped the leash around her hand. "But you can have another dog. I mean, if your mom says you can."

Shane shook his head and wrapped his arms around Dog's neck. "I want him."

Amber gave Charlie an apologetic look and pried the little boy's arms free. "Honey, he belongs to Charlie. If you want a dog, we'll go to the shelter after we visit Grandpa and find you one."

At that, the little boy began to cry. "But I want this one."

Dog gave him a worried look and lapped the pebbles of tears that rolled down the plump mounds of his cheeks.

"Here's your…"

Charlie turned to see Patch holding her coat. But her eyes were locked onto the scene on the floor. "Uh, hi, Amber. And this must be Shane."

Amber smiled. "Hi, Patch."

Patch looked at Charlie. "So…you guys know each other?"

"Uh, yeah. I kind of met Amber's husband and Shane's dad when I was…you know." She raised her eyebrows and gave Patch a conspiring look.

Patch didn't conspire back but looked at Shane, who had climbed onto Dog's back as if he were a little pony. Dog seemed to love his sudden change in species. "And these two?"

Charlie shook her head. "No, they just met. But Dog sure seems to know Shane."

Patch nodded slowly. From the look on her face she might as well have been chewing on a new dish, trying to figure out the ingredients by the taste.

"Is something wrong, Patch?" Amber asked.

"Uh, no. I just, it's quite the coincidence. I guess. I guess that's what this is."

Charlie looked at her. "What is?"

"Well…how can I put this…" She said it more to herself than anyone else.

Amber stood up. "What are you talking about?"

Patch sighed. "Oh, screw it. Charlie, whose dog was that before you adopted him?"

Charlie gave her a puzzled look. "Quinn's."

Then she followed Patch's gaze to Amber, who put a hand on the chair to steady herself. "Quinn McDonough? My husband's father?"

Chapter 26

It hadn't taken long to convince Patch to let them stay. But first, she and Amber wanted to talk to Quinn alone. Dog didn't seem to mind one bit, since Shane stayed with Charlie, too. Plus he got to go outside to lift his leg on every brittle bush along the drive, and do the rest of his business behind the privacy of an evergreen. Charlie knew she should find a bag to pick it up but doubted anyone would be having a picnic back there anytime soon.

She hung onto Shane's mitten with one hand and Dog's leash with the other.

"Why doesn't he poop out here?" the boy asked.

Charlie shrugged. "Privacy. Don't you close the door when you poop?"

Shane looked up at her, put his other mitten over his mouth, and giggled. A small stream of steam rose from beneath the knit fabric and hung in the frigid air over his head.

As if he knew his bowels were the topic of conversation, Dog suddenly reappeared to reclaim his dignity.

"Okay, let's get something to eat." She looked at Shane. "You hungry, buddy?"

"Do they have donuts?"

Charlie shrugged. "Maybe. I had my heart set on bacon, but a donut sounds good, too. I think I'll have both."

They walked toward the door just as Patch was emerging. "Quinn wants to see you. All three of you."

Charlie smiled at Shane and Dog. "Awesome."

Patch held the door, and then they all walked toward Quinn's room together. She reached for Shane's hand, but he shook his head and hung onto Charlie, looking over at Dog to make sure he was coming, too. "Can I hold his leash?" he asked.

Charlie looked at Patch, who raised an eyebrow. "Uh, no, we have to make sure he behaves. How about if you help me hold onto his leash?"

Shane nodded, moved to Charlie's other side, and put his hand over hers on the leash.

Patch smiled. "I think you have a new buddy."

"I think Dog has a new buddy."

When they got to Quinn's room, he was sitting up in his chair. His hair was combed and his face cleanly shaven. A breakfast tray sat nearby, but the food hadn't been touched. Amber was sitting in a folding chair across from him. Shane took one look at Quinn and ran for his mother. She pulled him into her lap and leaned into his neck with a kiss.

Charlie held onto Dog, who was straining forward. Patch touched her hand and nodded. Charlie unhooked the leash and he trotted first to Quinn, then the boy, and then curled himself into a ball on the floor between them.

"Well, Quinn, you're so popular we don't have enough chairs," Patch said.

He ignored her as he stared at the boy.

Shane wiggled uncomfortably under his gaze, whimpering and burrowing into Amber's bosom. She smoothed his hair.

"It's okay, son. Your grandpa just wants to meet you."

Shane slowly turned to look at Quinn, whose eyes were brimming with tears. "He looks so much like him," he whispered.

Amber nodded. "Yes, he does. It's why I sent the card and kept coming here to try to see you. I wanted you to be able to meet your grandson."

"Final said he'd have trouble shaving that cleft, just like his dad." Charlie's palms were sweating, and she'd chimed in so unexpectedly they all turned to stare at her—including Patch.

"What Charlie means is that—"

"Is that she saw my son when she was dead. Amber told me. Besides, I figured it out last night."

Charlie made a conscious effort to keep her mouth from dropping open. "You did?"

"When you said his name, I knew. Then I couldn't breathe."

Patch lifted an eyebrow at Charlie.

"Oh, leave her alone, Patch. She was trying to help. It's not her fault I was a lousy father."

Charlie took a step forward. "But he said he knew you were a good person."

Quinn looked at her as if she'd just told him he didn't have cancer after all. "He did?"

Charlie nodded. "Final told him—" She glanced at Shane, then Amber, who reflexively covered Shane's ears. "He told him your alcoholism was a disease, just like his drug addiction. And that it didn't mean you were a bad person. Shane said he knew that."

When Quinn began to cry, Patch extended her hand to Shane. "Let's go find a snack, buddy."

He looked at her doubtfully, then looked up at Amber. She nodded. "It's okay. I bet she'll take you to the room with toys, too."

At that, he scrambled off her lap and clasped Patch's hand.

Dog lifted his head and looked from Quinn to Shane as if unsure of his loyalties. Charlie clarified them for him. "Dog, you stay." Relieved he didn't have to make the decision, he lowered his chin back to the floor and let out a sigh.

Quinn blew his nose with a honk and looked at Charlie. "What else did my boy say?"

"He said he forgave you for the abuse."

The cleft of Quinn's chin began to quiver. His breathing grew more ragged as he closed his eyes and lowered his head. "I never meant to hurt him," he wheezed. "I was drunk. Always drunk."

Charlie flipped on the fan and aimed it toward Quinn's face. "He knew that. He wanted to see you."

Quinn looked up. His skeletal cheeks glistened with tears, and thin streams of mucous trickled around the oxygen nubs in his nose. His eyelashes were saturated enough to congeal into four rows of little black clumps which bobbed up and down when he blinked against the breeze of the fan. "He did?"

"He did. Final told him that when you tried to reconnect with him you'd gotten sober and changed. He said he would've agreed to see you if he'd known that."

Quinn's face screwed up with relief, and then he let out a sob. Charlie put a hand on his heaving shoulder, and Amber moved to sit next to him. "Charlie said he had a lot of regrets, Quinn. About me and Shane, too. It's why I wanted to see you. I wanted you to know Shane. I wanted you to see the son you loved in him."

Quinn pulled the prongs from his nose, gave a honk, replaced the oxygen, and took three deep breaths as if getting ready to jump from a plane. He looked out the window and didn't speak for several minutes. When he did, his tone sounded numb. "When I heard he died, I thought it was all over. That I'd never have my chance to say I was sorry."

Charlie flipped off the fan and set it on the table. "Well, Final told him for you, Quinn. Before he died, Shane knew that you loved him."

Quinn nodded and smiled the first real smile Charlie had seen since she met him. Then he frowned. "And the heaven or hell thing? Where'd he go?"

Charlie hesitated. "It was kinda dicey at first, but at the last minute, he said he wanted Jesus." Then she smiled. "Final said that was all he had to say."

Quinn watched her for a moment longer, then looked back out the window.

Charlie looked at Amber, who was gazing at her intently, urging her on. She took a deep breath. "But, Quinn?"

He continued to stare out the window. "Yeah."

"You don't have to wait till Final shows up to make your choice," Charlie said.

~

"I told you he might not be ready to hear all that." Patch held the door for Charlie and Dog as they stepped out into the cold.

Charlie pushed her shoulders back a little and lifted her chin. "I don't care. I'm still glad I told him. At least he knows about Final. And that his son forgave him."

"Well, he deserves to live out the rest of his time in peace. So don't bring it up again."

Charlie held Patch's gaze. "I'm not making any promises."

"Charlie…" Patch's tone was a warning.

"Hey, Spirit may not talk out loud to me, but I can still tell if he's saying something I'm supposed to listen to."

Patch sighed. "Whatever. You sure you don't want me to call your mom to come get you?"

"Not hardly. We can walk."

"And where are you walking to?"

Charlie shrugged. "We'll figure it out along the way."

As if on cue, her mother's black sedan pulled into the parking lot, crunching the morning's layer of salt under its tires. Charlie's heart dropped as if an elevator cable had snapped. Her mother wasn't alone. Stella was in the passenger seat. A white van pulled in behind them with "Ripple Creek Rescue" in bold red letters on the side. Lorna was behind the wheel.

"What the…? You have got to be kidding me."

"This should be interesting," Patch said. "The other one your boss?"

Charlie sighed. "Yeah, that's Lorna."

Stella climbed out of the car first. Charlie barely heard the door close behind her. But the slam of her mother's door echoed off every surface within reach. Lorna pulled to a stop, put the van in park, and left the engine running, as if she knew she should wait.

"Now, Beth, take it easy," Charlie heard Stella say. She put a hand on her mother's arm to slow the steaming locomotive heading in Charlie's direction. At Stella's touch, her mother stopped, and Charlie saw her shoulders rise and fall with the conscious effort of suppressing a scream. Then she nodded at Stella, and they walked toward Charlie and Patch at a slower pace.

"Any chance for a little help? I may need it," Charlie murmured.

Patch sighed. "If you didn't remind me so much of the younger me, the answer would be no. But…" She put an arm around Charlie's shoulders. "Since you do, I'll be right here."

Dog sat on Charlie's foot, apparently certain none of this could be good.

Stella smiled as they neared. "Good morning, Charlie. Patch."

"Morning, Stella," Patch said. Charlie responded by putting her hand on Dog's head and tightening her grip on his leash. Her mother glared at her, and she glared back.

"It's awfully cold out here. Patch, is there somewhere Beth and I could talk with Charlie over a hot cup of coffee?" Stella asked.

Patch nodded. "Sure."

"She's coming too." Charlie gestured toward Patch. "I want her there."

Stella looked at Charlie's mom. "Is that okay with you?"

"Yes, that's fine."

"What's she doing here?" Charlie pointed at the van.

"She called me this morning to apologize and I told her Dog needs a new home." Her mother's words were precise and unbending.

Charlie just wanted to spit on something. Or someone. "If he needs a new home, then so do I."

Stella held up her hands. "Okay, ladies. Everyone breathe." She looked at Patch and raised her eyebrows for some help.

"Right. Let's go inside. I think the family conference room is in use and my office mate is at her desk. But the chapel may be empty. Sorry, no coffee allowed in there, though."

Stella nodded. "Perfect. Lead the way."

When Charlie turned with Dog in tow, Stella stopped. "Why don't you let Lorna take him?"

Charlie shook her head and backed away.

"Not that kind of take him. Just let her watch him while we're talking."

Charlie had been focusing so much on everything she was going to say to her mother that she hadn't even heard Lorna get out of the van. She was standing about ten feet away, giving Charlie a sympathetic look. She held out her hand. "It's okay. You know he's safe with me. I won't go anywhere."

"You promise?"

Lorna nodded. "Promise."

Dog leaned hard against Charlie's leg. She bent and gave him a kiss on the snout. "It's okay, buddy. I'll be right back."

She handed off the leash and followed the parade of her apparent intervention.

Chapter 27

The chapel wasn't much bigger than her bedroom at home. It was cool and dark, but warm, too. A gathering of battery-operated candles flickered on the wooden table at the front, and the light from several others danced in their own shadows around the room. The aroma of incense rose from the dark tans of the industrial carpet beneath their feet, and four short rows of padded folding chairs stood ready to soften the falls of the grieving. Charlie expected harp music, but there was none. Just a thick and peaceful quiet. Even the soft hum coming from the pink lighting fixtures on the walls seemed intentional, a soothing chorus of electric life.

Stella pulled four of the chairs into a small circle and gestured for everyone to sit down. Once she settled into her seat, Stella closed her eyes, rested her hands in her generous lap, opened her palms, and just sat there. She'd taken off her coat, which made it clear her office wasn't the only place where she didn't wear a bra.

Of the other three, Patch was the only one who followed suit. Charlie examined the tightly looped pattern of the carpet and rolled her nose ring while she ignored the heat of her mother's stare.

When Stella let out a snore, Patch's eyes popped open. Charlie giggled, and her mother sighed with such force that if the candles weren't fake she would have blown them out.

Stella sat up with a startle and cleared her throat. "Sorry. Happens when I make myself relax." She looked at Charlie and then her mom. "So, you two figure things out?"

They gave her a simultaneous dumbfounded look.

"Us?" Her mother's bright red nail polish sparkled in the candlelight when she put her hand on her chest.

"Yeah, we were waiting for you." Charlie looked at Patch, who smiled as if this was just a Stella thing.

Stella yawned. "Well, I'm not the one who needs to talk. You two need to talk to each other so you can get to the real problem here."

Charlie's mom eyed her daughter. "I think we all know what the real problem is here. Rather, who."

Charlie's eyes went wide. "Me? I'm not the one who judges everybody. I'm not the one who never gives a person a second chance. I'm not the one who wants to kick her kid out of the house."

"I'm not kicking you out of the house. I said the mutt can't stay and ruin my nice things."

"Oh, your nice things. That's all that's important to you. Your stuff. Your pretty self and pretty things and pretty reputation."

"I defended you with Lorna. I stood up for you."

Charlie stood and jammed her index finger into the air in front of her mother's face. "That was all a show. You had no intention of letting Dog stay. And he's not a mutt. He's an animal with feelings who needs love. But you don't care, and you knew it wouldn't work. You just wanted to prove you could bully Lorna. You just wanted to prove your point. You just wanted to put me in my place and prove once again how wrong I always am. Your wrong, no-good, screwup daughter who will never be able to live up to your standards. Just admit it. Admit what all of this is finally about. Even if I died and came back from the dead. Even if Grace told me that God forgave me. You never will, Beth. You will never forgive me for having an abortion."

Charlie felt like she might pass out. She took a step back, fell onto her chair like a rag, put her face in her hands, and began to sob.

Patch put a hand on her back and a tissue on her knee.

Charlie was so spent she didn't think she had the energy to reach for it. She stared at the folds of the white tissue against the denim of her jeans and wondered why Stella wasn't saying anything. Or her mother. Her throat was raw from yelling and at that moment she wondered if Final and Grace and Spirit had been right about any of it. Maybe she'd made it all up. Maybe it was a dream. A nightmare. If life with God was so good, why did she feel like crawling back into that crumpled car to wait for Final one last time?

"I had one, too."

Charlie looked up. The voice was so small she thought a child must have come into the room. The look on her mother's face was as if she'd been startled by a presence she'd known had been there all along. There were no tears. Just the numb look of someone who'd been slapped.

"Mom?"

Her mother's nod was slow and intentional, like a bird figurine bobbing for water in a bowl.

"One what?"

"I had an abortion." The four wispy words hung in the air, changing everything.

Charlie's mouth hung open for so long she felt her saliva begin to dry.

"You had an abortion?" She looked at Stella as if the question were directed to her. But Stella maintained her poker-faced pose. "When did you have an abortion?"

Her mother looked into her lap. "A long time ago."

Charlie felt her heart pounding in her ears. "How long ago?"

"You were eight."

"Eight? How did I not know this?"

Her mom shrugged in a halfhearted way that was more unpleasant remembering than being nonchalant. "Why would you?"

Charlie stood so fast she knocked over her chair. "So was it my little sister or my little brother you killed?"

Her mother winced, and her face filled with the regret of knowing her admission had just unlatched Pandora's box. "Charlie, please."

She took a step toward her mother. "Was it a girl or a boy, Mom?"

"I don't know."

"How far along were you?"

"I don't remember."

"Who was the father?"

"I don't know."

Charlie inhaled so sharply she felt a pain in her chest. "You don't know?"

Her mom slowly shook her head.

It was as if the light of a hundred sunrises dawned on Charlie's world, revealing all the weapons she'd needed all along, simply lying there at her feet. "And you called me a slut." If words were spit, they would have showered the room.

"I didn't—"

Charlie put up a hand. "Save it, Beth. Your glass house is in ruins."

Her mom didn't say anything for a minute as she fingered one of her perfectly manicured nails. Finally, she looked up, her expression holding a new determination to defend herself. "Charlie, I know I've been too hard on you, but—"

"Hard on me? You've been a total hypocrite. You've been judging me for the same thing you did." Charlie put her hands on her hips and glared, punctuating her words with bitterness. "Exactly. The. Same. Thing."

Charlie watched her mother's resolve begin to crumble like an eroding cliff. She flicked her head back and forth and screwed up her face in attempts to will it away. But finally, a single crack in the fortress of her perfection trickled down her cheek. Then another. Then a muffled sob. Finally, the depth of her mother's pain took on a life of its own. Her shoulders heaved, and her sobs grew to a wail that pulled her to her knees. Charlie gave Stella a panicked look, but she didn't budge. She simply let her mother grieve on the floor beside her.

Finally, Charlie couldn't take it anymore. She knelt beside her mom and wrapped her arms around her. Then she too began to cry.

~

They must have been that way longer than it seemed, because when it came time to stand, Charlie's mom was too stiff to manage it. She started to get up, but then plopped back onto the floor. "Apparently, I'm getting too old for this."

Charlie reached up and touched her mother's face. Black rivers of mascara had carved a path down her cheeks, but her eyes were more peaceful than Charlie ever remembered. When her mother looked at her, it felt like the first time she'd been seen in forever.

"I love you, Mom."

She touched Charlie's cheek. "I love you, too, honey. I'm so sorry."

Charlie nodded. "It's okay. I understand now. And Mom?"

"What, Charlie?"

"He'll forgive you, too. You know that, right?"

Her mother's eyes shimmered, but she didn't respond.

Charlie took her mother's face in her hands. "When Final told me the Father named my baby Rose, I knew she was loved. But when I realized what I'd done, I hated myself and figured God hated me, too. But Grace said that wasn't true. She said God still loved me. And forgave me after I told him how sorry I was. God loves you, Mom, and he'll forgive you, too. And know your baby is with him. Named and loved and happy. And you'll get to be together again someday."

Her mother nodded as tears tumbled from her eyes. She wrapped her arms around Charlie and hung on. When Charlie looked up, both Patch and Stella were reaching for the tissues.

There was a light tap on the chapel door. A nurse stuck her

head around the edge. Her tone was reverent. "Patch? I'm sorry to interrupt. Can I see you for a minute?"

Patch got up from her chair. "Sure. I'll be right there." She smiled at Charlie and her mom and extended her hands. "Would you two like some help up?"

As they stood, Stella got up from her chair and stretched. "Well, I guess my work here is done."

"*Your* work?" Charlie said.

Her mom put her hands on her hips. "Yeah, we did all the work."

Stella smiled. "As I said."

They rearranged the chairs, gathered their things, and headed out of the chapel. As they neared the lobby, Charlie spotted Patch coming out of Quinn's room. She walked in their direction as if she had news.

"Did he change his mind? Does he want me and Dog to come back?" Even with all the good stuff that had just happened with her mom, she was still hoping for another chance with Quinn.

"Do you ladies mind if I steal Charlie for a minute?"

Charlie sighed as she followed Patch to her office. "Am I in trouble again? I can't take much more of this roller coaster day."

Patch stepped into her office, closed the door behind them, and then sat in one of the two chairs in front of her desk. Charlie assumed that meant the other was for her and sat down.

"Is he mad at me? I told you I'll—"

"Charlie, Quinn just died."

Although Patch said the words with a tone gentle enough to put a person to sleep, they had the effect of a shot from a taser. Charlie carefully pried the tendrils from her mind and took a deep breath. "He died?"

Patch nodded.

"When?"

"Just a little bit ago."

Charlie felt the familiar choke of confusion. "But he looked so good. We just saw him. He didn't look like he was going to die."

"Yes, sometimes it happens like that." Patch sounded like she was explaining the habits of an eccentric-but-cherished family member.

Charlie sat up with a horrified thought. "Was it my fault? Did I kill him? Maybe I shouldn't have said all that. Maybe it was too much for him. I thought I was doing the right—"

Patch put a hand on her arm. "Stop. You did absolutely nothing wrong."

Charlie exhaled. "You're sure?"

"Positive. On the contrary, I think you did everything right."

Charlie slumped back into her chair with relief. "I did?"

"Yes. When people have unresolved and painful things in their lives, it can be difficult for them to die peacefully. Quinn's relationship with his son was one of those things. You gave him quite a gift, Charlie."

"Really?"

Patch nodded.

"But what about Final? What about heaven and hell and Jesus? What'd he decide about that?" Charlie began to worry that she'd focused too much on telling him about his son and not enough about the whole ball of wax.

"I don't know for sure, but he did ask to see the chaplain after we left."

"He did?"

"Yes."

"What'd he tell the chaplain?" Oh, how Charlie wished she could've been a fly on the wall.

Patch smiled. "That he'd never prayed, and it seemed like a good time to start."

When they walked out of Patch's office, everyone was waiting in the lobby. Her mother, Stella, Amber, Shane, Lorna, and Dog. They gave her a unified look of sympathy. Her mother stood and gave her a hug. "I'm sorry, honey. Amber told us about Quinn."

Charlie nodded. "Thanks. I thought maybe it was my fault, but Patch said no."

Patch put an arm around Charlie's shoulders. "I told her she helped Quinn. She's a brave girl, and she gave him the gift he needed to die peacefully."

Dog came over and licked her hand. Charlie knelt beside him. He licked her face, giving special attention to the salty trails that covered her cheeks. She ran her hands down his back and buried her face in the fur of his neck. When she emerged, she blinked away tears as she held Dog's face in her hands and locked onto his gaze. As if he understood, he gave her face one more thorough bath and then went over to Shane, licked his hand, and sat at his feet.

Charlie looked at Lorna, who gave her a nod of approval.

"What just happened?" her mother asked.

Charlie gestured toward Shane, who had knelt to wrap his arms around Dog's neck and was smiling up at her. "Dog knows where he belongs."

Amber's eyes were wide. "Charlie, are you sure?"

Charlie's chin quivered when she nodded.

"But, honey, we can try again. I'm sure we can figure it out." Her mother's voice had an edge of panic to it, as if doing this might mean she would lose Charlie again.

Charlie held up a hand. "No. It's okay, Mom. It's not about that. It's not about me. It's about Dog. Shane is who he really needs."

Lorna stood and put her arm around Charlie's waist. "This girl knows her animals. Dog latched onto the wee lad because he has his master's blood in him. He senses it as clear as if it were written on his forehead. She's right. Dog knows exactly where he belongs. With the boy."

Shane looked up at his mom as if it were too good to be true. "I can keep him?"

Amber gazed at Charlie. "You're sure?"

Charlie nodded.

Then Amber put one hand on Shane's head and one on Dog's. "Yes, Shane. He was your Grandpa's dog, and thanks to Charlie, now he's yours." She looked at Charlie. "And we expect to see a lot of you."

Charlie smiled. "You can count on it."

Chapter 28

Two weeks later

It may have just been Charlie's excitement about the morning ahead, but the fact that the sun was shining brighter than anytime in recent memory seemed to be a sign that God was smiling on their plans. After an unseasonably warm week, the first buds of spring were sprouting in irregular patches of green within the fading brown landscape that zipped by her window.

When her mom slowed to turn into the park, the three balloons in the backseat bounced off of each other with playful thumps as if they also knew something good was about to happen. Stella's car was already in the lot, and the sight of her disheveled form sitting on a bench with her eyes closed and soaking up the morning sun made Charlie smile. She could've easily been mistaken for one of the homeless people who frequented the park. Charlie wondered where she and her mom would be without this ragamuffin who had so gently and lovingly led them to the forgiveness they needed for each other—and themselves.

After her mom put the car into park and turned off the ignition, she just sat there gazing at Stella, and Charlie was pretty sure she was thinking the same thing. When she finally looked over, the peacefulness in her face made Charlie want to take a picture.

"Ready?" Her mom asked.

Charlie smiled and nodded.

Her mom patted her knee. "Then let's do this."

When Stella heard their car doors close, she opened her eyes and slowly rose from the bench. The halting effort with which she did this, along with all Charlie had been through with Final, gave her a glimpse of the fact that although Stella seemed to be such a rock, she was as old as she often pointed out. The sudden realization that she wouldn't always be there nearly made Charlie forget the balloons.

She opened the car's backdoor and wrapped her fingers around the three thin strings, which made the balloons bob and squeak against each other, as if the children they represented were giggling together. The thought made Charlie smile as she tugged them into the sunshine and watched them pop toward heaven, two pink and one blue, since her mom didn't know if her baby had been a girl or a boy.

Charlie had asked Spirit for some insight into the matter, because her mom wanted to give her baby a name. Since she didn't get an answer, Stella suggested one of each color and a gender reveal in Heaven. She also said she was sure God wouldn't mind if her mom named her baby whatever she thought was best. While her mom seemed relieved at the thought, she said since it was Charlie's little sibling, she wanted Charlie to pick one out.

At first, Charlie hadn't known what to say, but then felt it was such a huge responsibility that she'd been online for a week, pouring over baby names, believing this was her chance to finally get something right. She'd made a list and obsessed over it, testing each name to see how it would fit into their now family of five. Dan, Beth, Charlie, Rose—

Of course, her mom helped her whittle down the prospects, since there were some that neither of them liked. Too normal. Too weird. Too not-really-us. Charlie savored getting to watch the expression on her mom's face with each name she read and then listening to her say it in the context of the rest of the family names to see whether or not it would work. Each time her mom said Rose's name, the granddaughter she hadn't yet met but had quickly come to cherish, Charlie's heart melted with love for them both.

It was Charlie's idea to get a new family portrait made for the front hall, since she was hoping for a completely different look. Instead of two strangers and the kid who didn't belong, Charlie wanted everyone to see a mom and dad and a kid who knew she was loved. Plus, she and her mom were each going to hold a single rose, so their babies could be included, too.

Finally, the moment had arrived when the perfect name appeared. When Charlie said it, her mom's eyes had lit up. And when she repeated it along with all the others, they both knew they'd found the perfect match. Dan, Beth, Charlie, Rose and *Lee*.

Of course, Rose was much younger than Lee, which meant her name should've been listed last. But Charlie loved having Rose right beside her. Plus, when she said the names fast enough, the last two sounded like Rosa Lee, as if they belonged together. That's how Charlie hoped things were in heaven for them, too.

Charlie whispered the babies' names into the gentle breeze that tugged at the strings in her hand. When her mom reached over and clasped her other hand, Charlie looked into the crystal blue of her eyes, which seemed to sparkle in the morning sun. Since that day in the chapel, Charlie had been savoring what she had wanted all along. Finally, she was finding out who her real mom really was—which gave Charlie permission to figure out who she really was, too.

Charlie leaned in, kissed the tear that trickled down her mother's cheek, and handed her two of the strings. Then they walked toward Stella as the balloons trailed behind them like children playing in their shadows.

As they reached her bench, Stella smiled and did something

she never did. She stepped forward and gave each of them a hug. "I'm so proud of you both," she whispered. When she pulled back, her eyes were rimmed in red, and her cheeks glistened in the sun. She pulled a tissue from her pocket and blew her nose with a honk.

Charlie had wondered if she might cry, too, but she didn't. Instead, she felt a surge of peaceful certainty. She gathered in her string until she held the pink balloon in front of her.

"I love you, Rose."

Then she kissed the balloon but didn't let it go. Instead, she looked over at her mom, whose cheeks were wet with tears. She followed Charlie's lead and pulled each of her balloons down for a kiss. When she clasped Charlie's hand and nodded, they both released the strings and watched the balloons drift toward heaven.

"You'll see," Charlie whispered to the disappearing ovals overhead. "One day, we'll be there to take care of you. Until then, the Father will do it for us."

Acknowledgements

So many people have encouraged me over this loooong journey to publication! I'm so grateful for the support and encouragement of: Mike Parker, my wonderful publisher who was willing to take on a new project from a debut author and welcome me into the WordCrafts Press family; Jennifer Odom and Marian Rizzo, for all their fabulous guidance and help; Diane Kitts, for her continual cheerleading, manuscript review, and eagle-eyed editing; Elizabeth Hurlow-Hannah, who is now with the Lord and was a soul sister in talking/writing about preparing for end of life; Katie Vorreiter, my God-ordained ACFW roomie who encouraged me to stick to my dreams, quickly became a life-long friend, and provided expert copyediting review; Ashley Schwartz, for her fabulous developmental editing expertise that helped me fix some glaring issues early on; Lt Col Douglas P Gracey Jr USAF (Ret), for his kind support and aviation expertise to help me avoid major flying fax paus; James L. Rubart, who generously took the time to discuss/review my manuscript and encouraged me to hang onto my writing dreams; members of the Ocala and Lake County Chapters of Word Weavers International, who provided many hours of essential critique and encouragement; our sweet boy, Blue, who is always at his "work station" at my feet, no matter the hour; my wonderful avid-reader-editor-teacher mom, who planted the love of words within me at an early age and cheered me on throughout the years; my incredible husband, Dave, who always supports my dreams no matter what the journey entails or how crazy they may seem; and of course, my Lord and Savior, Jesus Christ—the Great Shepherd and Champion of Rescues, Who never gave up on this wandering lamb.

About the Author

$\mathcal{S}$ue Montgomery has been a registered nurse for over 40 years in roles from staff nurse to administrator in critical care, hospice, the health insurance industry, and as a healthcare writer. She's a former certified hospice and palliative nurse (CHPN) and has extensive experience as a family caregiver. Through her business, Organize the Essentials LLC, she creates marketing and education content for clients—and is also the creator of Bibles & Bathrobes™, a short video/text devotional she sends out daily to subscribers.

Sue holds a Bachelor of Science in Nursing and a Master of Arts in Digital Journalism and Design. She has won awards for her fiction in various contexts—including winning Best Novel at the Florida Christian Writers Conference and being a top-10 finalist in the Christian Writers Guild's Operation First Novel.

Sue lives in Central Florida with her incredible husband, his sweet mom, and their precious rescue, Blue. *Final Moment* is her first novel.

Connect with Sue online at:

suemontgomery.org

Also Available From

WordCrafts Press

Down by the Riverbank
by Jennifer Odom

Paint Me Fearless
by Hallie Lee

Yeah, But I Didn't
by Ann Swann

The Legacy of Mrs. Cunningham
by Marian Rizzo

27 Words
by KL Palmer

www.WordCrafts.net